James A. St. John

Life of Sir Walter Raleigh

1552-1618 - Vol. 2

James A. St. John

Life of Sir Walter Raleigh
1552-1618 - Vol. 2

ISBN/EAN: 9783337388270

Printed in Europe, USA, Canada, Australia, Japan

Cover: Foto ©Andreas Hilbeck / pixelio.de

More available books at **www.hansebooks.com**

LIFE

OF

SIR WALTER RALEIGH.

1552—1618.

BY

JAMES AUGUSTUS ST. JOHN.

IN TWO VOLUMES.

VOL. II.

LONDON:

CHAPMAN AND HALL, 193, PICCADILLY.

1868.

LONDON: PRINTED BY WILLIAM CLOWES AND SONS, STAMFORD STREET
AND CHARING CROSS.

CONTENTS.

CONTENTS.

LIFE OF SIR WALTER RALEIGH.

CHAPTER XIX.

NEW POLITICAL COMBINATIONS.

THERE is in most matters of business much less interest than importance; it might consequently be tedious to attack the reader with a detailed account of the services performed by Raleigh for the miners, tinners, fishermen, and exporters of Cornwall and Devonshire. At the time, however, they were gratefully acknowledged by the persons concerned, who repaid with abundant attachment and affection the earnestness and assiduity which, as their Lord-lieutenant and Lord-warden, he displayed before the Queen and Council in their behalf.*

Towards the end of summer, while everything external, whether in nature or art, was gorgeousness and splendour, everything within, in the state as well as in the hearts of individuals, was ashes and poisonous dust.

* Carew, 'Survey of Cornwall.'

The false friendship between the triumvirs had risen and cleared away like a desert mirage, leaving bare and naked to the eye what had before been invested with beauty. Cecil beheld, in the slow decay of his father, the inevitable approach of the hour of supreme conflict for lead in the Government; Essex, in sullen discontent, conscious that the tide of his court influence was rapidly ebbing away from about him, laboured to concoct those schemes which would, he hoped, enable him to crush both Raleigh and Cecil; and Raleigh himself, looking through the long vista of policy, saw many of the dark preliminaries to Essex's fall, though these only formed the avenue to another fall which he did not then see.

On the 4th of August, the Lord-treasurer Burleigh, who by the toil of seventy years had climbed to the highest pinnacle of power in England, succumbed to the united effect of old age and disease. His remains, after lying in state like those of a prince for more than three weeks, were, on the 29th of the same month, interred with equal pomp. A few circumstances connected with his obsequies are thus glanced at by a contemporary:—

"The Lord-treasurer's funeral was performed yesterday with all rites that belonged to so great a personage. The number of mourners were, one with another, about five hundred, among whom was the Earl of Essex, who, whether it were upon consideration of the present occasion, or for his own disfavours, methought carried the heaviest countenance of the company. They say he means to remain at Wanstead, since he cannot be received at court, though he hath relented, and sought by divers means to recover his hold; but the Queen says he hath played long enough upon her, and that she means to play awhile upon him, and to stay as much upon her greatness as he hath done upon stomach. The Lord-treasurer hath left the Queen's coffers so bare that there is but twenty thousand pounds to be found. Of his private wealth, there is but eleven thousand pounds come to light, and that all in silver, whereof six thousand pounds, with eight or nine hundred pounds in land, is bequeathed to his two nieces of Oxford. His lands are not so great as was thought, for Mr. Secretary says, his own part will not rise to one thousand six hundred pounds a-year upon the rack. Sir Walter Raleigh and Sir John Stanhope are in speech to be sworn presently of the Council."*

Whatever countenance Essex might affect at Burleigh's funeral, his sadness by no means contributed to augment his wisdom. In eight days after Burleigh's obsequies, the jousts and tournaments which usually took place on Elizabeth's birthday afforded him an opportunity of putting an affront upon Raleigh, who on

* August 30th, 1598. MS. State Paper Office.

this occasion resolved to run at the tilt in honour of the Queen. The custom was, for the knights in imitation of the practice of chivalry to enter the lists dressed in particular colours, but otherwise disguised. Raleigh's colour was orange-tawny, and this having been made known beforehand, Essex resolved to annoy him by coming to the tilt-yard with two thousand followers all decked with the same colours. This was designed to make Raleigh, who had a smaller retinue, appear to be only a portion of the earl's suite. But either through excitement or over-eagerness to display his skill in Elizabeth's presence, Essex is said to have run very clumsily, so as to excite the ridicule rather than praise of the lookers-on. Next day, hoping to do better, he appeared upon the course in green, but ran worse than on the preceding day. A murmur of disapprobation passed through the company, and some one asked, why so poor a tilter should covet to appear twice? Only, replied the person spoken to, that the man in green might be thought more absurd than the man in orange-tawny.*

Court and country were still full of speculations respecting the new Lord-deputy for Ireland, and the name of Essex became every day more and more closely connected with the office.†

* Bacon, Apophthegms, 188. Clarendon in 'Reliquæ Wottonianæ,' p. 190.

† Letter of John Chamberlain, October 20th, 1590.

Raleigh's domains in Ireland being grievously infested by some rebel, he ordered his steward in that country to set a price upon his head, a measure for which he was first careful to obtain Cecil's concurrence. When it appeared likely however that the fact would be made known to the public, the wily Secretary showed much anxiety to escape from responsibility. In this affair as in many others I miss in Raleigh that astuteness for which he generally obtains credit, and discover, instead, marked proofs of the recklessness which so long turned the current of public opinion against him. "It can be no disgrace," he writes to Cecil, "if it were known that the killing of a rebel were practised, for we see that the lives of anointed princes are daily sought, and we have always in Ireland given head-money for the killing of rebels, who are evermore proclaimed at a price; so was the Earl of Desmond, and so have all rebels been practised against. Notwithstanding, I have written this enclosed to Stafford, who only recommended the knave to me on his credit, but for yourself who are not to be touched in the matter, and for me I am more sorry for being deceived than for being declared in the practice."*

The rebellion now raging originated partly in the misgovernment of the country by the English, partly in the hope of aid from Spain, which had equipped and

* Raleigh to Cecil. State Paper Office.

sent forth a large fleet to cruise about the British islands. To cope with this armament, a fleet was fitted out by Elizabeth, under the command of Howard, Mountjoy, and Raleigh, who gained some advantages over the enemy, though they came to no decisive engagement. Petty skirmishes took place at various points on the ocean in which success declared sometimes for the Spaniards, sometimes for the English. Much fear was at one time entertained that several important ships, the arrival of which at Plymouth was unaccountably delayed, had been captured by the enemy, but they all came in one after another, and the alarm of the fleet and of the country gradually subsided.*

Perplexed by the disturbed state of Ireland, the politicians of this country experienced great difficulty in determining what course to pursue. The two court factions, one headed by Essex, Mountjoy, Southampton, and their friends; the other by Raleigh, Cecil, Cobham, and such others as adhered to them, clearly foresaw that a final rupture was at hand, which could only be terminated by the headsman's axe. In such circumstances men naturally seek to put off the evil day, for though hostile courtiers think little of shedding blood, their eagerness is necessarily checked by the uncertainty

* Joint letter to the Earl of Essex from Lord T. Howard, Lord Mountjoy, and Sir W. Raleigh, October 29th, 1598. State Paper Office.

as to whose blood it is to be. To gain time was consequently the aim of both parties. If Essex could be sent to Ireland, his adversaries would enjoy leisure to destroy his influence which had become intolerable, while he on the other hand had enterprises in contemplation which were not yet ripe, and needed the freedom of a wide field for their development.

Never was the dark hand of Nemesis more distinctly visible in human affairs. The perdition of Raleigh, Cecil, Cobham, and many others had been decreed by the conclave at Essex House, the vast range of whose villainy included the cutting short in certain eventualities of the old Queen's thread of life. Essex's character seemed at this time to have undergone a complete metamorphosis. Instead of the gay lively man of pleasure, who charmed people by his easy manners, he had become the reckless plotter, sanguinary in aim, unscrupulous in the means. What that aim was will become evident as we proceed. Infirmity of purpose, however, was still predominant in his nature; repeated counsel and deliberation left him undecided as to whether he should repair to Ireland or attempt to realise his plans in some other way. He would once more consult Bacon, who had ceased to be his adviser for more than a year and a half.* That able politician appears to have understood the whole drift of his

* Birch, ii., 395. Mr. Dixon, Story of Lord Bacon, pp. 141, 142.

scheme, and wishing to preserve him from ruin, advised him first against the enterprise; then if he would persist, cautioned him against those excesses of conduct which he foresaw he would almost surely commit.

Advice and warning were thrown away upon Essex; who, having obtained the most ample powers ever granted to a Lord-deputy, together with an army of twenty-two thousand men, sailed for Ireland in the spring of 1599. With the particulars of his proceedings during his government I have no concern; but, in whatever business engaged, and how great soever the perplexities of his position, hatred of Raleigh, Cobham, and Cecil, predominated over every other feeling. Through them, he feared, Elizabeth would be enabled to form a just estimate of his conduct and motives, and therefore the sugared hypocrisy of his letters to her is thickly besprinkled with venom against them. "Is it not lamented," he says, "of your Majesty's faithfulest subjects, both there and here, that a Cobham or a Raleigh, I will forbear others (Cecil), for their places' sake, should have such credit and favour with your Majesty when they wish the ill-success of your Majesty's most important action, the decay of your greatest strength, and the destruction of your faithfulest servants."*

Through Cecil, if in no other way, these rancorous

* Birch, ii., 418.

attacks could not fail to be made known to Raleigh and Cobham, who, perceiving with what feelings they were regarded, adopted all possible means to ward off the consequences. With untiring perseverance, Essex went on labouring by insinuations as well as by direct charges to undermine them in the Queen's regards. Bearing testimony to his own virtue and that of his friends, he again writes: " Value such honest men as we, that undergo all hazards and miseries for your safety and greatness; and cherish such gallant and worthy servants as this bearer, who will take it for as great happiness to be sacrificed for you, as others whom you favour most will be to be made great and happy by you. Cherish them, I humbly beseech you on the knees of my heart; for they must sweat and bleed for you, when a crew of those which now more delight you will prove but unprofitable servants."*

The fulsome cant, addressed in these letters to her for whose " crooked carcase" he cherished so much contempt, and against whose power and life he was then plotting, enables us justly to appreciate the boasted chivalry of the writer. Who but must smile at his crafty interlacing of sentimental imposture with inexpressible malice? " If your Majesty," he continues, " whose parting with me so pierced my very soul, can be transformed by those sirens that are about you, then

* Birch, ii., 424.

think that you shall quickly hear that a brave death shall ransom from scorn and misery your Majesty's humblest servant." *

These puerile rhapsodies, which might have told with a girl of seventeen, failed to throw Elizabeth and her faithful counsellors off their guard. Essex's intrigues with Scotland had not remained wholly concealed, though their full scope was still unknown.

The suspicion, however, began to take root, that the twenty thousand foot and two thousand horse at the command of the Earl, with such forces as the Stuart could muster and push at a short notice towards the Border, might be simultaneously employed against the English government, under pretence of removing evil counsellors from about the Queen, and insuring the Scottish succession. A rumour was opportunely spread that a Spanish armament had put to sea, with the intent, it was assumed, to invade England. The alarm then displayed may doubtless have been caused in part by the naval armament which had just left Corunna; but there is reason to believe that the apprehensions of Elizabeth and her ministers were much deepened by doubts of Essex's fidelity. Whoever may have been the enemy that inspired dread, the whole kingdom was thrown suddenly into a ferment; large forces were levied in breathless haste, generals and other

* Birch, *ubi supra.*

officers appointed, a bridge was thrown over the Thames at Blackwall, heavy chains were drawn across the streets of London, lamps were suspended at night over the doors of private houses, and an army of six thousand men under the command of Lord Cumberland was charged with the protection of the capital.

Nor did preparations stop here. With unexampled rapidity a fleet was got in readiness to cope with the foe in the narrow seas, of which Lord Thomas Howard was appointed Admiral, and Raleigh Vice-admiral.* As the service, it was supposed, would brook no delay, Raleigh took leave of the ladies and his other friends at court, and repaired to the fleet, in the hope probably of finishing the contest commenced at Fayal.† The clouds, however, which had darkened the political horizon speedily dispersed; the Spanish fleet, whatever may have been its original destination, put into Brest; Essex and his friends, whether in Scotland or Ireland, either lost heart or upon examination found their strength unequal to the enterprise they had projected. No enemy consequently appeared, so that the land and sea forces which had been brought together with so much precipitation were disbanded or recalled, and the whole system of public affairs relapsed into its habitual calm.

* Winwood, i., 91.   † 'Sidney Papers,' ii., 112, 116, 117.

Encountering failure * and disgrace in Ireland, Essex, with a number of unscrupulous adherents, re-crossed the Irish Channel, and riding to Nonsuch where the court then was, forced himself into the Queen's bedchamber, "where he found her newly up, with her hair about her face," and threw himself at her feet. Taken thus unawares, Elizabeth suffered herself to be overcome by emotion, and was betrayed into some expressions of affection which the Earl interpreted into forgiveness. "Coming from her Majesty to go shift himself in his chamber, he was very pleasant, and thanked God, though he had suffered much trouble and storms abroad, he found a sweet calm at home." †

For some hours he was allowed to remain in this delusion; but in the afternoon, Elizabeth having enjoyed some leisure for reflection, changed her tone, reproached him with neglect of duty and misconduct, ordered him to give an account of his proceedings at once to such members of the council as happened to be present, and summoned all the lords to meet immediately at the Palace. This alteration in Elizabeth's behaviour was attributed to Cecil and that *party,* a phrase by which Raleigh and Cobham were signified.

On Michaelmas Day, on the eve of which he had

* Cecil to Neville Winwood, i., 105.

† Rowland White, 'Sidney Papers,' ii., 127. Winwood, i., 118—125.

returned, Essex appeared before the lords in the council-chamber, standing bareheaded at one end of the table, while Cecil, with the articles of accusation in his hand, stood at the other. His defence being deemed unsatisfactory, he was ordered back to his chamber; while the triumphant Secretary, who now beheld himself at the head of an immense following, sat down to a grand banquet with Shrewsbury, Nottingham, the Lords Thomas Howard and Cobham, the Lord Grey, Sir Walter Raleigh, and Sir George Carew.*

Essex's confinement still continuing, the public business of the country was neglected that the attention of Elizabeth and her ministers might be concentrated on his affairs. No hand has yet raised the veil which Cecil, Cobham, Raleigh, and their friends dropped at this time over their proceedings, which it cannot be doubted were all more or less regulated by the wish to deliver themselves from their arch-enemy, whose relatives and adherents shook the court with their intrigues; while his military retainers who had flocked over from Ireland disturbed the London taverns by their incessant brawls. Though the tragedy was to be long in performance, the curtain had been raised, and the actors were on the stage. Masks of the thickest dissimulation were put on by many of those engaged, from the terrible conscious-

* 'Sidney Papers,' ii., 129.

ness that they were moving through a labyrinth, the issues of which, whether they advanced or retreated, might be death. Essex's unappeasable hatred for his court antagonists had been fully revealed in his letters to the Queen, who had placed them in Cecil's hands: this fact must not be lost sight of. The true state of the case, therefore, was this: it was known that dangerous machinations had been carried on in Ireland while the army of which Essex boasted he was the soul,* seethed and panted for some employment, the nature of which remained unknown; numerous officers who had returned without leave,† hovered in mysterious sullenness about the capital, fretting and chafing at their leader's imprisonment; that leader himself looking upon what he suffered as a deadly affront, the desire of revenge for which was exasperated by every day that was added to its continuance. No art, no falsehood, no meanness, it was obvious, would be shrunk from which might appear to facilitate a reconciliation with the Queen, and then woe to the authors of his humiliation!

About the beginning of November, some indications of relenting towards Essex‡ supposed to be discoverable in Elizabeth, Raleigh, who had laboured to keep her firm to her purpose, and who knew the full scope of what the least weakness on her part boded to him and

* Birch, ii., 424.   † 'Sidney Papers,' ii., 131.
‡ Winwood, i., 254.

others, affected to be ill, and kept his room.* To convince him, however, that he misinterpreted her conduct, "her Majesty very graciously sent to see him."

Whether it were the air of the court, or the physical condition of the atmosphere, something at the same time occasioned much show of illness among the great. "Lord Nottingham," says White, "is sick at Chelsea, the Lord-keeper sick at London, Sir John Fortescue takes physic, Sir Walter Raleigh hath an ague."† Cecil himself, through hard work which saved him from the necessity of shamming, likewise fell ill, and was for several days unable to attend to public business. The capital, meanwhile, was from day to day troubled with sad stories about Essex's sufferings, which were described by his partizans to be so great that little hope could be entertained of his recovery. His gay sisters and his wife wore cheap black in the hope of working on the Queen by their mock humility; while London swarmed with libels, some for, others against the Earl—the latter supposed to be sharpened by Raleigh's pen—but all calculated to keep alive the general excitement.

Elizabeth had now an opportunity of learning how unwisely she had acted by elevating Essex through her favour to so great a height that his popularity over-

---

* Rowland White to Sir Robert Sidney, November 4th, 1599.

† 'Sidney Papers,' ii., 150. Rowland White to Sir Robert Sidney, December 13th, 1599.

topped her own. No intelligent person doubted that his maladies were counterfeit, yet eight physicians were found to certify their reality. The clergy in troops flocked to his bedside, or prayed for him as for the head of the state in their pulpits,* and having circulated a report of his death, caused the bells of their churches to be tolled. On the white walls of Elizabeth's own palace libels of the most shocking kind were written against her chief minister, while the tranquillity of her life was hourly disturbed by hosts of importunate solicitors whose earnestness made it evident that they postponed the interests of the kingdom to the private convenience of the Earl.

The year 1600 opened upon the state of affairs above described. Mountjoy having been appointed Lord-deputy of Ireland, looked to be made a privy councillor before his departure, and Cobham and Raleigh anticipated the same honour. Whatever at heart may have been the Queen's feelings, she entered with much apparent zest into the festivities of Christmas and the New Year, which were celebrated at Richmond, where Essex's brother-in-law, Percy, having quarrelled with Dorothy, was a perpetual courtier, cultivating assiduously the friendship of Raleigh, from which he many years afterwards derived consolation under totally different circumstances. It may be guessed, without

* " Their doubtful speech tending to sedition." 'Sidney Papers,' ii. 156.

unfairness to Cecil, that it was his influence which secretly barred Raleigh's promotion to places of trust, though he did not stand in the way of his reaping a harvest of credit, for the manning and victualling of Ireland were in a great measure ordered by his advice; the Queen likewise took him about with her when she went on visits, but otherwise did nothing towards the gratifying of his ambition.

Inferring from Essex's long imprisonment Elizabeth's resolution to employ him no more in state affairs, both Cecil and Raleigh appear to have viewed with less uneasiness the prospect before them; at the same time the latter found leisure to pay and receive visits; his niece Barbara, now Lady Sidney, had become an active politician, going about from one great person to another, in furtherance of her husband's business: from the house of Lady Leicester she flitted to that of Lady Buckhurst, or Lady Essex, or Mrs. Fytton. Occasionally she bestowed her presence on Sir Walter Raleigh and his lady, and found from both an agreeable welcome. As candidates for the same places, Raleigh and Sidney may sometimes have indulged those feelings which rivalry begets; but in the company of his wife and niece Raleigh's stern resolves melted away, at least in appearance, so that he professed his readiness to promote the interests of his frequent competitor.*

* February 21st, 1600. 'Sidney Papers,' ii., 167.

Little was for awhile thought of, either at court or in London, but the Earl's imprisonment and the manner in which it was likely to end. Conjecture was busy on all sides, yet few, if any, ventured to look forward to the actual dénouement. Sportive wits and superficial thinkers put their own constructions on events, while both Raleigh and Cecil beheld with anxiety the ebbs and flows of the Queen's humour, upon the stability of which it was impossible to count beyond the vicissitudes of the hour. Out of doors people indulged in all kinds of speculations, colouring according to their own leanings the prospects of Essex, who, in the course of March, was removed from the Lord-keeper's house to his own, which he found quite as far from court. "For, before he had the help of a friend at hand, whereas now he is left to himself, unthought of, and poor Sir F. Berkeley hath so strait a charge to be ever in his company, and to observe his doings, that it is a question which holds the other prisoner."*

In the meantime, perceiving that no speedy progress was made or likely to be made, either in his own affairs or those of Essex, Raleigh with his wife quitted London for Sherbourne. Unable, through the pressure of business, to watch over the education of his only son William, Cecil intrusted the care of him to Raleigh, who made him the playmate of his own Walter. The

* Dudley Carleton to Chamberlain, March 29, 1600.

whole party was received and entertained by Northumberland at Sion House; after which the journey westwards was continued.

In London the gossips were much perplexed to divine the object of this retreat from court; for which, being unable to assign any good motive, they assigned a bad one, setting it down to the sullenness of disappointment.* During Raleigh's absence, Elizabeth turned the beams of her favour on Sir John Stanhope, who could not remain two days away from court without being inquired for.†

Bearing in mind the plan agreed upon between Essex and his fellow-conspirators for the disposal of Elizabeth's crown and crooked carcase, the reader will be able to appreciate the nobleness of soul which inspired the following sentences:—"That I presume now again, most dear and most admired sovereign, to send my humble lines unto your Majesty's gracious, princely, and divine nature, the oppressions of mine own heart—breaking with such fearing and incomparable sorrow, the shrinking of my body, so as to fail of his wonted ability to do your Majesty service. . . . . To encourage me to be an importunate petitioner for myself, I have a lady, a nymph, or an angel, who, when all the world frowns upon me, cannot look with

* White to Sidney, March 15th, 1600.
† 'Sidney Papers,' ii., 188.

other than gracious eyes, and who, as she resembles your Majesty most of all creatures, so I know not by what warrant she doth promise me grace from your Majesty."*

The Earl enjoyed ample opportunities of trying the force of his epistolary style during the vicissitudes of his confinement, which, sometimes less, sometimes more strict, lasted till the 26th of August, when he was set at liberty, to weave the web of his last treason, and take, as he hoped, full vengeance on those whom he regarded as the authors of his humiliation.

It seems not improbable that this graceless favourite was confederate with those who drew up the artful and alluring scheme, which now began to be circulated through the kingdom, for insuring to Elizabeth a Catholic successor. Baits were held forth in it to all classes: the nobles were to be delivered from the oppression of wardships, the franklins were to be advanced to the rank of gentlemen; the common people, if they cheerfully co-operated in supporting the church's cause, were to have restored to them all the common pastures of which they had been deprived by grasping courtiers. Two other advantages were to be promised them: first, they were to be exempt from military service out of the realm; second, all foreign heretics —meaning Flemings and Germans—were to be ex-

* Essex to Queen, April 4th, 1600.

pelled, in order that the whole industry of the country
might revert into the hands of natives. A vast plan
of spoliation lurked dimly in the background—individuals of all ranks who refused to espouse the church's
cause were to be despoiled of their lands, which, by
way of reward for bloody service rendered, were to be
lavished upon active and zealous Catholics. If Essex
and his adherents were, as can scarcely be doubted, in
communication with the sacerdotal plotters, he may
have been the very orthodox prince* whom the
Jesuits intended to put forward as the rival of James
of Scotland.

While the court party, adverse to Essex, appeared
to have sunk into inaction, the rebellious Earl and his
accomplices were straining every nerve in the hope
of crushing them completely. In spite, however, of
these machinations, Raleigh, whatever may have been
the motive of his retreat, enjoyed at Sherbourne a
longer respite than usual from intrigue and toil. The
country in the south of England, in spring and early
summer, wears its sunniest and most soothing aspect—
the sweetest flowers known to our climate are then in
bloom, the nightingale fills the brief hours of darkness

---

* Two years later, the French ambassador, Beaumont, speaking
of the Jesuits, says, "they not only refused to acknowledge and
obey the Queen, but entered into conspiracies of all kinds against
her person, and into alliances with enemies of the kingdom, in order
to effect her downfall." Raumer, ii., 183.

with music, and if the soul be open to delight, it must experience it in that season. Raleigh was a man of many tastes, with an equal relish for the beauties of nature, the charms of poetry, the absorbing fascinations of metaphysics, the grand scenes of history, the excitement of politics, above all, for the fierce joy of conflict and victory.

To experience he knew not what, he was now suddenly recalled to London, which he reached probably about the day of Essex's private trial before the lords; when he shed tears which could hardly have been those of penitence.*

* Egerton, then Lord-keeper, observed dramatically in the Star Chamber, "that Essex confessed his fault with tears, saying that the tears of his heart had quenched all the sparks of pride that were in him." Chamberlain to Carleton, June 23rd, 1600. State Paper Office.

CHAPTER XX.

HIS PART IN THE ESSEX TRAGEDY.

THE siege of Ostend, which then concentrated upon the Netherlands much of the attention of Europe, was viewed in England with peculiar anxiety. The Cardinal Archduke Albert, recently married to Clara Eugenia Isabella, Infanta of Spain, was carrying on the siege at the head of an immense army. Prince Maurice, with the forces of the states, lay encamped near at hand to obstruct as far as possible the movements of the Spaniards. In the city, Raleigh's old antagonist, Sir Francis Vere, held the chief command, and gave proofs during the three years, three months, and three days * which the siege lasted, of valour, patience, and masterly soldiership.

* Reckoning on speedy success, the Infanta, in the hope of interesting heaven in the matter, made a vow not to change her linen till the end of the siege. She was as good as her word, so that her under garments assumed that tawny hue long known under the name Isabel. Raumer, i., 221.

No event of those times exhibited more characteristic features of Spanish policy: the Cardinal Archduke, being bent on the capture of the city, recked little of the sums of money or number of lives it might cost, for as the gold ebbed forth from the Treasury, fresh supplies were forwarded from Spain, while new levies from all parts of Philip's dominions marched to the camp over the graves of their predecessors. Eighty thousand bodies are said to have been interred in the surrounding swamps, and the deadly nature of the struggle having been widely circulated by rumour, fear at length began to pervade the ranks of the young recruits, and led to a formidable mutiny. In letters from Cardinal Albert and his wife Clara Eugenia to Philip III. and the Duke of Lerma, some found at Simancas, others in the Biblioteca Nacional at Madrid, we have a minute history of all the incidents of this contest. The German troops, it appears, at once badly paid and disheartened at the prospect before them, refused obedience to their general; the gentle means at first employed are described by the Cardinal, and alluded to by his wife; but we are indebted to a note, probably in the handwriting of the Duke of Lerma himself, for a knowledge of the fact, that a number of the mutineers, the writer says forty, had to be shot in front of the trenches, before tranquillity could be restored to the army.

To witness these proceedings, as far as they could be witnessed from the enemy's lines, Sir Walter Raleigh, Lord Cobham, and the Earl of Northumberland were sent over by Elizabeth about the beginning of June. Their mission aimed no doubt at something beyond the gratification of curiosity, and excited both in France and England a considerable amount of speculation.* Raleigh and Cobham executed their trust, whatever it may have been, noiselessly; but Northumberland, having much of Hotspur's blood in his veins, contrived to entangle himself in a quarrel with Sir Francis Vere,† which in the sequel occasioned him no little trouble. The visit of the three friends to the Netherlands camp, as well as to the beleaguered city, was brief; they may have been intrusted with sums of money for the use of the besieged, or instructed to attempt some negotiation with Maurice—whatever their errand was, it proved bootless, for after one of the most protracted and brilliant defences on record, Ostend fell into the hands of the Spaniards.‡

Early in July Raleigh was again at court, watching

---

* Sir Henry Neville, English Ambassador in France, attributed their visit to political motives, and was piqued at being kept in the dark. Winwood, i., 230, 231.

† Lodge, iii., 24. To this quarrel, Lord H. Howard refers in the rhapsodical letter published in Raleigh's Works, viii., 756: 'Secret Correspondence,' p. 69.

‡ Winwood, i., 371.

the efforts made by Essex's friends to obtain his freedom and restoration to favour. On the 26th of August the Earl, as I have said, was set at liberty, but forbidden to appear at court, and informed that he lay still under the Queen's displeasure. In these circumstances he proceeded on a visit to the house of his uncle, Sir William Knollys, at Graves, whence after a while he returned to Essex House, where his evil counsellors immediately began to flock about him. From this time forward his story becomes closely bound up with that of Raleigh, whose extraordinary favour with Elizabeth * formed one of the chief sources of Essex's discontent and hatred towards the Queen. All the court gossips, especially those who leaned towards the Earl, beheld with extreme envy the influence exerted by Raleigh over the course of public affairs, to which they constantly attributed the ill success of Essex's intercessors.

During the whole of this autumn Elizabeth was either at Oatlands or Nonsuch; but in order to afford Cecil an opportunity of enjoying the short leisure which he now found it necessary to allow himself from the cares and toils of office, Raleigh retired again to Sherbourne, where, in the beginning of September, he received his friend, who had at the same time the pleasure of being in the company of his little son. Even this short period of relaxation might have been

* 'Sidney Papers,' ii., 210.

fraught with ruin could Essex have obtained an interview with the Queen, who, in spite of the affronts and insults he had put upon her, might have proved too weak to withstand his eloquence and arts of cajolery. To circumscribe his power had now become a necessity, and therefore the Queen was prevailed upon to resist his importunities to have the farm of sweet wines continued to him,* which would have supplied revenues for multiplying his adherents. History abounds with frivolous apologies for princes who have suffered themselves to be led astray by evil counsellors; the same excuse is pleaded for Essex's crimes: Cuffe, Meyrick, Blount, Father Wright, and others, suggested to him, we are told, his desperate enterprises. This is false. He had entered upon the guilty course which led to his overthrow more than eleven years before, when he began his correspondence with Scotland, in which he designated himself the "Weary Knight." His enmity to Raleigh dated as early as the defeat of the Armada, and the incidents of every service in which they were engaged together only tended to deepen his resentment. At sea before Fayal he and his friends had openly discussed the policy of Raleigh's execution—this fact was never forgiven or forgotten by Raleigh—it clearly revealed to him what fate he must reckon upon if Essex and his faction ever again became predominant.

* Winwood i., 271.

The breach had now been widened, and the danger of a relapse of fondness on the part of the Queen infinitely augmented. Cecil, Cobham, Raleigh, and Stanhope never doubted that their necks would be soon on the block if they relented for a moment towards their remorseless enemy. They accordingly laid before Elizabeth a startling outline of the position she occupied; they showed her that Hayward's false chronicle of Henry IV., with the deposition and death of Richard II., only typified the contest between her and Essex; they may also have suggested that Shakespeare's tragedy on the same subject had been inspired by Southampton, and aimed at familiarizing the public mind with the deposition and murder of princes—a conviction to which she alluded when she inquired of Lambard, " Know you not that I am Richard ?"

On the other hand, Essex laboured to circulate the report that Raleigh and Cobham had entered with others into a conspiracy to cut him off, or even to murder him in his bed, if he attempted to approach the court; he affirmed also, and laboured to have it believed, that in conjunction with Cecil, they had formed the design of bringing in the Infanta as the successor of Elizabeth. Of this fictitious scheme he conveyed an account to James Stuart, pointing out to him with plausible minuteness the apt location of the conspirators for co-operating with Spain : Raleigh, he observed, was stationed in the west, Cobham in the east, Sir George Carew in Munster, Burleigh, Cecil's elder brother, in the north, while Cecil himself, commanding the Treasury, could dispose at will of the whole strength of the kingdom. Of these malignant and false suggestions the fruit afterwards appeared at Winchester and in Palace Yard; for the present, the current of events set in a direction exactly contrary to the views of the falsifier.

In some cases the animosity of the court factions broke out into acts of personal violence; thus Lord Grey of Wilton attacked the Earl of Southampton on horseback in the Strand, which led ultimately to a duel in the Low Countries; Sir Christopher St. Lawrence, son to the Earl of Howth, one of the ruffians brought over by Essex from Ireland, coolly proposed, in revenge of the affront offered Southampton, to murder Lord Grey upon the high road; the same St. Lawrence, seeking to get up a brawl at a tavern, drank to the health of Essex, then in prison, and said he would send his rapier through any man who refused to do the same; but when Raleigh's half-brother, Sir John Gilbert, who happened to be present, went to St. Lawrence's lodgings, and told him that he had refused to drink Essex's health, the bravo quibbled out of his threat.

In her partiality for Essex, Elizabeth had been grossly censurable; overlooking his incompetence, she had constantly raised him above superior men—had sacrificed or imperilled the interests of her country to gratify her personal preference—had squandered the resources of the state on her unworthy favourite, and had facilitated and smiled at the manœuvres by which he gained the popularity that made him dream of her dethronement, and his own succession to the crown. During the development of this plot, Elizabeth often unconsciously verged on her last hour. The policy of killing or sparing her was discussed by the conspirators as openly as any other incident of their drama, and one of Essex's myrmidons, more zealous or drunken than the rest, undertook with a recklessness exceeding that of the other conspirators to realise the wish of all.

Before matters however had reached this point, Essex had matured his scheme for insurrection in the capital. His house in the Strand, a lofty and spacious pile of building, opening on one side upon the river, with which it communicated by a broad flight of steps, and having on the other side a large court, divided from the street by a high wall and strong gates, had long been the resort of all the noblemen and gentlemen of his faction. In the chapel belonging to this fortress—for such in truth it was—seditious clergymen habitually preached to constantly-increasing audiences. Essex himself interrupted his licentious courses in order the better to work the lever of religion in the service of rebellion: his piety became the theme of popular admiration ; he prayed frequently, he associated through apparent preference with godly ministers, he went with them through numerous external acts of devotion ; while in the adyta of his mansion, Jesuits and other Papists sat in secret conclave, organizing the approaching movement which was to be consummated in the blood of Raleigh, Cobham, Cecil, Stanhope, Northumberland, and, if the necessity should arise, of the old Queen herself.

Blinded by their own confidence, the conspirators persuaded themselves that they carried on their operations as unnoticed as if they had possessed Gyges' ring. They forgot the sharp-sightedness of gold. Through the thick walls of Essex House the Government clearly saw their doings, and took measures which ought to have prevented the explosion of their madness. Before it was yet too late, Raleigh, knowing his cousin, Ferdinando Gorges, to be among the conspirators, sent him word that he desired to speak with him alone on the river, after which, not doubting that the gallant soldier would accept his invitation, he got into a wherry, and pushed towards Essex Stairs. This was on the fatal Sunday morning which had been chosen for the attempted insurrection ; Gorges disclosed Raleigh's desire to Essex, who in furtherance of the design of his bloody father-in-law, bade him go ; the meeting took place on the river, where Raleigh counselled him "to depart the town presently, or else he would be sent to the Fleet." Whereupon he replied, " Tush, Sir Walter, this is not a time for going to the Fleet ; get you back to the court, and that with speed, for you are like to have a bloody day of it. Whereupon Sir Walter again advised him to come forth from that company ; and then Sir Ferdinando shoved off the boat wherein Sir Walter then was, and bade him hie him hence—which he did, perceiving a boat to come out of Essex Stairs, wherein were three or four of the Earl of Essex's servants with pieces, who had in charge either to take or kill Sir Walter Raleigh upon the water."* On the same errand as that of Raleigh, Egerton, Lord-keeper, Popham, Lord Chief Justice, and Knollys. the Queen's Chamberlain, went from the Government to Essex House, in the hope of stifling the insurrection in its birth. The gates, however, had no sooner been swung open than the three peaceful envoys, on stepping into the court, found themselves in a throng of bravos and assassins, who with hoarse and threatening voices vociferated, " Kill them !" kill them !" By the leaders it was judged more politic to preserve their lives, at least for the moment, and to hold them as hostages. The massive gates were then once more thrown open, and out rushed the conspirators, in all about two hundred noblemen and gentlemen, in their doublets and hose, with rapier in one hand, and

* MS. State Paper Office.

pistol in the other. Making at once towards the City, they passed through Temple Bar, shouting as they went along that they were up for the defence of religion and liberty, against those who were plotting to sell England to the Infanta. Had it been hot weather, the contagion might have spread, but in that cold February morning their exclamations fell on deaf ears. Sheriff Smith having been deceived by Essex on the point of religion, had promised to join the conspirators with a body of citizens, but now found himself unable to keep his word. Everybody gazed in astonishment at Essex and his followers, as at a troop of brigands on the stage, whom it would have been madness to join. In vain they flourished their rapiers—in vain Essex harangued from a balcony—in vain he repeated the hackneyed falsehood, that his life was in danger from the daggers of Cobham, Cecil, and Raleigh : no one lent credence to what he uttered, no one sympathized with him, or raised an arm in his defence. It was soon perceived, therefore, that the game was lost, and the conspirators turning round, retraced their steps towards Essex House. Several of those who would not rise for them now rose against them—their retreat was attempted to be cut off—a fight ensued between them and their expected friends, in which Sir Christopher Blount, striking right and left, killed one of the assailants, but was at length disarmed, and conveyed, covered with wounds, to a place of safe custody. Essex escaped, and reached his own house by water.

Under no possible circumstances could the Earl have succeeded; Raleigh at the head of his soldiers guarded the palace; at Charing Cross and other passages through Westminster barricades were thrown up, while Nottingham, Cumberland, Grey, and other faithful noblemen were ready at all points to defend the Queen.* Essex himself, whatever show of valour he might have made on other occasions, exhibited none now. He was neither a Catiline nor a Pisistratus, to both of whom he was at the time compared, having neither the craft of the one nor the courage of the other. When Nottingham, therefore, dragging with him along the Strand a number of great guns, presented himself before the gates, and threatened, in case of resistance, to blow up Essex House, the rebellious Earl surrendered, and at three o'clock in the morning of the 9th, was, together with the earls of Rutland, Southampton, and Lord Sandys, conveyed to the Tower by his captor and Sir Thomas Garratt. Several of his accomplices, as the Lord Cromwell, Lord Monteagle, and Sir Charles Danvers, were on the afternoon of the same day conducted to the old fortress by Sir Walter Raleigh.†

The insurrection having been thus suppressed, the

* Birch, ii., 469. Cecil to Sir G. Carew. State Paper Office.
† MS. dated February 19th, 1601. State Paper Office.

eddies of danger might have been no longer supposed to revolve around Elizabeth—but she was never so near her death—the assassin Lea, to whom I have already alluded, now formed the design of delivering Essex and his accomplices from the Tower by means which would hardly have suggested themselves to any but an insane brain. Six ruffians were to meet about the close of evening at the door of the Queen's private apartment; to stab or otherwise dispose of the guard on duty, to rush into her chamber, seize upon her person, and by threats of instant death, to extort from her a warrant for the release of the prisoners. Experience had not revealed to them the character of the Tudor, who would have suffered herself to be cut to pieces in her chair rather than yield to men and menaces so base. Finding no seconds to his infamous purpose, Lea resolved to attempt the execution of it himself. Accordingly, repairing one night about nine o'clock to Whitehall, he succeeded in entering the palace as far as the lobby, from which there was a direct entrance to Elizabeth's chamber. How he acted the guard Poyntz, who encountered him there, shall describe: coming in out of the presence chamber, Lea, he says, " went to the further side of the lobby towards the privy chamber, yet stayed before he came to the door, and leaned his back against the closet, to which place I came also, and leaned my back as he did between him and the privy chamber door. He saluted me by name, and I him again, but methought his manner of usage towards me was very strange, for he moving himself near to me, did lean so hard towards me as he could, and looked earnestly upon me with a stern countenance; his colour very pale, yet so sweating, that many drops of sweat appeared on his face. After referring to the affair of the previous Sunday, Lea asked, 'Is not her Majesty at supper?' and I answered, that she was not; he paused awhile, and then asked 'Are not the lords yet come home?'"

The ruffian, it is evident, meant the worst, but being seized by paroxysms of terror, which paled his face and chilled his blood, could not screw up his courage to attempt at once the Queen's life. What he wanted was to incense the soldier to draw upon him, which might have seemed to justify his drawing also; a scuffle would have then ensued, in which he doubtless hoped to kill or disarm his antagonist, and then there would be nothing to prevent the carrying out of his design. The soldier's patience, however, proved more than a match for Lea's insolence: neither hustling nor thrusting could provoke him to draw his sword.

For the attempt thus made, Captain Thomas Lea, it is well known, was arrested, tried, and hung at Tyburn.

Upon Cecil and his friends now devolved the responsibility of dealing with the captive earl and his associates. To the offence they had committed, the punishment affixed by the law was death, though, owing to the relations in which the chief criminal had stood to the Queen, it was doubted whether her resolution to inflict the penalty would hold. This was a period of extreme peril to Raleigh. Essex had charged him with intent to murder; had put forward that intent as the cause of his rising in arms, and having thus pledged himself by word and deed to the truth of his accusations, it was not doubted that under any circumstances he would pursue the quarrel to its worst issues. At court, in the church, in the country, the offender's friends were numerous; his relatives also were high in power, and abounded with opulence; above all, the Queen herself, who constituted the mark shot at by his guilt, was connected with him by blood, and by other ties still stronger. For all these reasons it seemed not improbable that a course of leniency might be pursued, in which case the lives and fortunes of all who had reason to fear his after-vengeance would be compromised.

Cecil, though not wanting in courage, was less distinguished for that quality than for craft and caution. None better than he understood Elizabeth's nature, her yearning towards her kindred, her sudden changes of humour, her placability towards those whom she loved, her anxiety to avoid the charge of substituting vindictiveness for justice.   Considerations based on these facts might, it appeared to Raleigh, check the Secretary's ardour midway and betray him into a line of conduct fraught with ruin to himself and his friends.   Among writers who have undertaken to pronounce on the merits of this case there are not a few who shrink from according their full approval to the course that Raleigh now took; they forget who and what he was—forget that in force, breadth, and elevation of intellect he never perhaps had any equal among Englishmen—forget that he saw clearly the menacing front of danger which met his eye on almost every side, and that the study of his own position forced upon him the conviction, that by one path only, and that narrow and slippery, could he discern the least chance of escape for himself and those who acted with him.

So hemmed round by circumstances, he determined to act in conformity with the dictates of his intellect, at whatever decision his contemporaries or posterity might arrive.   To preserve Cecil from the wavering which he felt would be fatal to them both, he laid before him arguments the force of which no logic could parry :—

"I am not wise enough," he says, "to give you advice ; but if you take it for a good counsel to relent towards this tyrant, you will repent it when it shall be too late.   His malice is fixed, and will not evaporate by

any of your mild courses; for he will ascribe the alteration to her Majesty's pusillanimity, and not to your
good-nature, knowing that you work but upon her
humour, and not out of any love toward him. The less
you make him, the less he shall be able to harm you
and yours, and if her Majesty's favour fail him, he will
again decline to a common person. For after-revenges,
fear them not; for your own father was esteemed to be
the contriver of Norfolk's ruin, yet his son followeth
your father's son and loveth him. Humours of men
succeed not, but grow by occasions and accidents of
time and power. Somerset made no revenge on the
Duke of Northumberland's heirs—Northumberland that
now is thinks not of Hatton's issue. Kellaway lives
that murdered the brother of Horsey; and Horsey
let him go by all his lifetime. I could name you a
thousand of those, and therefore after-fears are but
prophecies, or rather conjectures from causes remote:
look to the present, and you do wisely. His son shall
be the youngest earl of England but one, and if his
father be now kept down, Will Cecil shall be able to
keep as many men at his heels as he, and more too.
He may also match in a better house than his, and so
that fear is not worth the fearing. But if the father
continue, he will be able to break the branches, and
pull up the tree, root and all. Lose not your advantage;
if you do, I read your destiny.

"Let the Q. hold Bothwell while she hath him, he will ever be the canker of her estate and safety. Princes are lost by security and preserved by prevention. I have seen the last of her good days, and all ours after his liberty.

"Yours, &c.,

"W. R."*

This letter has been variously interpreted, some affecting to believe that the earl's death was not urged, while others, with whom I agree, maintain that Raleigh argued for nothing less. In periods of violence, when the leaders of adverse factions have no choice left but to kill or be killed, the supreme law of nature determines their decision. Essex had long made it evident what fate he would assign to Raleigh should he ever acquire over him the power of life and death; and therefore Raleigh acted as a man instinctively acts towards the assassin whose dagger is at his breast. This must be his defence if he need any.

On the 19th of February Essex's trial took place in Westminster Hall, before twenty-five peers, with Buckhurst as Lord High Steward. His defence was as weak as it was false; he was sentenced to death, and being conveyed back to the Tower, was ordered to prepare for execution. He now retracted the charges against

* Murdin, Burleigh State Papers, p. 811.

Raleigh and Cobham which he had previously put forward as the causes which justified his insurrection. At his trial he expressed great contempt for death, but as the fatal hour drew near, his constancy deserted him, and he sank into a state of pusillanimous dejection. It is honourable to our nature, that sympathy with the fallen is almost universal among mankind, how guilty soever the sufferer may be. For Essex, extraordinary commiseration was felt; the people loved him for his pleasant countenance, winning manners, and easy affability towards all; even his enemies, now that he had been brought low, and lay at their mercy, shared the pity and unreasoning sorrow of the multitude.

We are all as familiar with death as we are with life; it is round about us at every moment, yet the preliminaries with their shadows and their mystery are sure, if we concentrate our looks on one who is dying, to sadden us profoundly. It is with a feeling, therefore, approaching disquietude or pain that we throw ourselves back to the evening of Shrove Tuesday, 1601, and read with Lord Thomas Howard, Lord Constable of the Tower, the following icy note from Cecil, preparing him for the reception of Essex's executioners:—

"Because we would fain have these two persons secretly conveyed into your Lordship's hands, and Mr. Lieutenant's within the Tower; where, when you have them, you are there to order them, and may with less suspicion make them provide their bloody tool, whereof I would there had never been occasion. We have sent these persons to you with Mr. Sheriff or his deputy: we send you two, because if one fail, the other may perform it to him, of whose soul, Almighty God have mercy. We will send you ere night some other directions; and her Majesty writes she will have seven or eight noblemen, named by her to be there, who shall bring our warrants to you; and therefore it is fit you leave some officer at the gates in the morning early to let them in, as also to let in some couple of divines who shall come with our letter or the Archbishop of Canterbury.

" Your loving friend,

" ROBERT CECIL."*

Soon after one o'clock in the morning, Essex was warned by the Lieutenant of the Tower to prepare for death. As the chill grey light of a February dawn broke over London, the lords Cumberland, Hertford, Darcy, Morley, Compton, and Byndon, who with the constable, Lord Thomas Howard, were to witness the execution, presented themselves at the Tower gate. About two hundred knights and gentlemen, actuated by various motives, likewise obtained admittance. Then

---

* Letter for the execution of my Lord of Essex, February 21st, 1601. State Paper Office.

at the head of a section of the guard came Sir Walter Raleigh, whose duty it was on such occasions to keep order and overawe the crowd.

The scaffold stood in the high court, above Cæsar's Tower, four feet high, and in breadth three feet, railed with small poles—the block was a piece of wood some half a foot over, and half a yard long, rounded at the upper side. The spectators sat on a form three feet from the scaffold; Essex, who wore a black-wrought velvet gown, and black satin suit, laid his head upon the block, being neither bound nor blindfolded. He cried with a loud strong voice: " Lord, into thy hands I commend my spirit!" not moving, though the executioner performed his office badly, in giving three blows.* At the last moment the Earl expressed a wish to speak and be reconciled with Raleigh, who had retired into the Armoury, whence in an agony of tears he saw without being seen; but no one conveyed to him the dying man's message, so that it was not until the moment of mutual forgiveness had gone for ever that he learned the desire of his adversary to die in peace with him.

---

* MS. State Paper Office. Compare Mr. Dixon's account of the treason and death of Essex. 'Story of Lord Bacon,' 4th edition, pp. 133—181.

CHAPTER XXI.

FINAL ECLIPSE OF HIS FORTUNES.

AFTER Essex's execution the trials of his friends followed rapidly, and they were successively dismissed to their account with little ceremony, and less pity.* Through Raleigh's interference two of the conspirators—Sir Edward Baynham and Mr. Lyttleton—were pardoned; but in conformity with the custom then prevalent, Raleigh stooped to accept money for exerting his influence with the Queen, and received, it is said, no less than ten thousand pounds from Lyttleton.

It has often been argued that the death of Essex proved fatal to Raleigh, who began, we are told, to foresee the ruin it was to bring upon him as he returned home from the Tower in his barge. But may not this be throwing too much subtlety into the reading of history? Had Essex lived, and been restored to favour, Raleigh's

* Birch, ii., 492.

lease of life would certainly have been short. It is possible that had the Earl not gone to Ireland, or engaged in a course of Scottish intrigue, his power at court might have sufficed to balance that of the Cecils', and thus have given Raleigh the opportunity of being a perpetual mediator between the parties. This position was of course rendered unnecessary by his overthrow, which may, therefore, have proved prejudicial to that extent; but, as will presently appear, the source of Raleigh's misfortunes lay in the union of Essex's surviving friends with Cecil, and those who favoured the Scottish succession.

Raleigh, as we are told by Bacon, used to say that the women about the Queen were like witches, who could do a great deal of harm but no good, and his own wife furnishes us, in a letter, with an illustration of this truth. Elizabeth, though she had taken Raleigh himself into favour, had never forgiven poor Bessy Throgmorton, who was incessantly made the butt at which calumny shot its arrows. We hear much of the Queen's discernment and knowledge of mankind, which, however, by no means included a knowledge of women, since she allowed some of the worst of her sex to hover about her, and libel the best. Thus we find Lady Kildare, an audacious intriguante, not only in high favour, but able, by malicious slanders, to inflict pain and injury on others.

"I understand," says Lady Raleigh, "that this is thought by my Lady Kildare that you should do me that favour as to let me know how unfavourable she hath dealt with me to the Queen. It is true that I should not have mistrusted so unhonourable a thought in her to me without good proof; but I protest, as you know, I never understood it by you; neither did I ever see or hear from you, since her Ladyship did me that good office; therefore, it was but her mistaking, which she useth too much. I only say this, that for the honour I bear her name, and for the ancient acquaintance of her, I wish she would be as ambitious to do good as she is adapted to the contrary. Thus ever wishing you all honour,

"I rest your assured poor friend,

"E. RALEIGH."*

Outwardly, Elizabeth bore up bravely against the effect produced upon her mind by the execution of Essex, though inwardly fed upon by the vulture that never ceased to prey upon her spirits till she was laid among her ancestors in Westminster Abbey:† yet, in the hope that by change of scene and the bustle of travel she might shake off the load which weighed upon her heart, she undertook a progress to the

---

* Lady Raleigh to Cecil, March, 1601. Burleigh Papers. B. M.
† See her Confessions to Beaumont. Birch, ii., 505.

southern coast, and was at Basing when Henri IV. arrived at Calais.* His object in this visit was to watch the movements of Cardinal Albert, then with a formidable army before Ostend. Desirous of maintaining a good understanding with the French king, Elizabeth sent over to him Sir Thomas Edmondes, charged to express her friendly feelings.† In return for this compliment, Henri despatched Marshal Biron. with a suitable retinue, to England; but instead of making their way to the Queen at Basing, the Frenchmen repaired to London, where, not being expected, no preparations had been made for their reception. By mere accident Raleigh, just then arrived in town, and learning how matters stood with Biron and his suite, took some pains to blunt the edge of their disappoint-

* Camden, 'Annals of Elizabeth,' ii., 642.

† Henri, however, either could not or would not repress the inclination of his Catholic subjects to vent their rancour against Elizabeth. In March, 1602, a species of tragedy, representing the death of Mary Queen of Scots, was brought upon the stage by certain low actors, which the English ambassador caused to be suppressed. Winwood, i., 398. A few months later, a new attack upon Elizabeth was meditated by some Italian performers, who covered the walls of Paris with placards, announcing their intention to bring forward a piece entitled " L'histoire Angloise contre la Reine d'Angleterre;" but Winwood stopped the play, and caused some of the principal actors to be imprisoned, though the Council objected to him that Elizabeth had allowed the performance of two pieces offensive to France,—"The Duke of Guise," and "The Massacre of St. Barthélemi."—Winwood, however, replied, that this was previous to the accession of Henri IV. Id. 425.

ment. By way of filling up the interval till horses could be procured, Raleigh took Biron and his friends to see the monuments in Westminster Abbey, and afterwards entertained them with an exhibition of brutality in the bear-garden, which, he says, "they took great pleasure to see."[*] When the post received the orders, without which they could not take up horses, the ambassador left London, and resting one night at Bagshot, arrived next day at Lord Sandys' mansion, " The Vine," where, on horseback in the park, Biron had his first audience of Elizabeth.

Some French historian alluded to, but not named by Camden, relates certain startling particulars respecting this visit. Elizabeth, according to that writer, carried about with her, by way of a keepsake, Essex's skull, which she exhibited to Biron, indulging at the same time in violent denunciations of his offences. She likewise intrusted him with a message of harsh counsel to Henri, pressing upon him the necessity of eschewing clemency in his treatment of rebels.[†]

The French noblemen and gentlemen, laying aside

* Raleigh to Cecil, September 6th, 1601. ' Burleigh Papers.' B. M.

† In Biron's case Henri certainly displayed no clemency. He was executed July 31st, 1602, in the court of the Bastille, where he fought with the executioner, and was at length cut down when in a state of extreme fury. To palliate this barbarity, Henri accused his victim of having slain five hundred persons in cold blood, and other enormities. Winwood, i., 427.

their usual style of foppery, appeared in sober black; and accommodating himself to their humour, Raleigh rode to London, got his tailor to make him a dress of black taffeta, and soon showed himself among the foreign gallants at "The Vine" as lugubriously habited as the best of them.

It was Elizabeth's wish that Lord Cobham, who probably spoke French fluently, should accompany Biron to Calais; but preferring the pleasures and gaieties of Bath, his Lordship felt strongly disinclined to accept the mission. Knowing how much any show of unwillingness on his part would grieve the Queen, Raleigh pressed him to comply: "I, that knew your Lordship's resolution when we parted," he says, "cannot take on me to persuade you; I will only say this much, it is but a day and a half journey hither; the Queen will take it exceeding kindly, and believe herself more beholding unto you than you think. The French tarry but two or three days at most. I will presently return to Bath with your Lordship. . . . . . It were long to tell the Queen's discourse with me of your Lordship, and pending it, I durst not say that I knew you were resolved not to come, but left it to the estate of your body. I need not doubt but that your Lordship will be here, yet I wish you to hold such a course as may best fit your honour and your humour together. If you come she will take it most kindly; if you come not, it shall be handled as you will have it."*

About this time the report of an expected invasion by Spain was once more spread, to end, as on former occasions, in nothing. Raleigh, when he heard of it, lay ill at Sherbourne, which set aside his intended visit to Cobham at Bath. He held still with Cecil a half-jocular correspondence, which wore the appearance of amity; dismissing the subject of the Armada, he says:—"I have by this bearer sent you the gloves; but it is intended that if they serve not your own hands, you must of your grace return them again." To inspire in Cecil the persuasion of a special preference, he afterwards adds: "Bess says that she must envy any fingers whatsoever that shall wear her gloves but your own."†

From the easy tone of familiarity observable in these letters, as well as from a variety of other circumstances, the inference might have been drawn that Raleigh and Cecil at least pulled the same way in politics; yet secretly it was otherwise. Owing, as he did, everything to the Queen, Raleigh, with an inexplicable lack of prudence, seems to have allowed the measure of her days to bound his horizon; whereas Cecil, though he

---

* Raleigh to Cobham, September 12th, 1601. 'Burleigh Papers.' B. M.

† Raleigh to Cecil, September 19th. 'Burleigh Papers.' B. M.

owed her no less, immediately upon Essex's overthrow, began to build up a new place of refuge for the future.

I have said that Essex's partizans, looking about for fresh engagements, betook themselves, not to Raleigh, but to the Secretary, who, wrapped in the mantle of impenetrable selfishness, cherished no enmities or friendships which appeared likely to interfere with his interests.

Among the Earl's forlorn clients was that notorious "ranter" Lord Henry Howard, whom all honest persons mistrusted, whom nobody loved, and who in the sequel proved a much greater miscreant than they who now thought worst of him could have believed. Nevertheless, Cecil soon made up his mind to employ him. Though Elizabeth was growing old in years, her fierce passions had done more for her than time; and Cecil, who watched her with the eyes of a lynx, detected all the noiseless footsteps of decay, whether in body or mind. Sentiment was out of the question with him. His worship was for the gods who had most to give, or who seemed likely to be longest in power. There can scarcely be a doubt that he carefully passed in array before his mind all the competitors for the succession—The Infanta, Arabella Stuart, James—and satisfying his mind that, upon the whole, the last was most likely, he determined, with due caution, to take the necessary steps towards an approximation to him.

Raleigh, Cobham, Northumberland, whom, in secret conclave, the "ranter" called a triplicity, were to be kept in ignorance of his northern tendencies; intelligence of which Howard, with the halter about his neck, undertook to make known beyond the Border. No date can be assigned to the first advance in this treasonable movement, which, like dawn on the Alps, first touched one elevation, then another; passing from Essex to his sisters, from his sisters to Lord Rich, from Lord Rich to Howard, from Howard to Cecil, till a long trail of glittering baseness could be traced from Richmond to Falkland.

It will be remembered that when Raleigh returned from Cadiz in 1596, he found that a trial pending when he left, between him and his former steward, Meeres, had during his absence been decided against him. The intricacies of this Meeres' affair are all but inscrutable; whether in success or failure, in favour or out of favour, at the head of a fleet, in the effervescence of court gaiety, or in the stagnant gloom of the Tower, Raleigh is still followed by the shadow of Meeres. At first he evokes him like a baleful exhalation from the Dorsetshire soil, develops his talent for business, intrusts him with the management of his property, awakens his yearning for wealth, and then hopes for gratitude. He had studied Machiavelli to very little purpose. The higher Meeres rose, the higher he wished to rise; and as he could do this at no one's expense so easily as at Raleigh's, he naturally took the most obvious course; and having entered on the career of a reckless pettifogger, laboured to strengthen himself against the day when the unveiling of his roguery might place him in antagonism with his master.

Nothing in history is more common than men who make their way to distinction by fraud; but Meeres had the peculiar good luck to work his way up over a splendid ladder—Raleigh, Essex, Lady Walsingham, and her sisters. Upon the whole, the groundwork of his manœuvres, as unveiled by Raleigh, is dark, but dotted with glittering points, which will enable the reader to make out the map for himself. Through a series of circumstances into which it would be tedious to enter, he, from a trusted servant, became a subtle and inveterate enemy, and, with his whole kith and kin, devoted himself to the carrying on of hostilities against his former master. A history of this legal crusade would be as prolix and perhaps as interesting as the famous Beaumarchais trial; but I must for the present content myself with transcribing one letter on the subject from Raleigh to Cecil, which contains information of the most extraordinary kind. "It is true," he says, "that Meeres is bound to the good behaviour by Sir George Trencher, Sir R. Horsey, and three or four other justices of this shire, but the recognizance is not above forty pounds, the rest that are bound with him are two or three rogues of the county, and when a councillor's commandment is laid, it serveth always for a *supersedeas*, and did it not, yet by me no advantage shall be taken. That his wife is a kinswoman to my Lady of Essex it is true, she was a poor man's wife of this country, but too good for such a knave, and being a broke piece that I think her, or would have had none of this knave, hoping thereby to have him upheld by the Earl of Essex, took her; but the Earl did not make show to like Meeres, nor admit him to his presence, but it was thought that secretly he meant to have used him for some mischief against me; and if Essex had prevailed, he had him used for the counterfeiter, for he writes my hand so perfectly as I cannot any way discern the difference. My wife writes unto my Lady Walsingham touching Meeres, for he took into his house a sister of his wife's, who had some two hundred marks' portion, which the knave hath cozened her of, and turned her off a begging: now that sister being as dear to my lady as Meeres' wife, she cannot esteem such a knave, who, if he respected her, would not so abuse her sister as he hath, who being unmarried and begotten with child in his house, is now by him thus undone, cozened and cast off; besides, I hope that my Lady Essex cannot say but in matters of more importance, it hath pleased you and your friends to do her service since her lord's death; but howsoever it be, if you should not think it fit that he submit himself, having used towards me many more cozenings and villainies than ever Daniel did to my Lady Essex, I shall be contented with your orders therein, and dare make my Lady of Essex judge in the cause. Meeres hath sent down sixteen subpœnas to me and other poor men since he was committed."*

The shadows, as we advance, close in more thickly about Elizabeth, and in the same proportion about Raleigh, for the thread of his good fortune, though not of his life, was interwoven closely with her existence. Cecil's star was in the ascendant, and there was an air of confidence in his bearing which they who knew nothing of what was transacting behind the scenes found it impossible to account for. Nowhere in history has the truth made itself more apparent, that greatness is often found to be no match for crafty littleness. Cecil, who soared over Bacon's head, likewise soared over Raleigh's, because there was no moral repugnance in his nature to employ any means which promised to attain the end he aimed at. His power was built on Elizabeth's weakness, of which he skilfully took advantage in those innumerable conferences which he enjoyed through the necessities of his place. Raleigh came to her more seldom, and often about unpleasant affairs,

* Add. MSS. 6177, p. 187, September 25th, 1601.

such as the designs of the Spaniards,* the struggles
going on in Ireland,† the raising of money, the restrictions to be put by policy on the freedom of trade.

In the autumn of 1601,‡ Elizabeth stood for the last
time face to face with her parliament, and connected
with this meeting there were circumstances which
rendered it peculiarly memorable and melancholy.
Her sensibilities were keenly alive, but her frame was
wasted, and her strength failing fast. Men viewed her
according to their leanings, with a throb of anxiety, or
with a sentiment of impatience. Let us accompany
her on her farewell visit to St. Stephens: being in the
House of Lords, and making her way towards the throne,
her knees tottered, and she would have fallen had not
two gentlemen stepped forward and supported her
while she ascended. Lord-keeper Egerton, in the
speech he then delivered, made one of those strange
allusions which sounded like a passage of a funeral
oration:—"I have seen her Majesty wear at her girdle,"
he said, " the price of her own blood; I mean jewels
that have been given to her physicians to have that
done unto her which God will ever keep her from; but
she hath worn them rather in triumph—though for the
price, that hath not been valuable."§

* Add. MSS. 6177, p. 201, October, 1601.
† Ibid., October 15th, 1601.
‡ October 27th, 1601. D'Ewes, Journal, p. 620.
§ Townshend, 'Last Four Parliaments of Elizabeth,' p. 130.

' The House having been adjourned, the Queen, with what feelings we may in part conjecture, descended from the throne and, "after room made, came through the Commons to go into the Painted Chamber, who graciously offering her hand to the Speaker, he kissed it, but not one word she spoke unto him, neither as she went through, few said, 'God bless your Majesty!' as they were wont in all great assemblies. And the throng being great and little room to pass, she moved her hand to have more room, whereupon one of the gentlemen ushers said openly, 'Back, masters, make room,' and one answered stoutly behind, 'If you will hang us, we can make *no more room;*' which the Queen seemed not to hear, though she heaved up her head, and looked that way towards him that spake. After she went to Whitehall by water."*

Raleigh in this parliament represented Cornwall. The questions which then came before the House were important and difficult, descending by various ways into the arena of political economy, and taxing all the energies of powerful minds, as yet unversed in its subtle mysteries. They were called on to determine how far the right of exportation ought to be extended, and where it should be stopped by considerations of State. It fell to their lot also to decide when the two branches of the legislature were brought into collision how the

* Townshend, p. 179.

contest should be carried on, and which should give way. The privilege of parliament had remained up to that time undefined, sometimes giving way before authority, sometimes venturing to assert the sacredness of its power, and referring obscurely to the great well-spring from which it was afterwards to derive supplies so profuse of authority and influence. Some alarm was felt and expressed by Cecil at the evident determination of the popular House to overstep the limits of its ancient practice, and interfere with matters supposed to lie beyond its competence, which he denominated a disputatious spirit. Afterwards, when the Commons took views different from those of the Lords—when he himself represented and interpreted the ideas of the body to which he belonged—he found it necessary to use some roughness with the peers in order to bring them to their senses. The occasion was this: having listened to the reasons of the Lower House, arranged and delivered by Cecil, Buckhurst, the Lord-treasurer, pronounced the views of the Speaker to be strange, improper, and preposterous. The Commons retired, Cecil harangued upon the insult, and was then sent back to point out to the peers the offence they had offered to the people's representatives. Cecil, keen, cool, and full at the same time of indignation, suggested by his language far more than he expressed, and wrought so salutary an effect on his hearers, that after humming and murmuring together for some time, they retreated from their position, and virtually acknowledged themselves to be in the wrong.

In a subsequent debate, when the House was clearing for a division, several members who desired not to vote at all made towards the door, when Mr. Dale, observing a friend in the retreating crowd, seized him by the sleeve and pulled him back, that he might afford his support to Dale's party. This gave rise to a fierce altercation, and several were inclined to censure very severely the member who had thus, according to their notions, interfered with the freedom of others. Raleigh, however, remarked aloud that he could not join with those who blamed the action, since he himself had often done the same; the Comptroller declared it was a heinous offence, and that the member who had been guilty of it, meaning Mr. Dale, ought to be called to the Bar of the House. Cecil, who with many others mistook the Comptroller's meaning, and thought he shot at Raleigh, said it would be most unseemly to have a gentleman of his place and quality called to speak at the Bar, by which the House was thrown into so great an uproar that it may almost be said to have resembled the French Convention during the stormy days of the Revolution.

While such was the aspect presented by the surface of affairs, the mysterious undercurrents to which I have alluded were constantly widening and running with greater violence northwards. Shortly after the execution of Essex, James, who had been at first restrained by fear of the disclosures which might have been made during the Earl's trial, despatched two embassies to England, both furnished with secret instructions, but aiming at different objects. The Earl of Mar and Edward Bruce, afterwards Lord Kinloss, were intrusted with the development of his secret designs; while the Duke of Lennox, a person of upright character, may be said to have had a mission of compliments.

Raleigh, Cobham, Northumberland, and their friends had been represented to James by Essex first, afterwards by Cecil and Howard, as men of desperate character, entirely hostile to his claims. But might not his informants have ends of their own to answer, prejudicial to his interests? He would send and see. Conscious of cherishing purposes which he dared not avow, he desired to discover whether or not suspicions of their real nature were entertained beyond the Border. In heart he was ready to become the Macbeth to a female Duncan; he could joke with assassins, suggest without betraying himself the work expected of them, and then insinuate how the wretches were to be dealt with; he could intrigue with priests and Jesuits, and arrange for a rising in conjunction with them in case of necessity; he could skilfully direct his agents to scatter firebrands among the multitude, or insinuate menaces at court against all such as opposed his succession, while they avoided advancing so far as to put themselves within swing of the axe.

Few transactions in our history open up to investigation a more obscure maze than the dealings now carried on between James and his dupes in England. Elizabeth, he perceived, through weakness partly, partly through weariness of life,* had allowed Cecil to become king there in effect, so that without purchasing his co-operation or putting him out of the way, his policy must encounter insurmountable obstacles. That he would have experienced no repugnance to have had recourse to the second alternative may be inferred from the assassination of Gowry; and that Lord Henry Howard would joyfully have become his coadjutor, the affair of Overbury may suffice to convince us. Cecil's murder was rendered unnecessary by the readiness he showed to become James's instrument and by his malevolent solicitude to vindicate to himself pre-eminence in baseness.

During two years James's accomplices at the English court compassed round Elizabeth with a girdle of fawning and treachery, maligning and neutralizing the influence of all such as might have opened her eyes; while with masterly craft and cunning they shaped the

* 'Secret Correspondence,' p. 6.

circumstances of the situation into conformity with the wishes of the Stuart. There were numerous competitors for the credit of these doings: Essex's sisters, Penelope and Dorothy, Cobham's intriguing wife, the Countess of Kildare, the Careys, male and female, the Earl of Nottingham, and Lord Thomas Howard, who all with more or less forwardness paid their devotions to the rising sun. The acrimony and hate by which the movements of Lord Henry and Cecil were directed appear at times to transcend the bounds of sanity. Yet motives for their conduct may be discerned. In splendour of appearance, in dignity of manners, in courage, in breadth and elevation of views, in eloquence, in intellect, Cecil inwardly recognised the superiority of Raleigh, and could not doubt that if he were allowed to bring to bear all these qualities and attributes upon the mind of James, the result would be absolute domination. The course dictated by such a conviction was obvious, and he resolved to pursue it. In Lord Henry the predominant sentiment was an unquenchable aversion for everything great or good, or a love of evil for its own sake. In this odious category he delighted to involve his whole kith and kin, maintaining that Nottingham would with more pleasure direct his great guns against Durham than he had against Essex House, and that the entire Howard family were actuated by the same feelings.

The means by which this treasonable correspondence was carried on indicate the consummate skill of the chief actor. When the letters left London, they followed no certain route, proceeding sometimes to Ireland, sometimes to France, sometimes to the western coast of Scotland, but always reaching Falkland or Holyrood without mischance. Yet there were various layers, so to speak, of agents and emissaries through whose hands they had to pass—spies upon spies—informers, assassins, some high, some low, English, Irish, Scotch, all governed by one motive which kept them steady in their treachery—the belief that when what they called "The Great Day"[*] should arrive, James's gratitude would be commensurate with their services.

Even upon Elizabeth's mind the hostile acts of Cecil were not without effect. Raleigh already found himself beginning to stand more and more in the shade; James had commissioned the Duke of Lennox to make an attempt upon his loyalty, a fact which Cecil interpreted into evidence that there existed some reasons for believing that loyalty to be incomplete. On this ground he counselled the man whom he still outwardly treated as a friend not to make known the circumstance to the Queen, who, he affirmed, would assuredly regard him as a mere pick-thank.[†]

* 'Secret Correspondence,' p. 8.   † Ibid., p. 48.

Cecil himself meanwhile walked every hour along the edge of a precipice. One day upon Blackheath, while driving with the Queen in her carriage, a courier rode up to the window with a packet containing secret letters from Scotland. Elizabeth asked to see them. Cecil felt a choking sensation as of the tightening of a rope about his neck; he would, however, make an effort to save his life :—" There may, please your Majesty, be infection in these papers," he said. " Permit me to step out and purify them in the open air before they touch your Majesty's hands." Elizabeth's eagle eye was upon him; still, with the dexterity of one who had performed a thousand acts of guilt and cunning, he contrived to extract the treasonable missive, after which the packet was submitted to the Queen.

As men approach the crisis of their fate they sometimes become conscious by instinct, rather than by foresight, that the cloud which is big with their destiny, though not yet visible, is nevertheless surging up towards the horizon. Under the weight of this presentiment Raleigh's mind was now bowed down. He was indeed liable throughout his career to the depressions and uprisings incident to a powerful and buoyant spirit, more addicted, however, upon the whole, to cheerfulness than gloom. But his hours were dark now; the dawn of his trials was breaking upon him; concern for his wife and son began to mingle with his public cares; he

learned to look upon his castles, his manors, his lord-
ships, his patents, his offices, as so many creations of a
desert mirage, and resolved to make an attempt, if his
overthrow should be sought, to provide himself with the
means of escape, or to realize something which he
might bequeath to his family. He was therefore disposed to listen to the counsel of Sir George Carew,
Governor of Munster, who, considering the troubled
state of Ireland, became convinced that an absentee
landlord stood little chance of realizing an adequate
income from his estate, since even resident landlords
were often stripped of everything, and beheld the waves of
rebellion roll up triumphantly to the very gates of their
castles. Richard Boyle, afterwards Earl of Cork, now
desired to become the purchaser of Raleigh's Irish
estate, and obtaining letters of introduction from Carew,
came over to England, saw Raleigh, and after the
necessary preliminaries, the transaction was completed
in the summer of 1602.

The event was now fast approaching by which
Raleigh's prosperity was to be finally eclipsed. Elizabeth, assailed at once by disease and remorse, and bearing upon her shoulders the weight of seventy years,
now began to stagger under the burden and exhibit an
inclination to lay it down and be at rest. She had out-
lived most of her friends, as well as most of her enemies ;
her heart, peculiarly prone to love, in the attempt to

secure which she had wasted her life, was now scorched and withered, and stung incessantly by fatal remembrances; pomp and state and flattery found no longer a welcome or an echo in her breast; she looked forth cheerlessly upon the world, which every day was growing more cold and chill, and as she possessed a keen insight into human motives and conduct, perceived but too plainly how many of those about her were impatient of her peevishness and longing to exchange the relaxing grasp of her good old hand for the advantages and honours which they confidently expected from her successor.* Among this calculating herd Raleigh was not to be found. He had owed everything to Elizabeth, and almost seems to have determined that his own star should go out with hers, though his reason could not but be convinced that since the interests of others were bound up with his own he was constrained to make what preparations he could against the coming change.

Centuries have elapsed since the death of Raleigh's

* It had not yet been determined who that successor was to be, and prodigious efforts were made on the Continent to insure the election of some Catholic prince. If, says Father Cresswell, "the two principal personages (Henri IV. and Philip III.) persevere in their apparent union to promote this affair, it is now in a better condition than ever. If it be managed prudently, the result is unmistakeable, but both will lose much by allowing the opportunity to pass." *Varios puntos de los avisos que dio el Padre Creswelo relativos à la eleccion del nuevo Rey de Inglatiera, 28 de Abril, 1603. Simancas.*

queen, yet we are still unable correctly to estimate her character. We move through the chill of mighty shadows created by ourselves, and instead of seeking to disperse them, suffer them irresistibly to influence our judgment. Such as she was, however, when death seemed to be preparing to lay his icy hands upon her form, the heart of all England thrilled with anguish.* During the forty-five years of revolution which cast down for ever the power of Catholicism in England, and inaugurated the reign of free inquiry, she had stood at the head of the British monarchy, bubbling to the brim as she was with fierce Celtic blood, and maintaining her position with indomitable courage, yet all the while hardly knowing what she did, since the fangs of the old church still griped her conscience, and regulated much of her conduct and modes of thinking.

Her struggles, however, were internal, or known at best to a few intimate friends. In the eyes of the people she had always appeared to be the type and symbol of Protestantism, that is, absolute freedom of belief and speculation, and therefore they hailed her presence among them almost as that of a religious

---

* Writing only five months before Elizabeth's death, Beaumont says that she was not merely loved, but worshipped; that her eye was still lively, that she displayed much spirit, seemed attached to life, and took great care of herself. Raumer, ii., 184. By the following March an entire change had come over her, both in body and mind, and the task devolved on Beaumont of chronicling her rapid decline and death.

Saviour.   Here, then, was a motive more than sufficient to justify the passionate ardour with which men of true English blood, with Raleigh at their head, clung to the old Queen.   They watched her looks, they reckoned with profound perturbation the years she had lived, and the probability that she could not live many more ; yet it was only by degrees, with strange aversion and reluctance, that they gave credit to the reports of her failing health, which nevertheless became more frequent and alarming, issuing forth like black midnight from the palace, and falling like the first symptoms of plague upon the bewildered nation.

It was at Whitehall that the symptoms of her fatal malady first became visible, upon which, by the advice of her physicians, she removed to the milder air of Richmond.*   But the conflict going on within her was not so much with disease as with Nemesis.   Essex may not have deserved the regret she felt, but this did not prevent her feeling it.   His enemies were about her, Raleigh, Cecil, Cobham, and nearly all the members of her privy council, who had regarded the Earl as a state criminal, while Elizabeth regarded him in a different light.   They approved what had been done, her reason approved it too; but affection, which

* During the illness of the Queen several meetings (of the Catholics) took place, with the design of seizing upon the Council, and proclaiming Arabella.   Relacion de Antonio Dutton, 18 de Mayo, 1603.   Simancas.

dominates in woman to the last, would not, and did not, approve it.

What her outward bearing may have been signifies nothing—she could for a while act as others have acted, and did act so as to impose even on the observing—but the torrent of feeling became at length too strong to be stemmed, and Elizabeth, relinquishing the endeavour, sat in hopeless dejection upon the floor, refusing to be comforted by man or woman, rejecting food and physic alike, and resolving to expiate the offence she believed herself to have committed by a voluntary death. Messalina lying dejected and deserted, waiting for the executioner in the gardens of Rome, presents a far less touching spectacle than the great English Queen closing her glorious career by suicide,*

* Of the circumstances attending Elizabeth's voluntary death we have the following account from contemporaries:—" I had good means to learn how the world went, and find her disease to be nothing but a settled and confirmed melancholy, insomuch that she could not be won nor persuaded, neither by the council, divines, physicians, nor the women about her, once to taste or touch any physic, though ten or a dozen that were continually about her did assure her, with all manner of asseverations, of perfect and easy recovery if she would follow their advice." Chamberlain to Carleton, March 30th, 1603. State Paper Office. A French letter in the same collection, dated April 4th (N.S.), 1603, takes precisely the same view, and adds, by way of explanation, that she refused food and medicine,—" Comme si l'apprehension et mepris de sa vieillesse ou quelque autre ressentiment secret qui l'on attribue au regret de la mort du feu Comte d'Essex l'eussent émeué à la chercher ou desirer elle-même.

for her abstinence from all that might have preserved her amounts to no less. Around her flitted her courtiers like spectres, with their thoughts half at Richmond, half in Scotland—the honest and earnest entreating her to take food, and preserve a life on which their own in many cases depended—but she had played out her part, and determined to close it then. When all but insensible, she was lifted from the carpet, and placed on a bed, where by the clergy present her thoughts were sought to be directed towards another world. Some endeavoured to wring from her the name of the person whom she desired to be her successor, and by interpreting what she intimated by dumb show according to their own wishes, obtained the recognition of James Stuart.*

Then the spirit of the great Tudor departed, and one of her kinsmen,† who, as a distinguished writer‡ remarks, had been hovering like a raven about her death-bed, effected his escape from the palace, and fled northwards with the welcome tidings. Never more perhaps in the experience of this country shall the death-bed of a sovereign be contemplated with so much solicitude. Equal affection others may perhaps inspire, but many feared lest with Elizabeth the light of truth and free-

* Earl of Cork, ' Preface to Carey's Memoirs,' p. 17.
† Chamberlain, March 20th, 1603. State Paper Office.
‡ Sir Walter Scott. ' Notes on Earl of Cork's Preface to Carey's Memoirs,' p. 23.

dom should be put out, and the nation be forced back, as on the succession of her sister, through torrents of blood, to the hated creed of Hildebrand and Leo X.

Raleigh himself looked on his dying mistress with more anguish perhaps than any other man. No discovery hitherto made impeaches the sincerity of his love for that grand old woman, who though she had stinted the growth of his ambition, was nevertheless the author of his fortunes; and by her profuse bounty had enabled him to found, at the expense of a quarter of a million sterling, that commonwealth beyond the Atlantic which has bestowed his name on two of its cities, and with whose history his memory will be for ever united.

With Elizabeth a whole order of things, half barbarous, half heroic, passed away, and England was destined to put on a new face, sterner and more sanguinary, though stained at the outset by licentiousness and riot, by unexampled folly in the prince, by incredible meanness in the people, or at least in that portion of the people who, not preserved by Puritanism, flocked around the Merry Andrew who came from beyond the Tweed to replace the woman who for forty-five years had ranked foremost among the sovereigns of Europe.

From Richmond Elizabeth's remains were brought to London,* where for several days they lay in state at Whitehall, while the metropolis rang with proclamations

* "The Council went on Saturday to Richmond, and that night brought the corpse with an honourable attendance to Whitehall

of the new sovereign. Very slowly, however, did the melancholy news travel to the distant parts of England, no one having any interest, and few the inclination to enlighten the common people respecting their loss. Preparations were meanwhile made for the funeral, at which Raleigh may be said to have performed the last public act of his life. Of all who had been elevated to opulence and grandeur by the Queen, few perhaps now sorrowed for her loss ; but the people, in whom death had revived all their ancient loyalty, thronged about the cortège with sobs and tears,* thinking, as the writers express it, " that the brightest sun that ever shone in England had set." They were right. With her to her resting-place went the greatness and grandeur of the sixteenth century, the glory of our heroic age, which had accomplished for England more than was ever accomplished in a period of equal duration ;† which had given the country a new religion, which had

where the household remains. The body was not opened, but wrapt up in cere-cloths and other preservatives." Chamberlain to Carleton, March 30th, 1603. State Paper Office.

* Yet in 'Items of Intelligence,' forwarded to Spain by Father Creswell, a Jesuit, it is suggested, that the only token of sorrow manifested by those present was the mourning they wore. He adds, that never was sovereign less lamented. 'Varios Puntos,' &c., &c. Simancas.

† Mr. Froude points out the weak and divided state of England at Elizabeth's accession ; and Coke, giving the result of her long reign, describes its flourishing state at her death. ' Detection of the Court and State of England,' p. 29.

prepared it for a series of revolutions of unexampled importance, and inaugurated those movements, political and social, which are still in full activity, throbbing through the heart of society at home, agitating all Asia and America, and foreshadowing to thoughtful minds the advent of an order of things such as the modern world has never yet looked upon.

To herald her to her grave with becoming solemnity and gloom, the plague broke out, and filled the whole metropolis with terror, achieving for London what Herod projected for Jerusalem, when he shut up all the nobles in the Senate House, with orders that they should be slain as soon as he should breathe his last. Elizabeth had no desire to imitate such a policy, but nature did it for her, signalizing the extinction of the Tudor line and the accession of the Stuarts by one of the most fearful pestilences that ever desolated a civilized country. The streets, the public places, the churches, were black with mourning, to which a deeper sable would have been added could the people have foreseen what the prince, whose coming they now looked for, was to bring upon them and upon their children. Elizabeth was at peace, but had bequeathed to many among her faithful servants persecution, imprisonment, and the axe, whose edge already glittered in the atmosphere, and was soon to fall on many an innocent and noble neck.

CHAPTER I.

SECRET ENMITY OF JAMES.

No period of transition in our annals is so fraught with difficulties as that which takes us from our heroic age to the age of brass. Under the Tudor queen, if there was cruelty, there was likewise grandeur; barbarism masked itself in pomp—vice wore a glittering livery—and if chastity laid aside her girdle, it seemed to be with the unconscious recklessness of the world's infancy.

In little more than one revolution of the moon an entire change passed over the face of England. Had an army of locusts marched from the Tweed to the Land's End, devouring every green thing as it went, and leaving everything behind arid and withered, the metamorphosis could not have been more complete. All that was poetical, all that was chivalrous, all that was beautiful in the intellectual aspect of the nation vanished like a dream, to make way for coarseness, selfishness, and those hateful enormities which blasted the Cities of the Plain.*

It was in the midst of this new order of things that Sir Walter Raleigh found himself, when, having laid his great mistress in her tomb at Westminster Abbey, he returned with the other mourners, to breathe the biting air which had just begun to blow from the north.† Of two unpardonable offences he already stood accused: he was said to have advocated in council the establishment of a republic;‡ or, if that should be deemed premature, that articles might be insisted on limiting the number of followers to be brought by the Scottish king into England.§ James, whose political creed was that of a Turkish Sultan,‖ abhorred all men who talked of liberty, and resented the limitation proposed by Raleigh and Fortescue as an audacious interference

* Raumer, a writer of ability and moderation, says, ii., 191, " that the greatest favour historians can show James is to skip his reign, in order to arrive at the more attractive period of the Civil Wars; but it is in the events of his reign that we must seek the causes of those wars, so that we cannot bestow too much study on that revolting epoch."

† Nichols, ' Progresses,' iii., 626.

‡ Aubrey, ' Lives of Eminent Men,' ii., 515.

§ Osborne, ' Traditional Memoirs,' ii., 7.

‖ On his journey from Scotland to London, he ordered a poor pickpocket to be hung, without judge or jury, at Newark. Coke, p. 33.

with his prerogative. He lived long enough to regret[*] that their views had not been adopted, when shivering on the brink of that gulf into which his breechesless retainers afterwards hurled his son.

Had Raleigh profited more by the study of Machiavelli, the writing of his life might have been a pleasanter task. The simplicity with which he fell into Cecil's net is provoking. Had he allied himself with Dorothy, with Lady Kildare, or with any one else who would have broken the weasel's neck,[†] instead of representing his grand white head bent by despotism to the block, we might have had to relate a story of successful intrigue, terminating in a dukedom. But the hero of the narrative would not then have been Raleigh. We might have been amused by the farce, but should have missed the tragedy; while his name, instead of glittering like some bright particular star over the dark waste of James's reign,[‡] might have glimmered obscurely among those of the Cecils, the Northamptons, the Nottinghams, the Suffolks, and the Doncasters.

---

[*] The English, in fact, immediately began to betray signs of discontent: "The King brings with him," says Father Creswell, "thirteen of the principal men of Scotland, together with five hundred of his nation, which is a cause of some murmuring here." 'Varios Puntos de los Avisos,' &c. Simancas.

[†] 'Secret Correspondence,' p. 21.

[‡] Hume, 'History of England,' speaks of Raleigh as "the only man in the nation who had a high reputation for valour and military experience," vi. 99.

Elizabeth's obsequies being over, Raleigh made ready in his office as Captain of the Guard to move northwards, in order to bring home his new sovereign, which filled his enemies with uneasiness; for in spite of all that had been done to prejudice James against him, they feared that the fascination of manner which had enthralled Elizabeth's imagination might produce a similar effect upon that of her successor. To guard as far as possible against such a result, Lord Henry Howard hastened to Scotland, that, being constantly about the new king, he might enjoy a monopoly of slander. In spite, however, of this precautionary step to back up the calumnies of the 'Secret Correspondence,' Cecil's cowardly heart still quaked with terror, to lessen which Lord Kinloss, at the instance doubtless of Lord Henry, addressed him in the following language: "Cobham and Raleigh are forlorn in our accounts, and I beseech you think not that any subject in England is able to win ground in us to the least disgrace of Sir Robert Cecil, for we are exceeding far inamorat of him, and you shall acquaint such as you love of Essex's friends, that if any of them have such business in head, or mean to follow such a rout, it will turn them assuredly to their ruin, for this is settled in the heart of King James. This is only to yourself."*

To provide against all probable contingencies, James

* 'James's Correspondence with Cecil,' edited by Mr. Bruce, p. 51.

despatched to London a number of blank warrants, to be filled up and used by Cecil at his discretion. Early in April Raleigh received one of these, containing a prohibition of his journey to Scotland, from which he might have divined the sequel. Having now been joined by Kinloss, Cecil wrote, in concert with that courtier, a triumphant account of the insult they had offered Raleigh to Lord Henry, for James's satisfaction.

"We think it not amiss," he says, "to move your Lordship to acquaint his Majesty privately with the contents of a letter which we have been fain to commence on one of the blanks, for staying the Captain of the Guard, who would have carried most of them that would have left this place with him; from which being dissuaded now, he resolved to be gone, and hath induced a great many gentlemen to accompany him—whom only by his undertaking to do great things for them,"* . . . he persuaded, as I infer from the context, to follow him.

From London, which the rush of noblemen and gentlemen to Scotland had left almost like a deserted city, Raleigh, with his family and a number of private

---

* The letter, a rough copy, blurred and blotted, scarcely legible throughout, becomes altogether unintelligible after the words "to do great things for them," though the sense requires some such conclusion as I have suggested. The document is endorsed, "Minutes from my Master and the Lord Kinloss to the Lord Henry Howard." Signed by Mr. Somerset—April 9th, MS. State Paper Office.

friends, repaired to Bath; while Lord Cobham, to ascertain the position he might hope to occupy in the new reign, proceeded to Edinburgh. As his father had been secretly a favourer of James's mother, he expected a kind reception,* being ignorant of the devices by which his brother-in-law had blasted his hopes; but meeting with the reverse, he retraced his steps in sullen discontent.† By undertaking this journey unknown to Raleigh, he clearly evinced an inclination to follow separate courses, though the ill success of his mission threw him back upon his old policy.

What at this time were Raleigh's expectations, or what were the designs he framed, it is now impossible to conjecture: like Burleigh‡ and his son Robert, he may have been inclined at one time to advance the pretensions of Arabella Stuart, though if he ever cherished such an intention, he must have speedily relinquished it when he beheld the incredible enthusiasm which a majority of the English nobles displayed in favour of James. Still, circumstances pressed upon him the necessity of adopting some measures in self-defence, since, from the tone in which he had been addressed by Cecil and Kinloss, he could not avoid

* 'Court and Times of James I.,' i., 5.

† "Lord Cobham has returned from the King very much displeased." 'Varios Puntos de los Avisos.' Simancas.

‡ This may be clearly inferred from a letter of Charles Cavendish. Miss Costello, 'Lives of Eminent Englishwomen,' i., 209.

perceiving that he stood in much peril. He had good reason to know how fertile in artifices the mind of the Secretary was, and with what sanguinary fervour he was always ready to sacrifice those who stood in his way. Having never been skilful in gaining friends or multiplying partizans, Raleigh now found himself so destitute of supporters that he could reckon with confidence—a confidence which soon proved baseless—on no man of high rank except Cobham. Rendered uneasy by the length of his absence, he urged his joining him and Lady Raleigh in anxious and affectionate language. " Here we attend you," he says, " and have done this fortnight, and mourn your absence the rather because we fear your mind is changed. I pray you let us hear from you at least ; for if you do not, we will away sooner. My wife will despair ever to see you in these parts if you come not now—we can but long for you all our lives." *

Upon James's arrival Raleigh necessarily came to town, to attend on him in his office. Upon his first presentation the King, we are told, punning coarsely upon his name, which he knew not how to pronounce, exclaimed, " By my saul, maun, I have heard but rawly of thee !" † To express the scorn that filled

* Raleigh to Cobham, April 29th, 1603. MS. State Paper Office.

† Aubrey, ii., 515. The new King is showing great partiality for his nation, and it is understood that he will give the principal offices

Raleigh's mind at hearing himself addressed after such a fashion would transcend the power of language. He saw, however, at a glance, all the bearings of his situation, and felt that the circumstances of that situation would constrain him to suffer—

> " The insolence of office, and the spurns
> That patient merit of the unworthy takes."

Various reasons urged Cecil and the Howards to undermine Raleigh's credit with the King: first, they were apprehensive lest, if he had obtained any knowledge of their doings during the interregnum, he might reveal it, and thus effect their ruin; second, even should he find it impracticable to accomplish so much, he might yet so far eclipse them by his transcendent abilities as to throw their fortunes into the shade. No one has ever raised the veil from what took place in the interval between Elizabeth's death and the instalment of James in London. The crown-jewels, the plate of gold and silver, the money in the Treasury, the ornaments, dresses, trinkets, and other valuables heaped up in the various palaces—all lay at the mercy of a few favoured families during six whole weeks, and it was afterwards more than suspected that the opportunity had been

---

to his countrymen. He has manifested displeasure towards Sir Walter Raleigh, the Treasurer, Lord Cobham, and the Chancellor, who feel very much aggrieved. ' Varios Puntos de los Avisos.' Simancas.

turned to good account. Fifteen years later, when James had been partially enlightened by experience, he sought to extort from Raleigh evidence against the favourites of his accession,* who had enriched themselves by his plunder, and been suffered in some instances to sink into the grave unpunished.

Except the flash of vulgarity displayed in Raleigh's first reception by James, no indication of the hate he cherished escaped the royal dissembler for some time. The actors in the plot felt that there need be no hurry, because the prey was completely in their toils, which were not the less sure because they were invisible. Out of deference, probably, to public opinion, it was thought best to let Raleigh down gradually, as if the process were regulated, not by any previous design, but simply by occasion of circumstance. The plan may originally have been Cecil's, but, in addition to the King, several noblemen and gentlemen had long been associated in the enterprise. We have seen the assurances of Lord Kinloss to Cecil that the destruction of Cobham and Raleigh had been resolved upon by James and his Scottish advisers before the death of Elizabeth, probably even before the Secretary and Lord Henry commenced that series of calumnies the last link of which was intended to be death. Still James seems to have experienced peculiar satisfaction in practically illus-

* Chamberlain to Carleton, Oct. 24th, 1618. MS. State Paper Office.

trating to the few who understood him his proficiency in kingcraft, of which among all his qualities he was the proudest. He loved to play with the fish before he hooked it. Raleigh was therefore not only received at court, but encouraged to ride out and jest with his assassin; who, as he gazed at his magnificent figure, martial bearing, and countenance beaming with intellect, chuckled inwardly at his resolution to send him sooner or later to the block.

Raleigh soon discovered, probably without much surprise, that Erskine, one of the murderers of Earl Gowrie,* was to be substituted for him as Captain of the Guard, though, by way of a set-off, the three hundred a-year he had hitherto paid Lord Henry Seymour, out of his salary as Governor of Jersey, were remitted to him.†

* Sir Henry Neville observes, in a letter to Winwood, that Earl Gowrie and his brother had been murdered in James's presence, and probably by his order. Memoirs, i. 249. He adds, in another letter, that Gowrie's brother was murdered on account of some affection between him and the Queen, which he believed to have been the real cause of the tragedy, *id.*, p. 274.

† Cecil to Windebank, May 21st, 1603. State Paper Office. Raleigh was made Governor of Jersey on the death of Sir Anthony Paulet, August 26th, 1600, his competitors being Lord H. Seymour and Sir W. Russell, to the latter of whom he offered, if he would withdraw his claims, the Lord-lieutenancy of Cornwall and the Wardenship of the Stannaries. Russell replied haughtily, that he would take what the Queen gave him, which he soon found to be nothing; but being unable, on account of his other duties, to reside in the island, Raleigh made Kemys his lieutenant, with a salary of a

For the time no farther change appeared to be contemplated, and Raleigh was permitted to mingle undisturbed among the other courtiers, while the machinery, the working of which was to produce his ruin and death, was preparing. The general state of things, characterized by turmoil and big with change, was favourable to the purpose of his enemies: conspiracies were afoot, some originating with their ostensible authors, others with the Government, which, by proving itself to be in the secret of several designs, sought to infuse the belief into the public mind that it held in its hands the thread and fate of all. As a man of mark, generally suspected to be little in favour, Raleigh was now looked upon by most of the plotters as a desirable ally; though in some cases he was reckoned among those who were to be immured in the Tower dungeons or cut to pieces. When throwing together the elements of their conspiracies, the difficulty of finding able leaders and agents led them to determine upon offering to him the command of the fleet, when they should have wrested it from the King; or if communications were opened with foreign powers, they judged him to be a fit person to conduct their negotiations.*

hundred marks a year. Kemys to Cecil from the Tower, August 15th, 1603. Add. MSS. 6177, f. 261. B. M.

* Compare Watson's Examinations, and Copley's Confessions. MSS. State Paper Office.

In the beginning of June Count Aremberg arrived in London * as ambassador from the Cardinal Archduke, ostensibly to congratulate James on his accession, but in reality to regulate secretly the movements of those plots and conspiracies the object of which was to re-establish Catholicism in England. Aremberg, fat, gouty, and slow of speech,† became at once an object of ridicule to James and his courtiers, who had yet to learn that under that unpromising exterior lurked one of the most subtle spirits in Europe. His instructions were drawn up conjointly by the Cardinal Archduke and his wife, who received from him and transmitted to Philip and Lerma at Madrid minute accounts of whatever was going on in England. The consequences of Elizabeth's death, says the Infanta, are likely to prove as prolific of mischief as any of the actions of her life. The blood of Mary Stuart still cries for vengeance before the Lord, yet the conversion of her son is to be hoped for, since his wife is undoubtedly a Catholic, together with many of his ministers.‡

James, however, who while doubtful of his future in

---

* State Trials, ii., 3.

† Lodge, iii., 10.

‡ " Su Mujer es sin dudo Catolica." Cartas Originales del Cardinal Alberto y su mujer desde 1598 hasta 1610. The letter in which the above phrase occurs is dated Brussels, April 16th, 1603. Biblioteca Nacional. Aremberg's own letters, together with those of the Duke and Infanta to Philip, are preserved in the Archives of Simancas.

Scotland had coquetted with the Catholics, now that he had won the prize discarded them with contempt. He perceived but too clearly, from the temper of the English people, that any attempt to interfere with the religion of the country would cost him his crown, if not his life; and this conviction had begun to dawn upon his mind before he left Scotland, which we learn from the narrative of a priest, who having borrowed ten pounds and a nag from a wealthy member of his sect, posted away immediately after Elizabeth's death to bear the joyful tidings to the King. Having, however, been forestalled by Carey, Ferrer, and many others, he found but a cold greeting at Edinburgh; and James, alluding to his offer of services as the delegate of his co-religionists, exclaimed contemptuously as soon as his back was turned, " Na, na, gude faith, we hae na need of the Papists noo."*

But the agents of Catholicism were not simple enough to lull themselves into the belief that Protestantism could be extirpated from the hearts and hearths of England by a few maudlin priests with their puerile conspiracies. Thoroughly to do the work of Rome and

* Your worship must anticipate every day worse tidings of the new King, because he is a heretic, every inch of him; and the Catholics who expect anything from him are deceived. He has said to several persons that he does not regard those as his friends who will not go with him to his church. Varios puntos de los Avisos que dio el Padre Cresuelo. Simancas.

the Escorial, Aremberg and his master knew that large sums of money would be needed, for which, therefore, they earnestly pressed Philip and the Duke of Lerma.* With the golden lever in his hand, the sanguine Count scarcely doubted of success. In all ranks of English society partizans of the old religion were still found, whose mental calibre rendered them capable of believing that when they knelt before a priest they were kneeling to God. Confessors and Absolution-mongers accordingly swarmed throughout the country, supported by devotees, male and female, whose imaginations were fired by the hope of enveloping their country once more in the darkness of the middle ages. Then as now, the decrees of Trent were adopted as a rule of belief by thousands, some of whom contentedly wore the livery of Rome, while others, more crafty, took refuge within the pale of the English church, which they polluted with their dogmas and their ritualism.

In war, great commanders have always reckoned it a gain to be delivered from the base and fainthearted, though they should swell the ranks of the enemy. It is the same in churches militant. No real loss is sustained by the desertion of the frail and ignorant, whose aim in life may be better answered by herding with monks and unmarried priests, than with upright clergy-

* Cartas Originales del Cardinal Alberto y su Mujer. Madrid y Simancas.

men, the fathers of families, respecting the sanctities of the domestic hearth, and by sharing the common joys and afflictions of humanity, better understanding how to rejoice with those who rejoice, and to sorrow with those who mourn.

But this reflection by no means suggested itself to Aremberg or his employers. In their view the conversion of nations could be best brought about by introducing the leaven at the summit of society, whence they doubted not it would work downwards. Christianity at the outset did not so work; it began with the poor, and threw its light upwards, dazzling principalities and powers, till they substituted Christ for Jupiter. It operated after much the same fashion in England, though not with exactly the same ultimate result; for Puritanism began with the people, rose into the middle ranks, passed upwards into the nobility, and then for a time compassed those who walked along the giddiest heights of power. There, however, the parallel ceases, for superstition in those airy regions soon supplanted religion, and being more reconcilable with royal modes of life, long continued to govern the consciences of our kings.

At the period of which I am speaking, conversion was only a means to an end: confession, absolution, celibacy of the clergy, monasticism, Jesuitism, chasubles, pixes, and wafers, were regarded only as a ladder over which some fortunate papist might mount the throne. Towards that point all the plots now in agitation tended. The first and most formidable was that of the Jesuits,* to be developed by infantry, cavalry, and great guns; to command which a sum equal to five millions sterling was in the course of being raised by the Catholics: the second was that of the priests,† the offspring of imbecility, which was to realize its object by seizing and killing the king—for it aimed at nothing less.‡ There was a third plot, partly Puritanical, partly Catholic, which meant to take James captive, and extort from him complete toleration.

In the midst of these projects there was another, of which we shall probably never know the nature, though the object, no doubt, was a change of sovereigns. This, laid in the Escorial, and sat upon at Rome and

---

* The Catholics have been ready ever since March in the hope of succour from Spain; but have been prevented from making large preparations by the necessity of keeping the secret among a few. They have however in readiness 3,000 horses, and might command all the horses in the kingdom if they had money or jewels wherewith to purchase them. Relacion de Antonio Dutton. Simancas.

† 'Watson's Examination,' August 23rd, 1603. MS. State Paper Office.

‡ The slightest resistance that might be made to the King of Scotland would place him in a dilemma, since he would not know whom to trust, and would think he was betrayed, and fly to Scotland if he could, because he would find no safety on this side Berwick. Relacion de Antonio Dutton, 18 de Mayo, 1603. Simancas.

Brussels, was to be hatched in London by Aremberg, with the aid of such other persons as he could purchase. It was in this mysterious transaction that Cobham and Raleigh were suspected of being engaged. Aremberg, on his arrival in London, took up his residence like other noblemen in a palace overlooking the river, with which, by a flight of stairs, it communicated. Both Raleigh and Lord Cobham resided in mansions similarly situated; communication, therefore, by water, and in the dark, was always practicable, and Cobham, we are told, in pursuance of some design the nature of which is still unknown, repaired secretly in a wherry to the Count's dwelling at two o'clock in the morning.* In those long days of June, light was already dawning over the Thames at that hour, so that his boat was visible as it glided along the shore, passing one flight of stairs after another. On some occasions he supped with Raleigh, and afterwards proceeded on his midnight visits.

We are now touching the end of the chain which connects Raleigh with the Bloody Tower, with his second Guiana voyage, and with the block in Palace Yard; yet it is not needful to linger very long over the circumstances of that dark and disastrous period. Every writer who has touched upon the subject con-

* 'Cobham's Examination,' July 19th, 1603. MS. State Paper Office.

fesses what is absurdly called " The Raleigh Plot " to be an enigma, the Œdipus of which has not yet been born. With the explosion of the other political machines, Raleigh's reputation is in truth no way connected; the priests' treason certainly glances at him more than once, but by no means in a way to compromise his character; and had it been otherwise, Cecil's connexion with that atrocious scheme would in any case suffice to explain his apparent complicity. Some years previous, Anthony Copley, a Papist living in exile, of which he had grown weary, made an offer of his services to Cecil.* Respecting the nature of those services it was not likely that he meant to be particular, since he spoke of them in the lump with a tone of debonnair rascality, indicating entire recklessness. Far-sighted as he was, it is yet possible that the crafty Secretary could not at once foresee how Copley might prove useful; yet he laid by his communication, so that he might know where to find him should his treachery be wanted. The time had now come. Copley was ordered up to town, and instructed to insinuate himself into the confidence of the disaffected among his co-religionists, learn the whole bearing of their designs, and then give the Government an equivalent for its permission to return to England. It would be heaping upon Cecil superfluous charges of guilt to make him

* Copley's ' Sketch of his own Life.' Lansdowne MSS.

the fabricator of the Watson and Clarke plot; the
credit of that wretched contrivance may be fairly left
to those poor priests, and their friends, Brooke and
Markham. But learning what was in agitation, Cecil
had very soon his representatives among the conspirators, for with Copley, Brooksby, Gifford, and Barneby
were at once associated.*

Though Cecil extracted out of this conspiracy a
pretext for effecting the destruction of his old friend, it
was only by the exercise of that subtle dexterity for
which he was known and dreaded by his contemporaries.
The real gist of the suspicions against Raleigh had
reference to Spain. To affect surprise at the discontent he cherished would be puerile, he could be no
other than discontented at finding himself besprinkled
with the fetid foam which the mere force of accident had
placed above him ; but that he never intrigued with
Rome or Spain seems all but certain. It would be
going too far to affirm that, in the immense mass of
documents preserved at Simancas and Madrid, no proofs
of such intrigues will ever be found ; but if they exist,
they not only escaped my own researches, but those of
the ablest antiquaries now in Spain, who declare
emphatically that the result of their investigations
was, that Guaterale, as they call him, was one of the

* Kinloss to Gifford and Barneby, Aug. 11th, 1603. MS. State
Paper Office.

most detested enemies their country ever had. They term him buccaneer, corsair, pirate, heretic, but never mingle with their objurgations the slightest intimation that he had at any time been friendly to their king or government. There is a series of original letters, in the highest degree private and confidential, extending over twelve years, and embracing the whole of this period, from the Cardinal Archduke and his wife to King Philip and the Duke of Lerma, in which I fail to discern even an allusion to Raleigh, though the letters in many cases are based on the reports of Aremberg; yet it is not to be denied that Lord Cobham was engaged in mysterious relations with the Count, that he was Raleigh's most intimate friend, and that he did reveal to him from time to time some of the wild schemes that flitted over his imbecile brain.

CHAPTER II.

ARREST AND IMPRISONMENT.

THE power to read the future belongs to few. Neither
Puritans, Catholics, nor Established Churchmen possessed it at the opening of the seventeenth century,
though they all sought to impress the character of
their respective parties upon the times. Lord Grey of
Wilton the son of him who ordered the slaughter at
Del Oro, now dreamed of reviving the practice of the
old barons, who used to present in arms their petitions
to the sovereign. But he lived too late or too soon;
the days of chivalry were passed, and the days of the
Long Parliament were yet to come. The Jesuits, by
locating their scheme in England, committed a geographical blunder, and the priests, with their project for
seizing the king at Greenwich or Hanworth, killing
him, or imprisoning him, and extorting from his fears
predominance for their religion, were guilty of an
anachronism. They shut their eyes to the mental

changes which Protestantism had effected in England—to the revolution brought about in philosophy—to the rapid spread of classical studies, which were silently moulding the generals and statesmen of the commonwealth—above all, to the influence of the Bible, which, pouring in upon fervid and impassioned minds, was generating that fierce system of theology which incited men at no distant day to abjure the name of Bishop and King, and to talk of the "Parliament of Heaven."

Events now flashed upon the world which were to present Raleigh to the public in a new light. The conspiracies in progress having been permitted by Cecil to develop themselves so far as to compromise the safety of their originators, a broad light was suddenly let in upon their secret movements, which startled their conductors into frenzy. Up to the moment of discovery, the conspirators were accustomed to meet at each other's lodgings, at the Temple, in the Strand, or in Westminster, where they occasionally sought to cool their heated brains by walking at night amid the cloisters of the Abbey. Copley appears to have stipulated that he should be thought to give his evidence on compulsion, or in the hope of saving his own life;* Brooksby, Barneby, and Gifford were less

* Proclamation for the apprehension of Copley, July 2nd, 1603. State Paper Office. Bancroft to Cecil, July 12th. Declaration of Copley, July 14th. Coke informs us that Bancroft was a stout

squeamish, and earned and took the wages of treachery with slight regard to appearances.

Though Cecil was from the beginning acquainted with the mechanism and working of the plot, he thought it for the credit of the Government that a discovery should seem to be made accidentally, and at a critical moment; his agents, therefore, came forward with their disclosures just in time to persuade James that his life had been saved by Cecil's sagacity, which he now learned to regard as a better defence against Catholic stilettoes than his padded doublet or systematic seclusion. As soon as news of the discovery reached the conspirators, the terror that seized upon them exceeded all bounds. They immediately dispersed, and concealed themselves, some in town, others in the country;* while proclamations were issued and despatched to the seaports, describing their persons with ludicrous minuteness, and peremptorily commanding all persons in authority to take measures for their apprehension.†

But how came the meshes of this wretched scheme to envelop Raleigh? No student of history will, I

----

foot-ball player, and an advocate of those political principles which brought James into general odium, and his son to the block, p. 60.

* "Stepped afield" is the phrase of Sir William Waade.

† Bancroft to Sheriff of Nottingham, July 14th, 1603.   State Paper Office.

think, be able to adduce a parallel case. The course of
reasoning by which suspicion was made to touch him,
manifestly implies in the mind of Cecil a foregone
conclusion. He had, in fact, for some years determined
upon Raleigh's overthrow, if not upon his death.
James, also, with Kinloss and Mar, had decreed that
Raleigh and Cobham should be forlorn as soon as an
opportunity presented itself, and for this they had all
along been eagerly on the look-out. Never did Red
Indian dip his arrows in a venom so deadly as that
which tinged the barbed calumnies of Cecil and Lord
Henry Howard. King, favourites, ministers, being
united in hatred, and aiming their shafts at the same
breast, it would indeed have been strange had success
not been achieved.

Throwing aside for the present what concerned the
priests and their accomplices, let us follow the chain of
incidents which led Raleigh to the Bloody Tower.
Among the worst of the plotters was Cecil's brother-in-
law, George Brooke,* a man deformed like himself
in body, and still more deformed in mind. He had
been driven into the ranks of the disaffected by an act
of injustice on the part of James, who had bestowed on
another a lucrative appointment of which Elizabeth

* Cf. Sir T. Edmonds to Cecil, July 13th. Answers and assertions of G. Brooke, July 17th. His Confession, July 19th. State
Paper Office.

had given Brooke the reversion. His habits being dissolute, his means were always unequal to his wants, so that he was ready to avail himself of the slightest chance of bettering his condition; and in the distribution of places, to be made after the contemplated revolution, no lower position had been assigned to him than that of Lord-marshal of England.*

While George was revelling in these dreams, the bubble burst, and he had to conceal himself. There is no hatred like the hatred of brothers: George hated his brother Lord Cobham, and Cecil, their brother-in-law, hated them both. They were accordingly arrested, and their family enemy prepared deliberately for vengeance. George, with his lame leg, took refuge in the house of his mother-in-law, Lady Burgh; Lord Cobham was arrested at Sheen. These things, however, were not done in an hour; Raleigh, with the rest of the world, heard of them one after another; he read the proclamations that were issued against the conspirators; he understood all the measures to which recourse was had for capturing and bringing them to justice; and he could not be ignorant of the animus with which the King, his courtiers, and ministers, would set about the business of making a thorough clearance of their enemies. Yet, with the confidence inspired by innocence, instead of attempting flight or concealment,

* Watson's ' Examination.'

he remained at court among those who rode out with the King for exercise or to the chase.

But Cecil had laid his plans, and proceeded leisurely to carry them out. Brooke and Cobham had been examined, and in the midst of their contradictory disclosures and confessions, Cecil detected some phrases which he thought might be made to criminate Raleigh. His platform of inference, as he himself explained it, was this: if George Brooke was guilty, his brother, Lord Cobham, could hardly be innocent; and if he were not innocent, how could Raleigh, who was his most intimate friend, be expected to stand in that category?* The exquisite logic of this process can hardly fail to excite admiration; upon the strength of it, however, Cecil determined to act. Walking to and fro on the great terrace at Windsor, now looking down on Eton's spires, antique towers, and fields so often loved in vain, and now at the walls and windows of the castle, he rapidly sketched the chart of Raleigh's destruction. While he was thus ruminating, his victim came forth from the castle, booted and spurred, in gorgeous cloak, with hunting-cap and feather, to ride abroad with the King. The two men, who had formerly been friends, met, the one with jovial unconcern, the other filled with deadly animosity, which could not fail to blanch his cheek and influence the inflections of

* State Trials, ii., 13.

his voice. He looked at the tall proud soldier, who had compassed land and deep in search of fame, and doubtless experienced that inward satisfaction which bad men feel when they are about to achieve a triumph over virtue. Addressing Raleigh, he said he must crave his company to the Council-chamber, where the lords were then sitting in deliberation. In that chamber, about twenty-six feet square, and very lofty, no lords now assemble to take counsel on any subject; it is appropriated to domestic uses, and there artists often sit when they take portraits of Queen Victoria, or any member of her family.

Instead, however, of palettes and easels, of sitters and artists, the apartment on that July morning was filled with statesmen, through whom a thrill of peculiar feeling passed when they beheld Raleigh enter with Cecil. On the proceedings of the hour a curtain is dropped for ever; but whatever they may have been, they resulted in the commitment of Raleigh first to his own house, and afterwards to the Tower. The meaning of Kinloss's phrase, " Cobham and Raleigh are forlorn in our account," was thus made clear, though it afterwards received still further elucidation. We have now accompanied Raleigh to the place which, with one short interval of absence, constituted his home for nearly thirteen years. Cecil therefore had him safe, to insult by formal examinations, by insolent interrogatories, by malignant suggestions, by holding up alternately before his mind prospects coloured by hope and fear; while day after day, and hour after hour, the Tower opened its ponderous jaws to take in new victims—Grey, Cobham, Brooke, Parham, Copley, Watson, Clarke, Gifford, Brooksby, Barneby, and others, some designed for the scaffold, others to aid in conducting them to it.

Through the examinations that followed of the plotters of various classes, nothing worthy the name of evidence was obtained against Raleigh; but Cobham being thrown by a dishonourable artifice into a fit of passion which overcame his reason, was at length betrayed into extravagant accusations. A portion of a letter was shown him from Raleigh to Cecil, which, apart from the context, read like a disclosure of Cobham's guilt, upon which he fell into the trap laid for him.* In the frame of mind thus produced, the two friends now lay, one in the Bloody, the other in the Wardrobe Tower. Raleigh, who had begun to comprehend the scheme of his enemies, felt the full importance of undeceiving Cobham, and obtaining from him a retractation of his falsehoods; but how were his explanations to be communicated? The medium that presented itself could hardly have been looked for. Sir John Peyton, Lieutenant of the Tower, was a solicitor for Raleigh's post

* Oldys, 'Life of Raleigh,' p. 373.

of Governor of Jersey,* which would become vacant by his attainder or death; he was therefore deeply interested in accumulating evidence of his guilt. But he had a son knighted and enriched by James,† yet nevertheless willing to risk everything by affording Raleigh the aid he needed to establish his innocence. For this purpose he voluntarily became the intermediary between Raleigh and Cobham, ministering to them what comfort he could, and conveying messages from one to the other. The business was perilous, as he afterwards learned to his cost; but with the high chivalry of youth, he despised the danger and persisted in his kind offices.

While matters were in this state an event occurred, or was said to have occurred, which will be admitted to be mysterious. At dinner one day, with many other guests at the Lieutenant's table, Raleigh, we are told, seized a knife and attempted to plunge it into his heart. The arm of the captive had not yet been weakened by paralysis; he was, on the contrary, in full strength, yet when the point of the knife struck against one of his ribs, and turned after inflicting a slight wound,‡ he threw it aside, and " there an end." Is this story true? and if so, how much of it, and in what

* Peyton to Cecil, July 30th, 1603. MS. State Paper Office.

† Grant to him of six manors in Herefordshire, Aug. 18th, 1603. MS. State Paper Office.

‡ Cecil to Sir J. Parry.

sense is it true? Men, not unworthy to be classed with Raleigh, have committed suicide without quenching the light of their fame—Brutus, Cato, Pætus, and many other Romans. If Raleigh was really ambitious to follow their example, I see no reason why his biographers should desire to screen him from the censure which such an act may be thought to merit. He stood by and looked on while his great mistress killed herself by voluntary abstinence, if not by a knife. Why should he shrink from what she had done? But the question is not respecting the character of the action, but the fact. A letter has been handed down to us, purporting to have been written by Raleigh to his wife *after* his attempt at suicide;* on the very day which witnessed the crime, another letter was written by the man who had wiped Raleigh's shoes with his cloak,† and who, nevertheless, as we are assured by one of his nearest kin,‡ was as eager to blow up Durham House with Raleigh in it as he had been to blow up Essex House. This man, I say, who thirteen years before had made James one of the persons of his infernal trinity, was now one of his most obsequious retainers. Papist as he was, he consented to become the medium of James's loathsome cant about good preachers, and that in

* Goodman, ‘History of his own Times.’ Edited by Mr. Brewer, ii., 93.

† Aubrey, ‘Lives of Eminent Men,’ ii., 511.

‡ Lord Henry Howard. ‘Secret Correspondence,’ p. 133.

language which reveals how keenly he sympathized with Raleigh's assassins. I give the document entire, as it may help the reader to estimate the Earl of Nottingham at his proper value.

"The king hath perused the letter your Lordship hath sent to me, and thanks you for your advertisement of your day's work, and doth desire very much that Raleigh may be now well examined, and that at the examination you would have some good preacher with you, that you may make him know that it is his soul that he must wound and not his body. The King's Majesty doth assure himself that as you have so wisely and well begun with Markham, so you will find out the bottom of this great wit's sore."*

In the forged letter published by Mr. Brewer, Raleigh is made to write as if he expected death from his wound; but three days after its supposed infliction, Peyton assured Cecil that it would be perfectly whole in a day or two.

Eighteen years earlier, a state prisoner, higher in the social scale than Raleigh, had been despatched in the Tower by what at the time was denominated suicide. Had the intention to imitate that transaction dawned upon the minds of James and Cecil? If so, was not the story of the dinner-table trumped up as a prelude

* Nottingham to Cecil. Palace, 11 at night, July 27th, 1603. MS. British Museum.

to what they meant should follow? Let this be another historical enigma to set beside that of The Raleigh Plot. Could the audacious fiction have been invested with anything like probability, would not Coke and Heale, and the other legal hirelings at Winchester, have gloated over it, and revelled in insults to their illustrious victim? And would not Sir Thomas Wilson, fifteen years later, together with Naunton and James himself, have been too happy to cast the obloquy of it in his teeth, when, if we may believe the witness who relates it, Raleigh did descant upon suicide as a Roman virtue? The last effort made by the English Government to give a wide currency to the report was the imparting of it to the Venetian Ambassador; who, receiving the relation from such a source, could do no less than forward an account of it, in language implying no scepticism, to his most cautious and scrutinizing masters, the seignory of Venice.

In the beginning of August, Peyton ceased to be Lieutenant of the Tower, and was succeeded by Sir George Harvey;* by whose appointment a marked change was effected in Raleigh's condition. Nothing further was heard of his melancholy. He rose early, combed his long hair like a Spartan, read or wrote for a few hours, and then went forth into the grounds to

* King to Sir George Harvey, July 30th, 1603. MS. State Paper Office.

play at bowls, and drink beer with Harvey and his officers. In the evening he generally supped at the Lieutenant's table.* At other times, however, when Cecil felt inclined to enjoy the luxury of triumph, Raleigh's days were passed differently: he had then to answer malignant questions, and to undergo the probings of Scottish divines, probably on the subjects of demonology, witchcraft, and tobacco.

Every day's examination must have convinced Raleigh that it behoved him to make careful preparation for his coming trial, at which nothing less would be aimed at than his life. The aspect of the times was as dark as his own prospects. Throughout London,† the Plague, with capricious footsteps, was scattering death among high and low,—now retreating to the farthest suburbs,—now coming back and knocking with skeleton fingers at the very gates of the Tower.

In those parts of the East where the Plague is a frequent visitor, its movements are regulated no one knows how. Commonly it seems to follow the track of the caravans, which bear with them therefore to great cities riches and death. Sometimes it travels in a mysterious way, over desert tracts, and little-frequented roads. A stranger arrives perhaps in the evening at a

* Examination of Edward Cotterel, February 4th, 1607.   MS. State Paper Office.

† The Plague of 1603 destroyed 30,578 persons.   Lodge, iii., 14.

Karavanserai; he looks ill, is scarcely able to attend to his beast, he does not eat, his turban falls down over his forehead, his clothes hang loosely about him, some disease has evidently shrivelled him up: he is dead before the morning, and his body is covered with livid spots. There is no mistake—he has died of the Plague. In the course of a few hours other deaths occur in the Karavanserai: the bodies are carried forth to interment; the clothes of the deceased are sold in the bazaar,—the contagion spreads, and scarcely a fortnight has elapsed before several thousands of the population have retreated to the narrow house. To this the belief in fate reconciles the survivors—it was written—God has called them to himself, and it is best so. No precautions are taken, the infection works its will, and the growth of population is thus kept within the limits of subsistence.

In England no belief in fatality interfered with the conduct of the authorities, or with the feelings of the people; yet through ignorance or negligence acts were perpetrated within the bills of mortality scarcely less censurable than the Eastern practice of selling the infected garments of the dead; for in Hampstead, Highgate, and the other villages around London, the old beds, mattresses, and straw of the beds of those that died of the sickness were thrown out into the highways, so that none could approach the capital without passing through the accumulated elements of infection.*

Throughout the metropolis the incessant tolling of the death-knell caused a rapid displacement of population, since all who possessed means fled into the country. All practicable precautions were taken to hinder the pestilence from making its way into the Tower, and snatching his business from the executioner. Yet the terror within the walls was great; one of the warders who had a house in St. Catherine's died there; another who lived near the Iron Gate in the farthest part of the fortress fell sick; alarmed therefore at the grim approach of danger, Harvey sent away his wife and children, though he determined to ride out the storm himself. Waade, intrusted, under the Lieutenant, with the special charge of the state prisoners, possessing less courage, took to flight, and tremblingly watched the spread of the contagion from his Hampstead villa. The courtiers, to whose lot fell the task of examining the prisoners, intermitted their visits to the Tower, so that all needful intercourse between them and their captive had to be carried on by fumigated letters. " Sir Walter Raleigh hath much importuned me," says Harvey, " to send these unto your Lordship, the contents whereof requiring no extraordinary haste, I am bold to commend them unto your Lordship by this bearer, Mr.

* Waade to Cecil, August 27th, 1603. State Paper Office.

Mellersh, wherewith (because many services belong to this place) I have thought it my duty to certify your Lordship, that, touching the sickness, the Tower standeth almost as it did at your last being here, until within these four days that one of the warders dwelling near unto the Iron Gate, the remotest place in all the Tower, fell sick, and so yet remaineth, as it is suspected of the Plague. One other of the warders sickened at a house which he had in St. Catherine's, and there died; but within the Tower, no contagion hitherto—praised be God—is entered, though in reason it may be feared. In the meantime I will use my best endeavour to keep it out."*

From this passage we make the discovery that something like a kindly feeling between Raleigh and his former friend had been re-established, for Mellersh was Cobham's steward, and conducted his most private business, both before and after his imprisonment.

* Harvey to Cecil, Sept. 7th, 1603. MS. State Paper Office.

CHAPTER III.

TRIAL AT WINCHESTER.

An astrologer would now have said that the stars in their courses fought against Raleigh.* Grown weary of prosecuting hostilities with England, and jealous of the ascendancy of France at James's court, Spain took decisive steps towards bringing about a peace; Juan de Taxis, Conde de Villa Mediana, with a suitable following, large sums of money, and a profuse assortment of presents, was in the month of August sent to England to co-operate with Count Aremberg.† James, in mortal dread of the Plague, was flitting hither and thither through his dominions, now resting for a while at Oxford, now at Windsor, Wilton, or Winchester, accompanied by the crafty and obsequious ministers of France

---

* Yet at this time Sir Thomas Edmondes remarked that it was expected all the prisoners except Raleigh would be found guilty, for that in his case positive proofs were wanting. Lodge, iii., 29.

† Lewkenor to the Council, Aug. 2nd, 1603. State Paper Office.

and Germany. Henri IV., to humour James's extrava-
gances, had accredited to him gentlemen who could at
least affect a passion for the chase, which insured them
opportunities of being frequently about his person.*

When Taxis arrived James was at Oxford, to which
city therefore the ambassador repaired, in the hope of a
speedy audience. Having come, however, from the
country in which delays flourish most luxuriantly, he
ought surely to have expected to meet with some few
specimens of the same plants in England. Whatever
may have been his anticipations, he certainly found
them. The French put in play all their talent for
intrigue to keep him from court, and were lucky enough
to find a powerful auxiliary; for the Plague breaking
out in Taxis's suite, furnished James with a fair pretext
for postponing an audience. Still civilities and promises
were lavished profusely upon the ambassador, who made
friends among the venal courtiers, male and female, by
distributing without stint the perfumed gloves,† laces,
bracelets, earrings, necklaces, and other jewels, with
which his master Philip had intrusted him; yet no
progress was made towards settling the business on
which he came. Instead of being admitted to James's
presence to see him gorge, thrust his hand into the dish
while the seneschal was carving, or drink himself into a

---

* The celebrated Duc de Sully was at the head of this embassy.
Cobham to the King, April 29th, 1603. State Paper Office.

† Lodge, iii., 25.

state of stupid intoxication with Greek wine,* Taxis
was sent to Southampton, which Lewkenor, master of
the ceremonies, affirmed to be the sweetest town in the
kingdom. Having an eye to possible contingencies, the
Spaniard wished to survey the ports and landing-places
on the Hampshire coast and the Isle of Wight, but was
put off with various excuses. To amuse his long
interval of inaction, the master-of-the-ceremonies had
recourse to sundry devices, sometimes amusing him
with banquets, dancing, and music; sometimes with
bull-baiting, which, reminding him of the amusement
he had enjoyed at home in the Plazas de Toros, delighted
him extremely.†

While the diplomatic agent of Raleigh's most persevering and most powerful enemy was slowly but
surely making way towards bringing about a pacification
between that personage and James, the attention of the
English public was divided between the Plague and the
preparations going on for the trial of the conspirators.
Much that then took place has been suffered to pass
into oblivion; the rack and the Scavenger's Daughter

* Raumer, ii., 200. Roger Coke informs us that James had no
taste for ordinary French and Spanish wines, but took to the wines
of Greece on account of their superior strength. He adds that his
own father, hunting when quite a young man with James, took a
draught from his cup, which not only disordered him for the time,
but left behind it a three days' headache, p. 78.

† Lewkenor to Cecil, August 23rd, and September 21st, 1603.
State Paper Office.

were actively employed to extort confessions from inferior prisoners, and once, we are told, the former instrument was significantly shown to Captain Kemys [*] by Northampton's or Cecil's order, in the hope of subduing the fidelity of that gallant companion of Raleigh's adventures in America. But Kemys was a man of Roman mould, whom neither the fear of torture nor its application could have subdued. It was wholly different with Cobham, his brother George, the priests, and their associates. These—cruel, cowardly, and effeminate—were ready to confess anything, and to accuse any one and every one, if they could only by so doing escape death. Not a plotter among them all, however, save Cobham, could even be supposed capable of giving the slightest evidence that could touch Raleigh. It was accordingly towards him that the attention of the Government was almost exclusively directed. No stage hero, no Claudio, no Hamlet ever conceived a greater horror at the prospect of being thrust into that undiscovered country " from whose bourne no traveller returns " than the wretched Cobham, whose soul sickened at the bare idea that, for indulging a few vain and frivolous hopes, he might soon be sentenced " To lie in cold obstruction, and to rot."

How far his weakness was purposely assaulted by such suggestions I know not, but it is certain that his

[*] State Trials, ii., 22.

worthless wife, with her whole kith and kin, desired that he should make a scapegoat of Raleigh.* Many a Roman slave has left in the records of history evidences of greatness of soul transcending even the conception of this English nobleman, who to prolong his miserable existence paltered, equivocated, confessed, denied, swore and forswore himself, till he excited the scorn and loathing of his very tormentors.

Not being able to foresee what course would be pursued by his enemies, Raleigh took all practicable steps for his defence. He had always been a diligent student, and possessing a searching and subtle mind, now applied himself to the reading of law, of history, scripture, and divinity, that he might be qualified on all points to deal with his assailants.

Lady Raleigh meantime laboured to have his cause removed from the ordinary courts to the Star Chamber,† a privilege for which she offered in vain the sum of five thousand pounds. Owing to the pestilence, it soon became evident that the trials could not take place in London, and various places in the country were, one after another, mentioned; but at length in the course of October the old city of Winchester was fixed upon. On the 26th the Lieutenant of the Tower received

* Lady Kildare to Cobham. October 29th, 1603. MS. State Paper Office.

† Sir Allan Percy to Carleton, Oct. 31st, 1603. State Paper Office.

orders to provide carriages, carts, and waggons for the conveyance of the prisoners, who with their servants and effects were to be conducted to their place of destination by an escort of fifty horse.*

Raleigh saw that the crisis of his fate was drawing near, while he remained wholly ignorant of the course which the only witness against him meant to pursue. Cobham had been tricked into a false accusation: had he retracted, or would he retract? In spite of the kindness of young Peyton and of Sir George Harvey himself, who often dined and supped with him in his apartment when all servants were excluded, Raleigh had failed to ascertain Cobham's intentions. After long and frequently racking his brain, he at length hit upon a device for conveying a solemn appeal to Cobham's conscience, which he hoped might awaken him to a due sense of the awful injustice and wickedness of his conduct.

In Raleigh's service there was a man named Cotterel, bold, ingenious, and for the time devoted to his master's interest; upon his shrewdness and fidelity he determined therefore to rely, as they offered the last chance of success in his design. November had set in with its fogs, its rains, its dark chill nights; an intimation was conveyed to the inmate of the Wardrobe Tower to leave open his window on such an evening. Raleigh wrote a letter full, we may be sure, of touching appeals, urging his

* Letter to Sheriff of Middlesex, Oct. 26th, 1603. State Paper Office.

old friend to retract his injurious accusations and state the truth. Cotterel was then called into Raleigh's chamber, and the all-important letter, twisted, and tied carefully about an apple, placed in his hands. It was about eight o'clock, an hour at which the old fortress was then still and silent. Cotterel emerged from the Bloody Tower, and gliding noiselessly through a labyrinth of narrow passages, which one who knew them well properly termed oblivious, drew near Cobham's prison. He looked up; a light was burning in the captive's chamber; the window was open. He took careful aim and threw the apple, which alighted at Cobham's feet. Then slinking back into some dark corner, he waited anxiously for that which he believed would convey the assurance of life or death to his master. For awhile the light continued to burn brightly in Cobham's apartment; but when at length it disappeared, Cotterel advanced stealthily to the foot of the Wardrobe Tower and beheld a letter pushed forth under the door: snatching it up, he returned cautiously and silently to Raleigh.* The letter thus obtained ran as follows:—"Seeing myself so near my end, for the discharge of my own conscience, and freeing myself from your blood, which else will cry vengeance against me, I protest upon my salvation I never practised with

* Cotterel's ' Examination,' February 4th, 1607. MS. State Paper Office.

Spain by your procurement; God so comfort me in this my affliction as you are a true subject for anything that I know, I will say as Daniel *purus sum a sanguine hujus.* So God have mercy upon my soul as I know no treason by you."*

On the 5th of November, a day afterwards made remarkable for a real plot, the old Tower became a scene of bustle and excitement; carts and waggons drove in, to be laden with the effects of the prisoners; a multitude of servants and of attendants assembled in the courts, or passed to and from the apartments of their masters; the officials of the fortress were likewise in busy motion, while the cavalry who were to guard the prisoners on the road pranced hither and thither in the outer yard. Early in the morning Raleigh's carriage drove up to the entrance of the Bloody Tower, and descending from his chamber with his usual defiant air, he passed through the ranks of spectators and enemies, and stepped into it with Sir Robert Mansfield, while Lord Grey of Wilton and Lord Cobham† were accom-

* He reaffirms the same thing in his letter to the Council of October 30th, 1603. Speaking of his communications with Aremberg, he says they had entirely ceased, and hopes for mercy. "My offence," he says, "being but a conceit acquainting nobody with it." MS. State Paper Office. To the same purpose is the whole of his letter to the King of the same date.

† Sir Thomas Vavasour was ordered to attend Cobham and Sir Richard Leveson Grey, but a different arrangement appears to have been followed.

panied by Sir George Harvey, Brooke by Sir William Waade, and Markham by Sir Robert Wrothe.*

In the past circumstances of this narrative the reader must seek the explanation of what follows. Sir Walter Raleigh, it will have been seen, had never up to that time been popular; his manner and bearing excited in his associates a feeling akin to fear; the false rumours circulated by the Government had now caused him to be regarded as an enemy to his country; his notorious hostility to Essex, whom the vulgar still looked upon as a martyr, kindled the hatred of many; but why on the morning in question the mob should have been so exasperated against him as, in defiance of their fear of plague, to make a rush at his carriage with the design of tearing him to pieces, seems all but inexplicable. The officers charged with his safe conduct harangued the rabble, conjuring them to let the King's prisoner pass in safety, but were for a while under strong apprehension that neither entreaties nor the swords of the cavalry would avail. Not being able to give vent to their fury in any other way, the populace threw at Raleigh's carriage tobacco-pipes, mud, brickbats, and stones, while he rode along with an air of contemptuous indifference, which augmented their indignation.†

* Tichbourne to Cecil, Nov. 13th, 1603. State Paper Office.

† Michael Hicks to the Earl of Shrewsbury. Lodge, iii., 74. Waade to Cecil, Nov. 13th, 1603. State Paper Office.

At length the suburbs of London were passed, and the cavalcade entered upon the miry roads, through which for days they were to plunge on towards Winchester. In every town through which they passed the demonstrations of hatred towards Raleigh were renewed by the scum of the people; and there were others belonging to the higher order of society who proclaimed their readiness to travel a hundred miles to see him hanged. Less than an hour and a half would now have conveyed the prisoners by express from London to their place of trial; the journey then took them nearly seven days, for it was not until late on the evening of the 12th that the last carriage, in which were Cobham and Grey, drove into the yard of Winchester Castle.

The differences, however, in the speed and mode of travelling of that period and ours were much less than the differences in moral feeling. The sight of a great man borne even justly towards his doom would in these days, instead of curses and execrations, excite in the populace the keenest feelings of sympathy and commiseration.

A remark made by Tichbourne, governor of Winchester Castle, afterwards knighted by James, shows that the descendants of the old Saxon Gewissy were not often called on to tenant their state prison; the accommodation supplied by the castle was, he says, so scanty that much difficulty was experienced in stowing away the captives, with their keepers and servants. On Cobham's arrival an incident occurred, characteristic of both jailer and prisoner: traitors being of course suspected of cramming treason into their trunks, it was one of the duties of a good Cerberus to hunt out the perilous stuff. No amount of experience sufficed to teach Cobham wisdom. When his coffers were brought up to the apartment where he stood talking with Tichbourne, the certainty he might have felt that his eyes were watched could not preserve him from casting a look of intelligence at the servants who had been with him in the Tower. That look was a revelation to Tichbourne. The prisoner's trunks, coffers, boxes, were immediately ordered to be opened, and in one of them was discovered a letter, which the governor seized and forwarded to Lord Cecil. Was not that the letter from Raleigh which had been thrown in at the window of the Wardrobe Tower?*

By some of Raleigh's superior attendants the man who had been employed to perform that delicate service was supplied with money and sent to Sherbourne, where he remained for years in the service of Raleigh's family. If, however, I rightly conjecture the character of the letter found in the trunk, Cobham's negligence had rendered this policy of no avail.

* Tichbourne to Cecil, Nov. 12th, 1603. MS. State Paper Office.

Raleigh, as I have said, reached Winchester on Saturday the 12th of November; the Sunday was probably consumed in arranging his papers and other effects, so that three other days only remained to make preparations for his defence, since his trial was to take place on Thursday the 17th.

Cobham meanwhile, growing more and more bewildered, as the awful day drew near, displayed so feverish an eagerness to escape from death that it became manifest he might be made to say or swear anything. Seven several times did this unhappy nobleman perjure himself—for he gave upon oath eight different versions of his testimony, of which one may have possibly been true. It is nevertheless clear that he fully understood the guilt of shedding innocent blood by bearing false witness, and yet to prolong his own existence during a few sad years was prevailed upon to take the responsibility; I say prevailed upon, because there remains in my mind no shadow of a doubt that his life was promised him if by perjury he would consent to destroy Raleigh.

At length the dawn of that memorable 17th of November broke upon the old city of Winchester, whose streets, lanes, and alleys ran with liquid mire, ankle-deep, while the chill moisture of the season hung thick and heavy upon window, door, and wall. The judges, and the jury—which had been packed overnight—took their places;* the apartment was thronged with spectators, all eager, all mute with hushed expectation. At a signal from the proper officer, Raleigh entered, his tall form erect, his countenance and attitude defiant, and for awhile stood confronting the judges, the jury, and the audience, among whom were some of the noblest persons in England. What they had come together to see was a sacrifice, and the victim was now before them. It may be doubted whether within those walls the accused possessed one friend. His judges were his enemies, personal in many cases, interested in all. The Attorney and Solicitor-general, Coke and Heale, who conducted the prosecution, were exact prototypes of Jefferies. Raleigh was his own counsel.

* No description of the appearance of the court at Raleigh's trial having fallen in my way, I extract from a secret letter of the Conde de Villa Mediana to Philip III., an account of its aspect at Cobham's trial. "The Lord Chancellor," he says, " who is here supreme Judge of Justice, was seated in a brocade chair under a canopy of the same, placed on a platform raised two steps above the level of the floor, on the sides of which were thirty-three earls and barons. At a table in the centre there were seated about twenty-four persons, and before the Lord Chancellor two keepers of the rolls ; at the sides, twelve Juris Consults, dressed in scarlet, and one—*inquisidor y reformador* of the kingdom ; all the rest were procurators and crown lawyers, the seat of the Attorney-general being directly opposite that of the Lord Chancellor ; and at the corners of the said table were four Kings-at-arms, with their maces, from whence they rose when ordered to make proclamation." Carta original del Conde de Villa Mediana, a Su Md. 8 de Diciembre, 1603. Simancas.

Of what did the prisoner stand accused? Of three things: first, that he desired to place upon the throne Arabella Stuart, a pert, smart, and fast young lady, who, though better than James, would have made but a sorry successor to Elizabeth; second, that he instigated Lord Cobham in behalf of this same Arabella to undertake a journey to Spain more wild and hopeless than any undertaken by Don Quixote, to obtain from the beggared sovereign of that country a sum equal to three million crowns of the present day, without security, without guarantee, without the slightest intelligible inducement beyond a verbal promise that he would try to convert a wayward girl into a queen; third, that out of this fabulous treasure Cobham was to bestow on him eight thousand crowns, together with a pension of fifteen hundred a year for supplying Philip with intelligence, and favouring a peace which both James and his ministers were eager to conclude with that prince. Of all this, how much was proved? Thus much—that Cobham related his dreams to Raleigh, who replied laughingly, "that it would be time enough to be serious when the treasure should pass out of the realm of fancy into that of reality." So much, and no more, was Raleigh's treason. He confessed he had listened to his old friend's development of his monstrous projects, had heard of his interviews with Aremberg, and ought to have denounced him to the Government.

I think he ought not, it was a reticence of which every gentleman would be guilty; but it amounted to what the law in its jargon denominates misprision of treason.

Raleigh had evidently apprehended from the first, that however trivial his offence might be, the Government would convert it into a pretext for taking away his life, if judges could be found to transform his honourable reserve into a capital crime, and if a jury of his countrymen, out of servility to the court, would consent to take the guilt of his blood upon their heads. From the commencement of the proceedings he was made aware of their true drift, and saw that he had to contend for his life. Amid the crowd of faces which looked down upon him from bench and niche, balcony and gallery, pale, eager, full of indefinite anxiety or expectation, he beheld few, if any, that were not hostile. The strength of the law, the influence of the court, the envenomed shafts of personal hatred, the unquenchable energy of revenge, the technical ingenuity of venal pleaders, the scarecrow shrinking of cowardice, the stupid prejudices of superstition, were all arrayed against him.

When Coke and Heale had drained their virulence and brutality to the dregs, he rose, with all the associations of the Armada and Cadiz, of the Island Voyage, of the Guiana Expedition, of the Virginia Discovery, of the Wars of Religion in France, of the quenching of rebellion 'in Ireland, of Elizabeth's brilliant court, of statesmanship of romance, of adventure, of poetry, of love, about him, and a universal thrill of admiration went through the thronged court, for all present felt that the man then before them was the greatest man living. Should they pull him down? Should they consign him to the block, and themselves at the same time to everlasting infamy? These were the questions that went like arrows through the consciences of commissioners, council, jury, audience. Raleigh's voice was not loud, but it was full of sweetness, and of that power which springs from commanding intellect. All the treasures of learning were his— philosophy, rhetoric, history, scripture, law, he had ransacked them all, and now, when pleading for his life, poured forth his eloquence in one grand ,flood, which, according to those who listened to him, seemed never to have been equalled before, and which drew tears from the eyes of many of James's noblest countrymen, whose refined sensibility proved them to be worthy of the elevated fortune they had reached.*

To make a show of deliberation, the jury remained shut up together half an hour, during which Coke, we are told in a very doubtful anecdote, went forth to walk in the garden. He was there battling probably with his own conscience, when one of his clerks came

* ' Court and Times of James I.,' i., 20.

running to inform him that the jury had found Raleigh guilty of treason. "Man," he replied, "thou must be mistaken! I myself only accused him of misprision of treason." Be this as it may, Raleigh having been pronounced guilty, the day was fixed for his execution, and the court broke up.*

The view taken of these proceedings by the representatives of foreign governments differed according to their tempers, and the amount of their knowledge of our institutions and national character. Familiar with conspiracies at home, they not only accorded a ready faith to the fact that a plot had existed, but accepting the assertions of the crown-lawyers as proofs, concluded all whom they accused to be guilty. Beaumont, the French ambassador, is said to have assured Henri IV.†

* Manuscript account of trial by Ortelio Renzo, Jan. 31st, 1604. State Paper Office. Arraignment of Sir Walter Raleigh attributed to Sir Thomas Overbury. Somers, 'Tracts,' ii., 409.

† Carte, iii., 718-721. Lingard, ix., 9. The impression made on the mind of Henri IV. by the despatches of his ambassador may be seen from the following extract of a letter from the minister Villeroi to Beaumont, dated November 16th, 1603. Having spoken of the intrigues of the Spanish agents in Germany, he proceeds thus: —"Quand j'en scaurai davantage, je vous en ferai pas, comme sa Majesté desire que vous fassiez de ceque deviendront les prisonniers de la cour, ne pouvant croire que l'on fasse mourir Rallé estant innocent seulement pour faire compagnie aux autres."

I fail to discover from Beaumont's letters any proofs that he was convinced of Raleigh's guilt, though he appears, like Napier, to have been sorely perplexed by the attempt to arrive at a satisfactory conclusion.

that he had seen two intercepted letters from Count Aremberg to the Archduke, by which Raleigh's complicity would have been clearly proved could they have brought the letters into court. That if he made this statement he lied, is clear from the subsequent conduct of James and his ministers, who, during the thirteen years of Raleigh's imprisonment, endeavoured by reiterated investigations to discover something like a fact which might even appear to justify their barbarous treatment of him.

I am not in a condition to prove that Beaumont did not make the statement attributed to him, though the following passage of a letter from a French gentleman of high honour and integrity satisfies my mind that no statement of the kind is to be found in the existing despatches of that ambassador:—"I have read," he says, "all Beaumont's despatches of November and December (1603) without being able to find the passage in question, and by way of proof, I have carefully transcribed every passage in which the name of Cecil occurs." This he did because Beaumont was said to have learned from Cecil what he wrote to his Government respecting the intercepted letters.

The Venetian ambassadors,* in conveying to the seignory an account of the Winchester trials, adopted

* Duodo and Molino, Dec. 1st (N.S.), 1603. MSS. Venetian Archives.

the current theory of the conspiracy, observing that its object was to kill the King, and raise Arabella to the throne. As it was assumed that the lady herself must have possessed some knowledge of what was to be accomplished in her behalf, she was constrained to be present at Winchester, where her fate would be decided by the disclosures made at the trials. Her innocence, however, might be inferred, they said, from the fact that when Lord Cobham sought by letter to involve her in treasonable correspondence with Spain, she carried the missive with the seal still unbroken to James, but how in that case she knew the dangerous nature of the proposal made to her is not explained. Her anxiety was at length, it is said, put an end to by Raleigh, who, after sentence of death had been pronounced against him, acquitted her of all participation in the conspiracy, but as he never admitted himself to have been cognizant of any conspiracy, his chivalrous declaration in favour of Arabella may safely be regarded as a fiction.

CHAPTER IV.

LADY RALEIGH AND THE COUNTESS OF PEMBROKE.

Around Thursday, November 17th, 1603, many incidents worthy of notice grouped themselves. Raleigh appears to have been informed immediately after his condemnation that he would be suffered to live eighteen days, during which time therefore it behoved him to close his accounts with Time, and prepare for Eternity.

It is easy, I am aware, to be stoical when it is another man's life, not yours, that is in jeopardy; yet with all my love for Raleigh's character, and profound reverence for his memory, I am unable to refrain from blaming the course he now pursued. He felt it was blameable, and blamed himself.* There was a violent struggle going on in his mind—he was ambitious, he felt that his life, if he perished then, might be looked upon by

---

* "It was for you and yours," he writes to his wife, "that I desired life, but it is true I disdain myself for begging it." Works, viii., 649.

posterity as a play not played out; he had a son, an only son, whom he dearly loved; he had a wife whom he loved still more dearly; and who, in spite of the hard usage she had met with from him in the outset, had proved herself the truest of true wives—her love rising as the tide of misfortune rose about them both, shedding its pure splendour over his dungeon, as it would, he doubted not, over his grave.

These were circumstances which could not fail to exert a powerful influence on his conduct, yet they should not have extorted from him the letter he wrote to James, entreating his forgiveness. He could not have forgotten that many of those Romans whom in secret he emulated, would not, when they knew themselves to be the victims of injustice, have stooped to ask their lives of king or emperor; their souls therefore—though it pains me to say it—were of nobler mould; they valued life no less than he, but when the inevitable hour presented itself, they bent their proud necks to the axe without a murmur.

Once and again in the course of his life Raleigh suffered the troubles of the hour to disorder his ideas, so that he was unable to discern clearly their relations and connexion. In such a frame of mind, hope interweaving itself with apprehension, and worldly considerations struggling with doubts of what might be beyond the grave—he may have cheated himself into the belief that he cherished something like love for the man who he knew could by a word reopen before him the grand vista of life, or consign him to a scaffold. This betrayed him into entreaties unworthy of his noble nature, and the memory of which still tarnishes his reputation.

While matters were thus with Raleigh, all his friends forsook him and fled; nay, not all—two women who still occupy a place amid the highest pinnacles of fame were found to sympathise with his sufferings, and drain their influence to the dregs in the endeavour to save his life. Of these, the first, by the laws of nature and of love, was the woman whom, as he says, he had chosen and loved in his happiest time: broken down with sorrow, and not knowing whom else to address in the blank desert in which she now found herself, this true wife, as he rightly terms her, attempted in her most touching language to soften the heart of Cecil :—

"If the grieved tears of an unfortunate woman may receive any favour, or the unspeakable sorrows of my dead heart may receive any comfort, then let my sorrows come before you, which if you truly knew, I assure myself you would pity me ; but more especially your poor unfortunate friend, which relieth wholly on your honourable and wonted favour. I know in my own soul, which something knoweth his mind, that he doth, and ever hath done, not only honoured the King, but naturally loveth him—and God knoweth far from him to wish him harm, but to have spent his life as soon for him as any creature living. I most humbly beseech your honour, even for God's sake, to be good unto him, to once more make him your creature, your relied friend, and deal with the King for him; for one that is more worthy of favour than many else; having worth, and honesty and wisdom to be a friend; pity the name of your ancient friend, and his poor little creature that may live to honour you, that we all may lift up our hands and hearts in prayer for you and yours. Bind this our poor family to praise your honour and wonted good-nature; let the whole world praise your love to my poor unfortunate husband; for Christ's sake, which rewardeth all mercies, pity his just case; and God for his infinite mercy bless you for ever, and work in the King mercy.

"She that will truly honour you in all misfortunes,

"E. RALEIGH.

"P.S. I am not able, I protest before God, to stand on my trembling legs, otherwise I would have waited now on you to be directed wholly by you."*

The other woman who now came forward was no less a person than "Sidney's sister, Pembroke's mother."

* MS. 'Burleigh Papers,' British Museum.

It is known that with nearly all members of the Sidney family Raleigh had lived from his earliest youth on terms of familiar friendship; but no trace I believe of his love for Mary, the inspirer of the Arcadia, is to be found, save that which now became visible. " I do call to mind," observes Dudley Carleton, "a pretty secret that the Lady of Pembroke hath written to her son Philip, and charged him of all her blessings to employ his own credit and his friends, and all he can do for Raleigh's pardon; and though she does little good, yet she is to be commended for doing her best in showing *veteris vestigia flammæ*."[*]

Two days after the date of Carleton's letter, in which the above passage occurs, the work of death commenced at Winchester with the two priests, Watson and Clarke.[†] Eight days later, Lord Cecil sent his brother-in-law, George Brooke, to the block, and circulated the report that in four other days, Grey, Cobham. and Markham should follow. Raleigh, who may have suspected, but could not certainly know the system of intrigue secretly going on, is said to have requested that Lord Cobham

---

[*] 'Court and Times of James I.,' i., 26. Carleton to Chamberlain, Nov. 27th, 1603.

[†] Up to the 15th of December (N.S.) it was generally believed that all the conspirators would be executed except Raleigh : " La sentenza è di gia stata esseguita contra li doi preti, et venerdi saranno fatti morire tutti li altre eccetto Rali." Molino, Despatch of the above date. Venetian Archives.

might be put to death before him, not doubting that when he should be on the scaffold, and see there could be no escape from the axe, he would, through fear of judgment beyond the grave, retract his accusations. Equally convinced that such would be the result, Cecil and James took care to defeat Raleigh's hopes by relieving Cobham from his apprehensions. When with Grey and Markham he was led forth as to execution, he knew that the whole was to prove a farce, and was able to play the hero accordingly.

Kept sedulously in the dark, Raleigh, who from a window in the Donjon Keep beheld a scaffold erected in the court below, and saw the prisoners led towards it between their own coffins, gave a serious interpretation to what he witnessed, especially when he observed the scaffold to be strewn with straw, the block set up, and the executioner standing beside it with his axe. Markham first mounted the steps, which he did with manly firmness, refusing the napkin offered by a friend to cover his face, saying he could look on death without blushing. When Raleigh saw him removed, and Grey ascend, he may have thought that the inferior offender had been reprieved from the penalty which would yet be inflicted on the superior. Grey, who supposed Markham to have been executed, spurned the straw aside with his foot as he walked towards the block, to discover if there were any traces of blood. When time had been allowed him for his devotions, he also was led away, upon which the spectator in the Tower must have begun to suspect the real nature of the exhibition. Cobham was brought out last, and prayed so loudly, and with so much apparent fervour, that he excited the jests and laughter of those who stood around in the rain, and were probably in the secret. Then followed one of the tricks of the stage—the three offenders were brought together on the scaffold, the King's pardon was announced,* the spectators shouted, the apparatus of death was swept away, and Raleigh, who must have been sorely perplexed by the aspect of the whole proceeding, was left to ponder, in what frame of mind may be conjectured, on the fate which the scene he had witnessed boded to him.

As no one knows what life is, whence it comes, or how, so no one can conjecture what elements concur to make up the life's experience of another. Forward from that day to the 29th of October, 1618, Raleigh stood every moment on the steps of the scaffold. While we move in the light, it costs us few pangs to reflect that we must sooner or later shrink behind the curtain of darkness, which death stands ready to draw over us; neither do we appear to witness anything strange, when

* King to Sheriff of Hampshire, Dec. 7th, 1603. MS. State Paper Office.

as we walk along the course of life the grim spectre snatches away one companion after another from our side; but it would cost us some effort to advance during fifteen years check-by-jowl with the grisly phantom, always visible, whether we paced the floor of a dungeon in the Tower, wrote 'Histories of the World,' navigated the Atlantic, or lay fever-stricken amid the bogs of Guiana.

I have said that Raleigh was to have been beheaded on the 12th of December, and it is currently believed that on the night of the 11th he wrote that magnificent poem "The Soul's Errand." The authorship of this piece is matter of doubt, as well as the date of its production, some attributing it to Sylvester, others to Raleigh. If we are moved by the force of analogy, we shall hardly accord to the translator of 'Du Bartas' credit for having given birth to so vigorous and daring a poem, every line of which is in perfect harmony with Raleigh's character :—

> "Go, since I needs must die,
> And give the world the lie."

For fixing the period at which it was written, we have no data, but that it is the offspring of fierce misanthropy cannot be doubted. We know of no occasion on which the gentle Sylvester could have been inspired by such a feeling; but Raleigh lay in the Tower in

1592,* and was then as likely as at any other period to have said—

> "Tell potentates they live,
>   Acting by others' actions:
> Not loved, unless they give;
>   Not strong but by their factions:
> If potentates reply,
> Give potentates the lie."

This was meant for the Tudor; in the blindness of his rage he might then have written—

> "Tell love it is but lust."

Eleven years later, he could not have uttered such a blasphemy against truth, in face of the holy zeal he had witnessed in Elizabeth, Throgmorton, and Mary Sidney. Indeed, with the shadows of death hanging over him, he retracted the slander against human nature, in that outpouring of his soul's agony, to her who had shown him by acts of the loftiest devotion that love is something better than lust, and who by her conduct during upwards of fifty years demonstrated the same truth still more strongly to the world.

On the 9th of December, Tichbourne received a warrant from James, to deliver up to the Lieutenant of

---

* Hallam in his 'Introduction to the Literature of Europe,' ii., 224, is doubtful to whom this poem should be attributed, but rejects the claim of Sylvester. Campbell says he had seen it in a MS. collection of 1593, which puts Pembroke's authorship out of the question, but makes in no way against Raleigh.

the Tower, Sir George Harvey, then at Winchester, certain State prisoners named in the document, including Sir Walter Raleigh.* On what day they departed from Winchester I have nowhere seen stated, but as they reached the Tower on the 16th,† they probably set out on the 10th; for it took them seven days to perform the journey down, so that we can hardly allow them less than six to return. The events of five weeks had wrought a wonderful change in public opinion respecting Raleigh. We hear of no mobs greeting him with execrations on his way back to the Tower; it is indeed probable that the populace had begun to share the sentiment of him who declared, that although while he knew not the man, he would have gone a hundred miles to see him hanged, yet after having his imagination kindled by witnessing his bearing in court, and hearing him pour forth his eloquent and convincing defence, he would have gone a thousand miles to save his life. Exactly so it seems to have fared with the London populace; for when the great prisoner emerged from his cell, and stood to take the air on the Tower

---

* King to Keeper of Winchester Castle, Dec. 9th, 1603. State Paper Office.

† Carleton to Chamberlain, Dec. 21st, 1603. State Paper Office. According to the accounts of the Lieutenant of the Tower, examined by Mr. Collier, Raleigh was sent to the Fleet about the Christmas of 1603, and remained above a fortnight. 'Notes and Queries.' No. 107, p. 7.

wall, multitudes thronged reverently to gaze at him, as at a martyr; while he, it is said, looked down forgivingly upon them.*

The current of public indignation began from the same date to set in steadily against those who had been engaged in his overthrow, and in history, and national feeling, has gone on increasing in force ever since. Who now pronounces with pleasure the name of Anderson or Gaudy, Coke or Heale, Suffolk or Northampton, Cecil or James? while the name of Raleigh is never repeated without enthusiasm, and the halo of glory with which it is encircled goes on brightening from year to year, and will go on as long as our English annals shall continue to be studied by the honourable and upright of mankind.

The winter of 1603 was severe and gloomy, sharp frosts alternating with fogs and rain. As the courtiers passed by Wilton on their way back to town, they beheld its pleasant walks rendered almost impassable by mire, and were greeted at their return by dense mists in which lurked the virus of the Plague.† Nations, vicious at other times, seem to grow more reckless in vice during periods of public calamity: Athens, Florence, London, furnished each in its turn an illustration of

* Waade to Cecil, Dec. 9th, 1605. 'Burleigh Papers,' British Museum.

† Carleton to Chamberlain, Jan. 15th, 1604. MS. State Paper Office.

this truth, and James's court appeared desirous of out-
doing the rest of the population. Plays, masques,
feasting, and revelry, mocked at the Plague, though
there was not one among the gallants, male or female,
who did not shiver in secret at the spectre on the pale
horse. What the foreign diplomatists thought of James
and his doings we know from the accounts they forwarded to their respective governments, and what by
the English was thought of them we discover no less
clearly from the contemptuous gossip of the times.
Three ambassadors, those of Spain, France, and Poland,
disturbed the company at Hampton Court by their
jealousies and quarrels for precedence, so that they had
often to be excluded from the royal banquets through
fear of bloodshed.*

In imperial times, when the effigies of the great men
of the Republic were borne in procession through Rome,
the people, we are told, gazed more earnestly at the
gap in the series which should have been filled with the
statues of Brutus and Cassius than at all the rest of the
exciting show. So it was at Hampton Court, where all
thoughtful eyes glanced painfully at the place that
should have been occupied by Elizabeth's old Captain
of the Guard. He had now taken up very different
quarters, where, instead of mirth and revelry, he was to
become acquainted with solitude, and such thoughts as

* Id., ubi supra.

it inspires in the great. He saw the sword of Damocles over his head, he felt its point at times touch his scalp, and made magnanimous resolutions, to which he generally, though not always, adhered. The whole world of science, literature, and philosophy, lay before him—to what department should he devote himself? Science first presented itself, and he became absorbed by the wish to become a great chemist, to extract the virtues out of physical substances, and with them to fabricate medicines for the cure of diseases and the prolongation of life.

The sixteenth century had been mentally a slave to the alembic, which, wrapped in clouds of mystery, had descended from the middle ages upon it. Both the Bacons, Roger and Francis, worshipped this type of physical philosophy, and Raleigh knelt no less reverently by their side. Whether or not he dreamed of the fluid which should turn all metals into gold I am unable to say; but he did certainly hope in the loneliness and stillness of his laboratory in the Tower to extract from the secret forces of nature an elixir which should subdue all diseases, and sometimes combat successfully even with poison. Upon his spirit thus confined broke in at times the salt spray of the ocean, upon whose billows he could not avoid hoping he should once more ride in triumph. Could he not therefore turn his present troubles into a source of solace and refreshment for mariners ? When he had been their companion on far-off seas, beneath Canopus and the Magellanic Clouds, he had witnessed with keen pain the sufferings they often endured through lack of fresh water. Could he not bring the alembic to their aid ? In what was called his "Still-house," erected in the Lieutenant's garden, he commenced a series of experiments, which resulted in the discovery of the means by which sea-water may be made sweet; and thus, in addition to the potato and tobacco, became a benefactor of man. Unfortunately very few particulars of this discovery are on record ; but when late in the eighteenth century Dr. Irving obtained from parliament five thousand pounds for the invention of his method of sweetening sea-water, he appears to have done little more than revive Raleigh's process. Of this all we know is derived from the following passage from the record of his conversations with Sir Thomas Wilson in the Tower :—

" This day Sir Walter Raleigh fell to discoursing of the wonders he had done for the benefit of the kingdom ; how much he had spent for the service thereof in discoveries; and after fell to tell me of his inventing the means to make salt water fresh or sweet, by furnaces of copper in the forecastle, and distilling of the salt water as it were by a bucket, putting in a pipe, and within a quarter of an hour it will run by a spigot, so that he had by that distilled water given two hundred and forty men every day quarts apiece, and the water as sweet as milk."*

When men enter on any course of study they seldom limit their researches within the bounds of mere utility, but push forward their investigations to the utmost of their power, leaving to chance the application of the results. It was thus with Raleigh, whose chemical extracts were so many and so various that the physicians and apothecaries of his time considered them beyond the reach of analysis. Wilson, a profligate and profane instrument of the court, placed about Raleigh to study and report upon his actions and language, regarding with astonishment the multitude of his bottles, vases, jars, and phials, said he believed " they contained all the spirits in the world except the Spirit of God."

In producing these spirits and essences Raleigh took so much delight that he seems to have often spent whole days in his laboratory, which stood in the garden opposite the entrance to the Bloody Tower, on a spot now gravelled over, and forming part of the place of exercise for the garrison.

James, who took credit for extraordinary clemency because he had not put to death a man whose guilt had not, to say the least of it, been proved, amused the public in the spring of 1604 by one of those displays of mock generosity which he hoped would render him

* MS. State Paper Office, September 29th, 1618.

popular among the English. Setting out from Westminster in his barge with the Queen and Prince Henry, attended by the whole body of his ministers and courtiers, in a little fleet of boats, he dropped down the river to the Tower. As his intention had been made known, vast multitudes had collected to behold the royal cavalcade, and so thronged all the approaches to the fortress, especially the Tower Stairs, that the King and his suite experienced much difficulty in ascending.

The act he came to perform would, had it been complete, have well entitled him to popular applause, since it was nothing less than to throw open the door of every dungeon and cell, and give liberty to the captives. Now therefore the public doubtless expected that the old Captain of Elizabeth's Guard would be withdrawn from his laboratory and favoured with congenial employment on the ocean. Such, however, was not James's method of proceeding. On the day before his visit to the Tower, Raleigh, with the other conspirators, had been removed to the Fleet and other prisons. This surely was keeping the word of promise to the ear but breaking it to the hope. However, if the great prisoner had been sent to languish elsewhere, the rabble and the monarch were entertained by bull-baiting, by fights between other fierce animals, and by feasts and shows which gladdened the hearts of the thoughtless, but suggested dark forebodings to the minds of reflecting men.*

It was well for Raleigh that he could take refuge in study from the blows now aimed at him by fortune. The conviction was pressing on him that he might soon have to say with Job, "Naked came I forth from my mother's womb, and naked shall I return to the womb of earth." The blue-bonneted gentlemen from beyond the Tweed, together with sundry rivals on this side the Border, were beginning to take note of his feathers, and considering where they should begin to pluck. Fortune in Elizabeth's time had led him by the hand up to the very pinnacle of her high places, lavished upon him castles, manors, patents, monopolies, wardenships, lord-lieutenancies, governorships, distinguished rank in army and navy, with privileges at court accorded to few. To advance from the highest point is to descend; and Raleigh, as we have seen, had been for some time on the downward path. His fall was now to become more rapid. Early in July he received from the King an order to deliver up the seal of the Duchy of Cornwall, upon which he addressed to his persecutor one of those servile and profane effusions which constitute the greatest blot upon his memory.

"I was of late sent unto," he says, "for the seal of

* Nicol Molin to the Senate, March 26th (N.S.), 1604. Venetian Archives.

the Duchy of Cornwall, which, together with the seal of
the office of warden and chancellor, I received at the
hands of my late sovereign.   This seal appertaineth not
unto me to dispose, but unto your Majesty only, and
therefore I have entreated my Lord Cecil to present the
same.   For myself, I have interest in nothing but your
Majesty's mercy only—God, who knows what faith I do
and have ever borne to your Majesty, move your imperial heart to perfect graces begun.   If I be here restrained until the powers both of my mind and body be
so enfeebled as I cannot hope to do your Majesty some
extraordinary and acceptable service, whereby I may
truly approve my faith and intentions to my sovereign
lord, God doth know then it would have been happiest
for me to have died long since ; for the everlasting
God doth bear me record it is to no other chief end
that I desire to live a day.   I most humbly beseech
your Majesty, even for the love of our Lord Jesus, to
think that I can never forget the mercies of the King
that hath vouchsafed to lift me out of the grave, being
then friendless. lost. and forsaken of all men.   Pardon
me, most renowned King, but to say thus much, that
if it shall please your Majesty to have compassion on
me, while I have yet limbs and eyes, that your Majesty
shall never have cause to accuse or repent your Majesty's
mercies towards me."*

* Raleigh to the King, July 31st, 1604.   MS.   State Paper Office.

In blasphemous extravagance such as this Raleigh's enemies might have found some colour for the charge of impiety which they constantly brought against him. But his capacious mind, agitated by irregular and undisciplined emotions, chafing and panting with the longing for action, and not yet voluntarily chained to the car of thought, only betrayed in such phrases the force of its internal agony. Still, interpret them by what rules we may, they are so essentially despicable that it is impossible to avoid blushing as we read. It is true that James's conduct towards Raleigh had not been all bad; from a natural impulse of humanity, through deference to public opinion, or through apprehension of future judgment, he exhibited towards him fitful relaxations of cruelty, leaving him in constant expectation of death, yet restoring to him much of the property and sources of income forfeited by his attainder. chief among the latter of which was his wine-patent. From this indeed he derived so large a revenue—all vintners in the kingdom excepting those of the City of London paying to his receivers one pound a year— that it was deemed impolitic to leave him in possession of it much longer, and accordingly in the following December it passed into the hands of Raleigh's great enemy, the Earl of Nottingham, James's cousin by marriage.

The evils resulting from the unrestrained influx of

Scotchmen into England soon began to appear.* Losing sight of the political advantages of the Union, the English suffered themselves to be chafed by the rough barbarism of the strangers, who, with something like the insolence of conquest, jostled the Southrons in street and palace. Difference in dress, speech, and manners is the source of that antipathy which foreigners cherish for each other; and in London the Scots of that period were exclusively regarded as foreigners, since they neither understood the English language nor could all at once adopt English habits. National dislike accordingly boiled over, not only in ribald songs and stinging epigrams, but in the flash of dirk and rapier, the clash of which, accompanied by oaths and a rush of gutturals, often rang at night through the streets of London. To James's national partiality and desire to put a stop to these outbreaks must be attributed the blackguardism of the following proclamation :—

" Whereas certain loose people, commonly called swaggerers, and of the damned crew whose names are hereunder written, have of late raised many quarrels against the subjects and servants of the kingdom of Scotland, and be the occasion of much trouble to the disturbance of the peace of this kingdom if it be not prevented : our pleasure therefore is that you shall cause these fellows to be apprehended, and any other of

* Raumer, ii., 196.

like quality whom you shall be . . . . of by other means
and put them under . . . . of the peace towards all our
subjects, and these shall be your warrant."*

When the necessity of inaction is first experienced
by a man of energetic character he is sure to overrate
its effects upon mind and body. Raleigh, therefore, in
the first dawn of his captivity feared for his health—for
his reason—for his life ; and though the company of his
wife and son in some degree mitigated the anguish of
seclusion, he never relinquished his endeavour to recover his freedom, even though it should be coupled
with exile from England. One of the worst features of
adversity is that in some situations it necessitates dissimulation. Raleigh thoroughly understood Cecil's
policy, which was to keep him out of the way without
destroying him ; yet as to give evidence of this knowledge would only have been to blight his own hopes, however frail they might be, he kept the mask of hypocrisy
perpetually before his visage, in the vain hope of warding
off the penetrating glance of his false friend. By the
same motive was the minister likewise actuated. What
he had accomplished by the ' Secret Correspondence '
had been then disclosed only to the King and his intimate friends, and he vehemently desired to escape the
condemnation of which he would have been certain had

* This was addressed to Sir John Popham, Chief Justice, April
15th, 1604. MS. State Paper Office.

his villainy been revealed to the public. To prevent if possible even a suspicion of the fact from becoming general, he always affected a friendship for his victim, and so was constrained to pursue a line of conduct not wholly irreconcilable with such a profession.

Buoyed up by hope, Lady Raleigh now made the most strenuous efforts to obtain her husband's enlargement, which Cecil, to whom her applications were chiefly addressed, suggested should be solicited through the instrumentality of some other courtier. Something in the behaviour of the Secretary intended to produce such an impression awakened in Raleigh's mind the belief that his deliverance might indeed be at hand. At the bare prospect all the faculties of his soul started into activity; he formed a thousand projects: restricted liberty at home—exile to some foreign country—the chances of war—the endless resources of maritime adventure: to be at large, to plunge into some scheme that might absorb his thoughts, and give full scope to his genius, there was no sacrifice he would not make, no humiliation to which he would not stoop. Up to this time his lands had not been wholly secured to the use of his wife and child, and he therefore strove earnestly to bring about the necessary settlement; he then touched upon the subject of his pardon, and entreated that he might not owe it to the interference of any one but Cecil, not being as yet able to conceive the weary years through which he should solicit it in vain, and the fact that the block alone would put a period to his solicitations.

"If I have a pardon," he says, "I may, notwithstanding, be restrained or confined. If I may not be here about London, I shall be most contented to be confined within the hundred of Sherbourne, or if I cannot be allowed so much, I shall be contented to live in Holland, where I shall chance get some employment upon the Indies." Should he fail in obtaining this privilege, he sought to have revived in his favour one of the practices of Elizabeth's time, and suggested that he might be delivered into the safe keeping of some nobleman or bishop, or be intrusted with the care of one of Cecil's parks. Confinement, as he then believed, threatened to undermine his health, to restore which he entreated the King's permission to repair to Bath. He could not as yet persuade himself that James meant, not merely to undermine his health, but to bring his life also as soon as possible to a close; though he at length found, after twelve years longer of insidious endeavour, that his captive's constitution would not yield to the rigours of imprisonment.

Raleigh's entreaties being unheeded, he was fain to derive what solace he could from study, and the company of his wife, who, in the spring of 1605, brought him a second son, whom, in honour of his brother, he christened Carew. Not long after, we find the unhappy mother appealing earnestly to James in behalf of herself and her children.

"I beseech your Majesty, in the name of Jesus Christ, to signify your gracious pleasure concerning myself and my poor children. That, whereas, your Majesty hath disposed of all my husband's estate to the value of four thousand a-year, and that there remaineth nothing to give me and my children bread but one fee-farm, held of the Bishop of Sarum, which your Majesty bestowed upon my husband during his life. That it will please your Majesty of your abundant goodness to relinquish your Majesty's right in the reversion of that farm, and suffer those poor harmless children to enjoy the same, in imitation of the most just and merciful God, who, though he punisheth the fathers, yet he gave the land to the guiltless, innocent children; and we shall ever pray to God for the increase of your Majesty's dearest comforts."*

Cecil, raised to the Earldom of Salisbury, May 4th, 1605, signed the draught of a warrant drawn up in reply to this petition.

"Whereas, we understand that, by rigour of law, the reversion of Sir Walter Raleigh's lands may come into our hands, yet, seeing his conveyance was made in the Queen our sister's time, as also because we have given

* MS. 'Burleigh Papers.' British Museum.

himself those lands for his own life, our pleasure is, that you cause a grant to be drawn for us to sign, wherein all our title and interest may be passed over unto his said wife and children, that we be no more troubled with their pitiful cries and complaints for that business."*

* MS. 'Burleigh Papers.' British Museum.

CHAPTER V.

RE-IMMURED IN THE BLOODY TOWER.

OWING to the unwearied exertions made by Lady Raleigh, who understood nothing of the real feelings or designs of Salisbury, the belief prevailed throughout this summer in Dorsetshire that James's government was about to relent. Impetuous and hopeful, Bessy made two journeys to Sherbourne, where, amid various other improvements and alterations, she caused two new walks to be cut through the grounds, fully persuaded that, before those walks should be strewn with autumn leaves, she should enjoy the supreme happiness of strolling with her lord in those sweet solitudes as of old. Grief had for two years turned her energies in a different direction; scarcely one day during that period had found her free from anguish, since she could never be sure that the next would not be the last of her husband's life. Fear, therefore, kept her constantly hovering about the court or the Tower, importuning the ministers, or endeavouring by all the arts of affection to mitigate the gloom of the Bloody Tower. Sherbourne Castle had been consequently neglected; cobwebs hung from the walls; rust gathered on the armour; the chambers remained unswept, the beds unmade. A gleam of hope now illumined the interior of Raleigh's dwelling; his armour was taken down from the wall and polished, his books were arranged in order, and all that a wife's care could accomplish was done to cheer him at his expected return.

Captain Kemys had been intrusted, after his release from the Tower, with the wardenship of Sherbourne Castle, of which he took as much care as could be looked for from an old naval officer. All Raleigh's companions and dependents made this place their home when they had no other. Among these was Captain Nichols, a learned mathematician and able engineer, whom Raleigh, when thrown into the Tower, recommended to the Earl of Northumberland, who employed him as inspector of the works at Sion. Cotterel also, it will be remembered, the bearer of Raleigh's letter to Cobham in the Tower, obtained an asylum at Sherbourne, where he yet remained, and was known in the neighbourhood under the nom de guerre of Captain Sampson.*

The summer wore away, autumn with its mists and damps approached, and Raleigh still lay captive in his

* Cotterel's 'Examination,' Feb. 4th, 1607. MS. State Paper Office.

unwholesome cell. Sorrow often embitters the sweetest tempers, and renders the noblest minds incapable of guarding at all moments against the inroads of peevishness. Few men have loved as Raleigh loved his wife; no woman ever loved more passionately or enduringly than that wife loved him. Yet perpetual conflict with disappointment, the heart sickness of hope deferred, the falling away of friends, the triumph of enemies, the incessant fretting which they felt in common, now threw a shadow over their lives. What blame there was rested neither on wife nor husband, but on both. Bessy's powers of endurance appear to have given way first; exhausted by long journeys, by incessant solicitations, by correspondence, by harsh rebuffs, she became wayward and angry, so that she seems to have been betrayed for a moment into unkind reproaches towards the man whom, nevertheless, she had enshrined for ever in her heart of hearts. Wounded by her words, Raleigh became unjust in his turn, and complained of her both to Waade and Cecil.

Public affairs were in some way interwoven with Raleigh's domestic sorrows; suspicion of having been concerned by conference, or through the intermediation of his wife, with the men of the 5th of November, now weighed upon him. His intimate friend, the Earl of Northumberland, seems to have been acquainted beforehand with the design of the Jesuits; and other individuals, who, if not actively engaged in the conspiracy, certainly tampered with its elements, had interviews with Raleigh, though the nature and object of their intercourse have never come to light. It seems possible that Lady Raleigh, a woman of strong passions and fierce spirit, who cherished, as she was justified in doing, a deadly hatred of the King, may not have kept quite clear of all connection with the plotters. However this may be, Raleigh believed her about this time to have unwittingly exposed him to fresh attacks from the Government. All who bear in mind the part played by Waade in Raleigh's story will know how to interpret the language in which he maliciously describes Raleigh's professions of innocence.

"It is not possible," he says, "for any man to protest more ignorance in the matter than he doth; laying all these rash errors and frantic parts on the folly of her whose imperfections he should conceal."*

The biography of a perfect man yet remains to be written; Raleigh made no claims to be so considered. He was a man of many failings, defects, imperfections, vices; but he was also a man of sorrow, and acquainted with grief: as such, let us proceed with him on his way, censuring where we must, excusing where we can. In the agony of his tribulation, he now unburdened his

---

* Letter to Salisbury, Dec. 13th, 1605. MS. 'Burleigh Papers. British Museum.

heart to Salisbury, having no one else to whom, as he believed, he could speak with so much freedom.

"I lay before your Lordship the true causes of my importunities. The one is, which I speak in the fear and presence of God, that I am, every second or third night, in danger either of sudden death, or of the loss of my limbs and sense, being sometimes two hours without feeling a motion of my hand and whole arm. I complain not of it, I know it is vain, for there is none that hath compassion thereof. The other, that I shall be made more than weary of my life by her crying and bewailing, who will return in post, when she hears of your departure, and nothing done. She hath already brought her eldest son in one hand, and her sucking child in another, crying out of her and their destruction, charging me with unnatural negligence, and that, having provided for mine own life, I am without sense or compassion of theirs.

"These torments, added to my desolate life, receiving nothing but torments and outcries where I should look for some comfort, together with my consideration of my cruel destiny, my days and times worn out in sorrow and imprisonment, is sufficient either utterly to distract me, or to make me curse the time that ever I was born into the world, and had a being, did I not hope that God will be pleased to accept those miseries in this world, which my neglect of Him and my offences against Him have deserved. I beseech your Lordship, as you must one day beg comfort of God, and cry unto Him for his abundant mercies, that you will be pleased to spare the time, and to push and effect in some sort your heart's intents towards me. If I could either help or blame their cries and impatience, I would, for myself, leave all to God and your Lordship; but if your Lordship spare one thought towards this estate of mine, I cannot but hope for some happy end, which I leave your Lordship to resolve of."*

Raleigh in the above letter uses, it will be perceived, no expressions which could have justified the language of Waade. On the contrary, though his wife's reproaches could not be other than bitter to him, he yet took the circumstances of her situation into account, and admitted that, though unjust, they were extremely natural, and therefore no way deserving of blame.

Few examples are on record of the struggles through which a powerful mind turns from action to speculation. Raleigh was naturally framed rather to make history than to write it; but reflecting in his solitude that there are more ways of serving mankind than by policy or war, he plunged from the sphere of action into that of thought, and gradually formed the design of reviewing the entire story of the world, from its conception in the mind of God to the moment at which it came in contact

* MS. 'Burleigh Papers.' British Museum.

with the historian's individuality. In this purpose he was strengthened by some changes which had been recently made in the society of the Tower. In the England of those days, spirits too restless, too daring, too vast, to be easily dealt with, were usually sent thither till the Government could discover some means of neutralizing their influence, or some feasible pretext for cutting them off. Henry Percy, ninth Earl of Northumberland of his family, though by no means a great, was yet a remarkable man, mingling science with politics, and Ovidian * effeminacy with the intrigues of a Catiline; he now naturally found his way to the Tower, where his father had been assassinated, and where the most illustrious of his friends was then awaiting assassination. Northumberland's means were large, and the liberality with which he shared them with his friends shed a lustre on his name. Science had not yet been clearly discriminated in popular apprehension from magic and other occult studies; and accordingly Percy's application to what the vulgar deemed unlawful investigations procured for him the name of the Wizard Earl.† Some credit is due to James and his ministers for the forms which society in the Tower was sometimes allowed to assume—I say sometimes, because indulgence

---

* His Treatise on love, more reprehensible than that of Ovid, still exists in MS.

† Wood, 'Athenæ Oxonienses.'

occasionally gave place to extreme rigour, which in particular instances degenerated into cruelty. In Percy's case lenity was so predominant that, but for his being restrained from changing his place of residence, he might have been said to be as much master of the dwelling as he would have been at Sion. He had apartments whenever he chose for his son or his daughter, he kept there open house for his friends, and when any female prisoner of rank and beauty came thither, no matter for what crime or enormity, he enjoyed access to her apartments, and made love to her after his wonted fashion.

By sending genius and learning to the Tower, James now converted it into a sort of rival to " the groves of Academe." Shakespeare was probably too politic to risk the loss of court favour by visiting the new academy —unless when Southampton, whom James suspected of familiarity with his queen,* came to breathe malaria for a while amid his old enemies ; but Ben Jonson, more jovial and reckless, obeyed the attraction of good cheer, and dined and drank with Raleigh and the magi, whose perilous speculations inspired him with no alarm. What those speculations were we may in part conjecture from the obloquy then cast upon them. Thomas Hariot, the man who had surveyed Virginia, now ranked with Hues and Warner among Percy's magi ; †

* Birch, ii., 394.   † Wood, ' Athenæ Oxonienses,' i., 460.

and as he lay open to the suspicion of scepticism, helped to fasten the same charge on his associates. Machiavelli, Giordano Bruno, and Vanini were then commonly read by philosophical students; and as Raleigh now began to carry back his thoughts to "the womb of nature, and perhaps her grave," he yielded to the temptation which, sooner or later, involves all thoughtful men in the sweet bewilderment of metaphysics.

But if Raleigh's days were often rendered cheerful by the society of men with minds so capacious, with fancy so fertile, with thoughts and ideas so diversified, the hours of the night were too frequently consumed by the precursors of paralysis, which periodically attacked him in the darkness; while dank exhalations from the river and the Tower ditch filled his chamber. All they to whom meditation is happiness receive the visit of the brightest ideas at night. It is a grand poetical conception that in the impenetrable gloom of chaos the Spirit of God moved upon the face of the waters. Man also struggles with chaos in the night, and sends his spirit forth over its limitless expanse to gather creative force; but Raleigh, than whom no man was ever more fitly framed for enjoying this delight, received in the spring of 1606 a check which seemed to threaten a sudden termination to his studies. The paralytic symptoms he described to Cecil went on increasing, till, on the 26th of March, he obtained leave to consult a physician. At court his complaints of illness were probably looked upon as fictions, but they were now backed by the authority of Dr. Turner, whose certificate was addressed to the Lords of the Council:—

"Sir Walter Raleigh's complaining is in this manner —all his left side is extreme cold, void of sense and motion, or numb. His fingers on the same side beginning to be contracted, and his tongue taken in some part, insomuch that he speaketh weakly, and it is to be feared he may utterly lose the use of it.

"Peter Turner, D. Physic.

"In respect of these circumstances, to speak like a physician, it were good for him, if it might stand with your honours' liking, that he were removed from the cold lodging where he lieth into a warmer, that is to say, a little room he hath built in the garden, and joining his still-house."*

Whether any improvement took place in Raleigh's lodgings in consequence of Turner's representations does not appear, though the dreaded apoplectic seizure kept aloof. He stuck close, however, to his studies, borrowing by the aid of Dr. Burhill, from the Hebrew, Syriac, and Chaldaic, all such glow-worm light as those languages throw on the world before the flood. His

* Medical certificate of Dr. Turner in Sir Walter Raleigh's behalf. MS. State Paper Office.

connection with the outer world became yearly less and less observable, until he, who upon the theatre of action had long attracted the whole world's gaze, shrank into an erudite recluse, exerting a visible influence little wider than his cell. Through accidental rents in the pitiable drapery of public affairs we catch a glimpse of him now and then, though of the most indistinct and unsatisfactory kind; as where Salisbury involves himself in a quarrel about him and his fellow-captives with the Spanish ambassador, or when James's queen's brother, Christian IV. of Denmark, seeks to obtain his liberation, that he may make him Admiral-in-chief of the Danish fleets. But these momentary glimpses obtained, the curtain falls again upon the Bloody Tower, and leaves imagination to picture to itself as it pleases all that is taking place within.

In the beginning of 1607 an attempt was made by the Government to obtain some new evidence which might appear to justify Raleigh's protracted imprisonment. The reader is already acquainted with Edward Cotterel, who, in the November of 1603, was sent to Sherbourne, where he seems to have gradually conceived the ambition of becoming a miniature Iago. Having contrived to make his whereabouts known to Salisbury, he was sent for to London, and instructed in the part he was expected to play. Lady Raleigh, it has been seen, had been permitted to join her husband, but under restrictions, for at a certain hour of the evening she had to leave the Tower. To be near at hand, she had taken a house on Tower Hill, from the windows of which she could see Raleigh when he went forth in the early morning to walk and meditate in the Lieutenant's garden. To stand by the site of that house and look across the open space to the lawn dotted with copses which represents that garden, is almost to glance across the centuries that separate us from Raleigh. To this house and this open space came Cotterel in the February of 1607, in the hope of making some discovery which might further the design of his employers. Having behaved in a way to excite suspicion, he did not proceed directly, as an honest servant would, to the house of his mistress, but lurked about while Morgan and Saunders, two of Raleigh's domestics, went forward to learn what reception he was likely to meet with. Having been put upon her guard, Lady Raleigh refused to admit the traitor to her presence, and while he paced to and fro in vexation at the failure of his plan, she left her house, walked down the hill, and entered the Tower. Completely baffled, Cotterel was taken back to the house of the Chief Justice, where he made it evident that nothing criminating his master could be extracted out of him.*

* 'Examination of Edward Cotterel,' February 4th, 1607. State Paper Office.

If any proof were needed that the trial at Winchester was a sham, and that James and his ministers knew it to be so considered by the public, the reiterated attempts they made to obtain fresh evidence against the prisoner would supply that proof. Could they have brought themselves to regard the sentence as just, they would not have hesitated to carry it into execution. If they did not know, they certainly feared it might be otherwise, and hence their repeated efforts, the examinations, the investigations, the confronting of witnesses, the schemes, contrivances, and intrigues, resorted to in the hope of imparting some appearance of justice to their iniquitous proceedings.

The process of civilization in modern times has generally identified itself with those subtle contrivances by which the poor are made poorer, and the rich richer. In old times every city, town, and village, was surrounded by its mark or belt of common-land, on which the humbler classes fed their cows, sheep, and poultry; but in proportion as the political condition of our island divorced the mass of the population from military habits, social helplessness succeeded to sturdy independence, and the common-lands passed from the hands of the poor into those of opulent proprietors. From the accession of James, these agrarian spoliations had gone on spreading and multiplying, till they goaded the people into insurrection, as was the case in the year 1608.

No spendthrift proprietor could look with a more covetous eye on the immemorial domain of his humbler neighbours than did James Stuart on Raleigh's castles and manors: having by the Winchester sham consigned the owner to paralysis, fever, and ague, in the Tower, he had for a while abstained from laying his hands on the property set apart for the maintenance of his victim's wife and children; but the growing necessities created by his vices now urged him to set aside his own act and deed, and plunder the captive of his property. The crown lawyers were therefore commissioned to scrutinize the instrument by which the Sherbourne estates had been conveyed by Raleigh to his son, and, as might have been foreseen, a flaw was immediately discovered in it. The Caledonian Antinous, by whose beauty James was now fascinated, wanted an estate to satisfy the cravings of his prodigality, and to gratify him, James had directed Popham to discover the flaw above mentioned. To ward off approaching ruin, Lady Raleigh made her way to the palace, leading her two sons, Walter and Carew, by the hand, and entering the Presence Chamber, knelt before the King, beseeching him in most passionate language not to deprive those little ones of bread. James's reply was characteristic: "I maun hae the land," he said; "I maun hae it for Car!" The blood of the Throgmortons was fiery in Bessy's veins: maddened by injustice, she lifted up her hands to heaven, and scorning the tyrant's power, imprecated Divine vengeance on the plunderer of her children.*

But, brutalized by licentiousness, the Stuart cared neither for heaven nor earth: having borrowed his ethics from Nero and Caligula, his humanity naturally took the same stamp, and he gaily proceeded therefore in his project of spoliation. Nevertheless, to blunt the sharp tongues of the Puritans, who took their morals from God, he devised, in conjunction with his lawyers, a scheme which he doubtless hoped would shield him from public condemnation. Sherbourne was worth five thousand a year—he would purchase it—what objection could be made to that? Not much, provided the lands were justly valued, and the purchase money honestly paid. No land agent would have estimated the value of the Sherbourne estate at less than one hundred thousand pounds: James determined to give her whom he meant soon to make a widow little more than one year's rent—that is, eight thousand pounds.

Raleigh had seen enough of minions to know of what qualities their characters were generally made up, and might therefore have spared himself the humiliation of seeking by an eloquent and touching appeal to turn the edge of Car's avarice. In the interest of his wife and children, he would nevertheless try what potency there

* Carew's narrative in Lord Somers' 'Tracts,' ii., p. 454.

might be in words, and therefore wrote the curled and scented favourite a letter, which, persuasive as it was, he himself could hardly have hoped would weigh with a young profligate against a large annual revenue in gold. Among others, the letter contained these words:—

"For yourself, Sir, seeing your fair day is but in the dawn, and mine drawn to the evening, your own virtues, and the King's grace assuring you of many favours and much honour, I beseech you not to begin your first building upon the ruin of the innocent, and that their sorrows with mine may not attend your first plantation."*

The affair of Sherbourne, which if related at length would make a little history of itself, went on spinning its dark thread of fraud and cruelty through the length of two years, bringing lawyers, bishops, ministers, favourites, princes, upon the stage, but at length ending in the defeat of Raleigh. An old bishop in far back times had amused his sacerdotal leisure by composing a piece which he called 'The Curse of Sherbourne.' It was certainly a restless property, flitting from the church to the crown, from the crown to a favourite, from that favourite to the crown again, and so on by a zig-zag route to the Digbys, with whom it became stationary.

Some incidents connected with its transfer to Car

* Letter to Car. Works, viii., p. 650.

may be worth a cursory notice. When the chaos of Raleigh's affairs was shaping itself after the trial at Winchester into a new sphere, the Bishop of Sarum entered into negotiations with him in the hope of recovering Sherbourne for the church. He now opened a correspondence on the subject with Salisbury. It might not have been displeasing to this astute statesman to check the efflorescence of James's vices, which he could not doubt would soon throw him into the arms of some new favourite whose greed might prove no less ravenous than Car's. To soothe therefore the rapacity of that prodigal whose star had not yet emerged from behind the moon, Salisbury desired to retain something in hand, if he was not actuated by the wish to prevent the minion's wings from overshadowing himself. At any rate, he desired the bishop to transmit to him Raleigh's deed of surrender of Sherbourne to the church, and was informed in reply that the deed, being long, would take a considerable time to copy, but that, if his lordship pleased, he might command it out of the Records, where it was enrolled.*

This ecclesiastical episode appears to have exerted no influence on the main action; for James would not be diverted from his purpose by church or law. Commissioners went down to Dorsetshire to survey and

* Bishop of Sarum to Salisbury, Jan. 17th, 1609. State Paper Office.

estimate the value of the estate, and these, knowing what was expected of them, made such a report as suited James's views. Ere the prey had fallen into the minion's fangs, Prince Henry, who held Raleigh in admiration, and detested the injustice from which he suffered, went in a passion to the King, and dwelling on the strength and beauty of Sherbourne, entreated that it might be withheld from Car, and bestowed on him.* But if James had not given, he had promised it ; yet, as he could not refuse the boon demanded by the prince, he is said to have satisfied Car's rapacity with the poor equivalent of twenty-five thousand pounds.

While Sir Griffin Markham, Raleigh's old companion in the Tower and Winchester Castle, was fighting duels in his shirt in the Low Countries, and learning that his lewd lady, having committed bigamy, was doing penance in a white sheet at church doors, Raleigh himself, under the direction of Nemesis, was forging additional links in the chain that bound him to Guiana. In 1604 James had permitted Captain Leigh† to attempt to settle there as in a British colony ; again, in 1608, the same privilege had been granted to Robert Harcourt ; and in 1609 Raleigh, without let or hindrance, despatched a ship in search of treasure, which returned towards the

* Somers' 'Tracts,' ii., 454.

† Captain Leigh to the Council, July 2nd, 1604. State Paper Office.

close of the year with a cargo of yellow ore, supposed to be gold. Had the conjecture proved true, Raleigh's imprisonment would have been of short continuance; but the ore turning out upon examination to be nothing but a species of ochre, the enthusiasm of the adventurers again collapsed, and Raleigh was left to proceed in peace with his 'History of the World.'*

It seems highly probable that Prince Henry, who like his mother had warmly espoused Raleigh's cause, paid visits more or less frequent to the Bloody Tower, which led him to make the significant remark that, "no man but his father would keep such a bird in a cage."

* Chamberlain to Carleton, Dec. 30th, 1609. MS. State Paper Office.

CHAPTER VI.

INTERCOURSE WITH PERCY, BEN JONSON, AND THE MAGI.

In the calm of a literary life, as it is led by a fortunate few, there may be inexpressible sweetness, the delight of creation mingling itself imperceptibly with the irradiations of future glory into the soul. It may be that Raleigh sometimes tasted of this happiness, the footsteps of which seem to be traceable on many a page of his 'History of the World.' But all such joys, like those that visit us in sleep, terminate in fruition; for when we emerge from the dream, whether sleeping or waking, the grim realities of life rush in resistlessly upon the mind, and compel it to renew the contest which identifies itself with so large a portion of human life.

At what Raleigh laboured we know, but we do not know how he laboured, or exactly where; for though the apartments of the Bloody Tower were appropriated to him, he walked about in garden and gallery, dined, talked, read, and perhaps wrote in Northumberland's apartments, which appear to have been almost as free to him as his own. When study became wearisome, he had his wife and two boys to converse and play with. Bessy was young and handsome still, Walter was sixteen, and little Carew between five and six. Accordingly, he had companions with whom to chat about the past, to whom to impart living knowledge, and principles for the guidance of the future; or whose pretty sports and lispings, by touching the tenderest elements of our nature, could from time to time drown the sense of present evils in the overflowings of paternal love. There was besides nearly always a choice though small society to be found in the Tower, consisting of distinguished men and noble ladies, whom the jealousy or vindictiveness of power condemned to ventilate its chambers with their sighs, or to moisten its courts with their blood. Everywhere on wall and wainscot appeared the mementoes of guilt or suffering, affected stoical maxims, sweet expressions of piety and resignation, outpourings of love, or indications of blank and desolate despair; which, read by the dim light creeping down between massive walls, or glimmering in through small windows, could hardly fail, sooner or later, to bring the imagination of captives into dismal harmony with the character of the place.*

* Mr. Hepworth Dixon, 'London Prisons,' pp. 54, 55. Lord de Ros, 'Memorials of the Tower,' pp. 96, 97.

Time and the hour, which wear through the roughest day, bring us at length to the summer of 1611, when Lord Thomas Grey of Wilton once more presents himself to us, not proud and fearless as at Winchester, but broken and subdued by eight long years of confinement, scanty fare, and want of exercise. His case appears to have been marked by peculiar hardships, which originated in James's fears lest, if more liberty were allowed him, he might make some impression on the susceptible heart of Arabella Stuart. It is true she was now a married woman, but her union with Seymour being pronounced illegal, she was free according to law to enter into any new contract. In obedience to James's apprehensions of the frailty of his niece's virtue, Grey petitioned for leave to walk in the gardens before the ladies were up, though he could not be ignorant that the effects of his dangerous wooing might not be thus neutralized, since the ladies had female attendants, and windows to their chambers.

The other great state prisoners were not subjected to equal hardships: Northumberland enjoyed permission to walk on the hill; Cobham had a garden of his own while to Raleigh were allotted both a garden and gallery, wherein to stroll and meditate on the laws of the twelve tables or the decalogue, the Persian expedition, or the Punic war. Grey's mind, never perhaps very capacious, had been so dwarfed by captivity that considerations of the pettiest interests filled it. Under Elizabeth, James had called Cecil King of England in effect; he was still more so now, since he arbitrarily managed the affairs of the whole realm, while his nominal sovereign, stuck like an inanimate lump on the back of a horse, with his hat askew, scoured the fields after hares or foxes. To this King " in effect," Grey addressed his pitiable complaints. " In all my distress," he writes, " your lordship under God is the sanctuary under whose shade I seek to shroud me."*

I have already observed that, throughout the continuance of Raleigh's imprisonment, the court gave from time to time fresh proofs of its belief in his innocence, or at least of its doubt of his criminality, by reiterated examinations. Grey was hastening towards his dissolution, with his only sister lying sick near him; the descendant of a long line of Percies was losing his animal spirits together with the fine edge of his faculties; but Raleigh, according to the confession of Northampton, his bitterest enemy, still preserved that indomitable pride which, with a few occasional lapses caused by disease, accompanied him to the scaffold. From a half-naked adventurer, Car had now, for his feminine figure and portentous licentiousness, been made Viscount Rochester, and thrust occasionally between even Salisbury and the King. To him were

* Grey to Salisbury, June 26th, 1611. MS. State Paper Office.

subjected for wanton interrogation the most illustrious commanders and the highest nobles in the land, while a member of the house of Howard degraded himself into his tool.   Having taken the sceptre out of James's hands, Car sent Northampton to question Raleigh and Northumberland, the latter of whom, after six years' imprisonment, had just been assailed with fresh accusations by a fraudulent steward.   It is with surprise that we learn—if we can credit the witness—that, " whether by the distemper of his diet, or the disorder of his hours, or the disquiet of his mind, God knows, but I never found so great a change in so short a time, his conceit being exceedingly blunted, and his spirits weakened." Then, with characteristic vulgarity, he proceeds to give the minion an account of his next undertaking.   " We had afterwards a *bout* with Sir Walter Raleigh, in whom we find no change, but the same blindness, pride, and passion, that heretofore hath wrought more violently, but never expressed itself in a stronger fashion."   He felt himself, however, unequal to deal with Raleigh's arguments, or to describe his bearing, so breaking off suddenly he says, " But hereof his Majesty shall hear when the lords come to him."

For some exhibitions of atrocity, in the tragedy soon afterwards acted by Northampton and others in that State prison, the reader may be in a measure prepared by the language of this letter.   For the administering of poison, for the application of secret torture, and other enormities, the closest confinement would, the writer knew, be needed, so he goes on to say, "the lawless liberty of that place, so long cockered and fostered with hopes exorbitant, hath bred suitable desires and affections in the braver sort of the prisoners." *

James's camarilla, flagitious as that of Tiberius, now restrained the "lawless liberty" complained of by Northampton. Up to this time, Percy had been served in the Tower by thirty-two attendants,† and been allowed the society of Raleigh, Ben Jonson, and the magi. All this was at once changed. Many of the retainers were dismissed, the intercourse of the captives restricted or prohibited, while such other measures were taken as appeared best calculated to augment the evils of captivity. The fact is known that James's queen cherished a strong friendship for Raleigh, in which her eldest son Henry participated; but many documents which might have thrown a light on the progress and extent of that friendship have been suffered to perish. To her, as to his most powerful friend, he now addressed his complaint, both of the rigour of his imprisonment and of the King's refusal to

---

* Northampton to Viscount Rochester, July 12th, 1611. MS. State Paper Office.

† John Bennett to Dudley Carleton, July 15th, 1611. State Paper Office.

allow of his undertaking a new expedition to Guiana. From the whole aspect of the times, which he had enjoyed ample leisure to study, he apprehended that James's compliance with his request might only end in misery and death; yet believing that the expedition he projected would promote the extension of our colonial empire, he still pressed eagerly for permission to undertake it. All offices of authority in the Government being still however in the hands of his enemies, he entertained little hope of success. "The desire that led me," he says, "was the approving of my faith to his Majesty, and to have done him such a service as hath seldom been performed for any king.

"But, most excellent Princess, though his Majesty doth not so much love himself for the present, as to accept of that riches God hath offered him, thereby to take all presumption from his enemies, arising from the want of treasure by which, after God, all states are defended, yet it may be that his Majesty will consider more deeply thereof hereafter, if not too late, and that the dissolution of his humble vassal do not precede his Majesty's determination therein; for my extreme shortness of breath doth grow so fast on me, with the despair of obtaining so much grace as to walk with my keeper up the hill within the Tower, as it makes me resolve God hath otherwise disposed of that business and of me."*

* Raleigh to the Queen, July, 1611. MS. State Paper Office.

I have said that in the friendship of the Queen for Raleigh, her eldest son participated. He appears in fact to have regarded him as the greatest statesman and commander of his age, and to have looked up with something like filial reverence to his counsel on matters closely connected with his personal happiness; for when a marriage was proposed between him and a daughter of the Duke of Savoy, instead of suffering himself to be guided by his father, or his father's official advisers, he consulted the prisoner of the Bloody Tower, and with respect both to himself and his sister Elizabeth, shaped his course by the advice he received. No fact in history is better known than that James and his wife cherished the deepest hatred for each other, and that, upon the whole, Prince Henry sided with his mother. To lean to and stand well with them, therefore, was obviously to be in antagonism with the King; so that Raleigh, even had no other causes been in operation, would for this preference alone have been regarded with aversion by James. He further incurred his dislike, by labouring to infuse into his son's mind feelings of hostility towards Spain, by which James was now strangely infatuated, partly perhaps because he thence received a pension of three thousand a-year* for permission to import English ordnance, and partly because he had already conceived the hope of obtaining the

* Lodge, iii., 228.

hand of the Infanta for his son. The Queen, meanwhile, stood secretly at the head of the French party in England, going so far as to grant private audiences to Marie di Medici's agents and encouraging Raleigh to wield his powerful pen in support of her views. The two short essays he wrote in favour of a French alliance, and against an alliance with Savoy, may be fairly looked upon as the basis of the scaffold in Palace Yard. In them he offended Spain past forgiveness, pointing out the heinousness of her policy, which he regarded as so little scrupulous, that it would readily, to compass a favourite design, take off any number of princes by poison. This stung James to the quick, and afterwards, when Prince Henry was commonly believed to have been so taken off, rankled still more deeply in his mind.*

Raleigh himself was about this time complimented with the suspicion of being a poisoner. His chemical studies and fondness for medical investigations caused him to be looked upon by many as a great physician, especially when it became known that the Queen, in a dangerous fever, had consulted him, and believed herself to have been restored to health by his prescriptions. Following the example of her royal mistress, the widowed Countess of Rutland, only daughter of Sir Philip Sidney, being seized by a fever, applied to Raleigh for medicine ; but either because his advice

* Works, viii., 221, 237.

was taken too late, or through not seeing the patient for whom he prescribed, the pills he sent were vulgarly believed to have caused her death.*

Raleigh's hopes and preferences, identical at this time with those of the Puritan party, centred in Prince Henry, whose fate, however, contrary to expectation, was more imminent than his own. For reasons the consideration of which belongs to history, the Prince of Wales and the King by no means lived in the harmony which becomes the relation of son and father. An heir-apparent has often in England, as elsewhere, a number of persons about him who call themselves his friends, and seek to show their attachment by blowing up into a flame every spark of discord between him and his father. Prince Henry was so surrounded, only in that case the nobler and better natures adhered to the younger because of his superior mental and moral qualities. Still, dissensions in families, whether high or low, are painful things to witness, and rather derogatory than otherwise to the actors. James was not a person qualified to inspire respect in any one, yet few could have withheld from him their sympathy when, accompanied by a scanty number of followers, he beheld his son on the racecourse at Newmarket encircled by a brilliant cortège of nobles and gentlemen, who, elated

---

* Chamberlain to Carleton, August 11th, 1612.   MS. State Paper Office.

by the preference of the son, scarcely deigned to show
common respect to the father. James, who had not
laid aside the absurd practice of maintaining a pro-
fessional fool at his court, where his presence was
surely not needed, had his attention directed to the
galling contrast by that silly personage; upon which
he burst into tears, for which he afterwards made
several of those who caused them pay dearly. The
fool, on the other hand, met with chastisement from
the Prince's friends, who seized on a suitable opportunity to toss him in a blanket.*

The rivalry between father and son was soon brought
to a close. Agreeably to Raleigh's counsel, the idea
of a Savoyard match was laid aside, and the Elector
Palatine of the Rhine, whom the Prince favoured, and
whose interests Raleigh had espoused, arrived in England
as a suitor for the Princess Elizabeth's hand.† At this
period the Prince sickened, and his malady having
been declared by the court physicians to be a fever
of the most infectious kind, his friends, and especially
the Princess Elizabeth, were rigorously kept away from
his bedside. But the affection of the sister was not
easily daunted. Repelled in female attire, she is said
to have put on that of a man, and to have vainly endeavoured thus disguised to make her way to her

* Osborne, 'Traditional Memoirs of James I,' ii., 122, 123.
† Chamberlain to Carleton, Oct. 22nd, 1612. MS. State Paper Office.

brother's room.   Almost in despair, the Queen now applied to Raleigh for that cordial which she always believed had saved her own life.   The medicine was immediately sent, with a letter expressing the writer's persuasion that the cordial would prove effectual against the force of any fever unless caused by poison.   The prince took the medicine and died; which, it was thought, suggested to his mother the idea that it was to poison he owed his death.   This belief, however, was far from being confined to her.   It prevailed so widely, and among those, too, whose opinions carried with them so much weight, that, in order to stifle their conviction, a post-mortem examination of the prince's body was ordered.   But the report of those who made it is of little value, since, knowing what was expected of them, they would not have ventured, whatever might have been their real opinion, to return any other than an exculpatory testimony.*

In the Tower itself a crime was committed which, at the time, sent a thrill of excitement through the whole kingdom, the vibrations of which have not yet entirely ceased—I mean the murder of Sir Thomas Overbury. Into the history of this case it is not my intention to enter.   Overbury, a man of some talent, who wrote mediocre verses and excelled in intrigue, had been mixed up with the adulterous connection of Car and

* Chamberlain to Carleton, Nov. 12th, 1612. MS. State Paper Office.

the Countess of Essex; he had likewise contrived to get employed by the minion in a way less disreputable, yet not such as a man of high honour would have chosen—examining correspondence, and writing letters in the name of another. A quarrel arising between him and his associate, James was brought into the affair, and agreed to commit Overbury to the Tower. From that moment his doom was sealed. Car, now Earl of Somerset, put in play the most complicated machinery for his destruction: the Countess of Essex, her uncle Northampton, the Lieutenant of the Tower, with a rabble of conjurers, chemists, sellers of philters and other infamous persons, who aimed in concert at the prisoner's life. While Overbury, covered with blains, blotches, and yellow spots, was yielding slowly to the effects of poison, he experienced violent pains in the side, to allay which he applied to his fellow-prisoner Raleigh. Raleigh gave him plasters, not knowing the nature of the venom which was revelling through his system; the plasters proved useless: Overbury's body fell to pieces almost before his death, immediately after which it was thrust *like carrion*—the word is Northampton's—into a hole in the earth. Before the discovery which might, it has been thought, have delivered over Northampton to the hangman, the hoary assassin sank in agony to his grave. Had it been otherwise, there would have been no halter for him; for since the principal was cognizant of some secret, by holding which *in terrorem* over James's head he escaped the gallows, it would not have been possible to execute his accomplice; that is, if of noble rank; for the minor instruments were hanged without scruple.*

To the readers of history the Countess of Essex and the Earl of Somerset are well known, though some of the incidents in the latter part of their career have not been much dwelt upon. When, after trial and sentence, they found themselves in the Tower, Overbury's cell was vacant, and it was proposed by the authorities to appropriate it to his murderers. Her nerves, however, through proof against the horror of shedding blood, were not sufficiently tough to enable her to face the spectres and phantoms which imagination would have called up in the darkness in that dreadful place. In agonies of remorse and terror she therefore besought the Lieutenant to assign to her some less fearful lodgings, and Raleigh's apartments in the Bloody Tower being then untenanted, they were given up to her and her partner in guilt.† Car's apartments were at one end of a gallery, his wife's at another; so that, though they were sentenced to be separately confined, they

* Dr. Rumbold, 'Works of Overbury,' Introduction. Amos, 'Great Oyer of Poisoning,' *passim.* Archbishop Tennison, 'Baconiana,' Speech of Lord Bacon.

† Chamberlain to Carleton, April 6th, 1616. MS. State Paper Office.

might, as the doors were left open all day, be still said to live together. The concession, however, proved no boon, since their connection having originated in lust, not love, they now, the flush of passion being over and the consciousness of crime mingling with their sensuality, regarded each other with aversion, and frequently passed their days in mutual recriminations and revilings.*

Beauty, even in a murderess, still possesses for some persons irresistible fascination. Northumberland now became Somerset's rival for the favours of the fair prisoner, whose conscience, by whatsoever recollections burdened, seems to have been by no means unwilling to add to the load; for when the wizard Earl detained with him in the Tower his daughter, Lady Lucy Percy, to prevent her from dancing Scotch jigs, as he expressed it, with Lord Hay, he found, as he might have foreseen, his assassin mistress endeavouring to corrupt her morals. It was to guard against a similar influence that he desired to keep her from her profligate mother; but perceiving he could find for her no safe asylum, he exclaimed, "The young courtesan is just as bad as the old," and sent back Lady Lucy to court; where she soon became the wife of Lord Hay.†

* Sherburn to Carleton, July 25th, and Chamberlain to the same, Aug. 24th, 1616. State Paper Office.

† Chamberlain to Carleton, March 8th, and May 24th, 1617. MS. State Paper Office.

CHAPTER VII.

In the year 1614 Raleigh, to the amazement equally of friends and enemies, published his 'History of the World.' To enter into a minute analysis of this work, or even to indulge in a protracted criticism, would be to go beyond the limits of biography. Raleigh's performance is *sui generis*, more remarkable for those portions in which the writer is not a historian than for the story itself. Nothing can exceed the grandeur of the opening, since it begins with God, in a strain of lofty speculation, as worthy of the subject as anything ever written by man: the reason of its brevity and obscurity, by which we cannot fail to be impressed, may be discovered in the temper of the times, and in the belief which he knew to prevail very widely concerning himself. What he writes, therefore, is rather suggestive than explanatory. God, he appears to have thought, being essentially a creative power, there never could have been a time when the universe was not;

though the intellect of man has been always striving to fix upon some period when it ceased to be a mere idea in the mind of God, and began to exist, so to speak, outside of the Divinity.

If God be infinite, he not only fills and penetrates the universe, and clasps it round, so that, in the language of the Hebrew prophet, he may be said to hold it in the hollow of his hand, but regulates everything within it, intellectual as well as physical. We think, therefore, as well as exist in God: yet if freedom of thought and action be a prerogative of our being, our immersion in the Divinity implies no restriction of that freedom; for with the idea of existence the idea of justice is inextricably linked; so that to give birth to all the varied beauty of which an infinite universe is susceptible, every being must be suffered freely to develop its intellectual forces in order to be responsible for the result. Closely connected with this question is that of the existence of evil. In space distances exist so immeasurable that deviations of millions of miles from the right line cease to be recognizable when compared with the space passed through in travelling from star to star. Nay, if we advance in imagination to the farthest star discoverable by the telescope, and look thence into the abysses of space beyond, we shall discover new stars and planets which never have been or can be visible from this earth; and so on in succession for ever: no end to space, no limit to the universe. It is the same with what we call moral good and evil. Let good be the right line, and evil the deviation : that deviation is so minute that it becomes imperceptible in the infinite protraction of the line of existence through eternity. In this way, if we may be permitted to say so, we may regard the evils which afflict mankind as of absolutely no consideration if we attribute to the soul an eternal duration, *a parte post,* as the schoolmen say.

Giving Raleigh credit, however, for much grandeur of thought and unshackled speculation, we shall yet find as we advance through his work proofs of narrow and invincible prejudice. There are luminous bodies in space which we call periodical stars, the movements of which are regulated by laws hitherto unknown to science. Apparently they move in orbits so vast as to defy calculation, and only become visible to us while passing through some small portion of their periphery, outside of which we in this part of the universe stand. In our intellectual world there have appeared some few minds resembling those luminous bodies—vast, obscure, inscrutable—problems to be for ever studied, never solved. The list is short: Menes, Menu, Minos, Zoroaster, Lycurgus, Solon, Socrates, Plato, Mohammed. To these few men the laws, the institutions, the beliefs in religion, the theories in philosophy by which the whole human species is governed, trace their origin. In the brief period of their lives they stamped their impress upon humanity, which retains it still, and will probably continue to retain it through thousands of years. Raleigh, predominated by the notions of the sixteenth century, contemplated human affairs from a comparatively low point of view, and misunderstood them accordingly.

Instead of treating the inhabitants of the earth as an aggregate of nations, grouped by their beliefs and languages into several families each independent of the others, he subordinated the whole story of the world to that of one section of mankind, curious and instructive in itself, but entirely distinct from that of other races. This is the fundamental error of his book, which lacks the freshness, fervour, and sublimity it might have possessed could he have freed his mind from the leading idea of his age, and persuaded himself that the Arabic race, though vigorous and influential, had limits set to its power and influence by other races, still fuller of energy and intellect.

Consistently with his scheme, and with the leisurely style of speculation prevalent in his time, he discusses and determines to his own satisfaction the geographical position of Eden, a fact thus sportively alluded to by Butler :—

> " He knew the seat of paradise,
> Could tell in what degree it lies,
> And, as he was disposed, could prove it
> Below the moon, or else above it."

All drawbacks however being made, Raleigh's history is a great work, sparkling with brilliant philosophical reflections and political truths. Contrary to the strict laws of historical composition, but fortunately for us and for his own fame, he occasionally escapes from Tubal and Phut, Chedorlaomer and Methuselah, to treat of topics more germane to the interests of modern times; speaks of his wanderings on the banks of the Orinoco, of some incidents in his French campaigns, of coracles, and old countesses in Ireland; mixes up Prince Henry and Sir Philip Sidney with the Kings of Judah; dissertates on the defences of countries, inland and maritime, on poetry and conjectural history, on the state of kings and the evil fortunes of military men, on Don Antonio's expedition to Portugal in which he himself was engaged, and on several particulars of the Island voyage, especially the taking of Fayal, putting forward a modest defence of his own conduct.

These things inspire us with regret that he never wrote the second part of his History, in which he would have found himself more free to deal with characters and events; and that he would have used his freedom we may certainly infer from his Essay on War. There, though through no strict necessity, he sketches the history of the papacy, from its starting point to the period in which he wrote; remorselessly unveiling its policy and distributing severe censure on all those states which identified their cause with that of the popes.

Several writers have at various times attempted to deprive Raleigh of the credit of being the real author of his history, which, like the Iliad and Odyssey, they represent as a bundle of fragments tied together by one master hand.* The Tower, according to them, was a sort of literary factory, where poets, doctors of divinity, mathematicians, statesmen, philosophers, and soldiers co-operated in producing under Raleigh's eye a great composite performance, which when completed he illuminated and vivified with broad flashes of eloquence. This theory appears to me altogether unfounded. Ben Jonson, as Drummond tells us, laid claim to the history of the Punic War,† and other persons probably, after Raleigh's death, likewise took credit for other parts of the work ; but I fail to discover in Jonson's dramas any modes of expression, any force of thinking, any vastness of conception analogous to what we discover in Raleigh's elevated and masterly narrative. Able as he was, Jonson misunderstood himself when he sought to place his intellectual power on a level with that of Raleigh, which, had he lived two hundred years later, he would have shrunk with proper modesty from attempting. Jonson's style, though strong, is artificial, strained and contorted; while Raleigh's, amid the greatest displays

* Disraeli ('Curiosities of Literature,' v., 233) advanced this opinion, which Bolton Corney ('New Curiosities of Literature,' p. 65) and Napier ('Edinburgh Review,' cxliii.) have completely refuted.
† 'Notes of Conversations of Jonson with Drummond,' p. 15.

of nervous energy, elevation, and grandeur, rolls along easily and sweetly, with a murmur and a cadence like that of some mighty river in its flow.

Raleigh's history appeared at an inauspicious moment, when men's minds were too much absorbed by discords between James and the House of Commons to be able to bestow much leisure on the transactions of Jews or Gentiles. It was beginning to be suspected that an armed contest with the Stuarts for liberty must sooner or later be entered upon: the House of Commons rang with what were denounced as seditious speeches; James was told that Canute, when he had made up his mind to settle in England, sent back his Danes to the Baltic; and he was advised to imitate that tyrant's policy, to preserve his countrymen from a repetition of the Sicilian vespers.* For these and similar suggestions, Neville, Chute, Hoskins, and Wentworth were added to Raleigh's circle in the Tower. The moment, however, had not yet come for resenting the insults heaped upon the people's representatives; the four members fretted during a whole year in prison, and no effort was made to deliver them. Raleigh, Bacon, and many others, instead of denouncing James as an infringer of the privileges of Parliament, laboured to conciliate him by fulsome adulation, and met with ruin in the one case and death in the other for their pains.

* 'Court and Times of James I.,' i., 321, 322. Raumer, ii., 197.

Raleigh, however, proved but a clumsy flatterer; his language was too transparent to conceal his motives, and James, chuckling at his own shrewdness, only resolved to push still farther the humiliation of his great enemy. What Raleigh wrote on civil war was at once intended as an apology for the King's cowardice and for the nation's slothfulness and long-suffering; but in spite of his historical special pleading he suffered to peep forth here and there the great truth, that the sovereign power, by whatever forms, ceremonies, and glitter it may be sought to be disguised, lies inalienably in the people. In an evil hour he undertook the task of sketching a history of the conflicts that had taken place in England between the Parliament and the King.* He wished to subordinate in appearance his real to his pretended opinion, but failed egregiously In spite of all his arts and subterfuges, his enmity to despotism glowed so brightly through the whole dialogue that lawyers, courtiers, minions, and all discerned it clearly, and on the very day therefore of its appearance the book was called in.†

During the whole period of his imprisonment Raleigh had cherished the design of fitting out and conducting a second expedition to Guiana, and had kept up at great

* See the original in the State Paper Office, Sept. 30th, 1615.

† Chamberlain to Carleton, January 5th, 1615. State Paper Office.

expense his connection with that country * by despatching thither almost every year a ship or two, for the purpose partly of prosecuting the search for gold ore, partly to keep alive in the minds of its inhabitants the expectation of his return. In 1595 he had brought back with him two or three Caciques to be educated in England, and, incited by this example, his subordinate commanders brought over from time to time other natives, some of whom resided with Raleigh for a while in the Tower. Obviously he must have entertained the belief that James would ultimately relent and set him at liberty. His enemies were sinking one after another into the grave, or suffering the blight of infamy—Salisbury, Northampton, Somerset; while a new generation was rising at court, not likely, as he hoped, to inherit the rancorous hatred of their predecessors.

Few inducements as Raleigh had had to form a favourable estimate of James's character, he still seems to have cherished a better opinion of him than he deserved, though not without many doubts and misgivings, which rose up powerfully at intervals to blast his expectations: almost everything he wrote, whether for the public or to his friends, bears indubitable evidence of his uncertain state of mind, tossed to and fro by incessant fluctuations—now buoyed up by hope,

* To which he sent a ship annually, or every other year. 'Apology,' p. 52.

now smitten by despondency, now striving to think well of his persecutor, and now contemplating him in his true light as a cowardly, cruel, and treacherous despot. To this mental condition must be attributed the contradictions in his language and his conduct. He could not certainly know that James secretly intended all along to put him to death, whether he conceded to him an interval of liberty or not, and whatever might be the use he should make of that liberty. When, yielding to the seductions of hope, he gave a happy interpretation to the King's policy, his heart brimmed over with loyalty ; when anxiety and apprehension took the lead among his thoughts, he shrank away from James, nay, even from England, and longed for some other place of refuge.

In this frame of mind he found himself when, towards the close of 1615, he recommenced his negotiations for deliverance with additional chances of success. Villiers had succeeded to Car as the object of James's passion, and the new favourite was surrounded by hungry relatives, who would undertake any service for a bribe. By a felicitous coincidence also, equally rare and unexpected, an honest man had become Secretary of State—I mean Sir Ralph Winwood—who appears to have entertained, in common now with the greater part of the nation, a lofty admiration for Raleigh's genius, united, as was natural, with a warm sympathy for his sufferings. In

James's venal court, however, virtue by itself exercised but little influence. To give its exertions full efficacy they must be winged with gold. Villiers, as I have said, had relatives needy and unscrupulous; and two of these, Sir William St. John and Sir Edward Villiers, his uncles, undertook for fifteen hundred pounds to accomplish Raleigh's release and entire pardon. Only a moiety, however, of that sum was paid, and therefore the release was conceded, but not the pardon. It was believed at the time that Raleigh neglected to complete the transaction through the persuasions of Bacon, who represented to him that the money would be better laid out in preparations for his voyage, since the royal commission with which he was to sail would in all respects be equivalent to a pardon. But the story rests on too slender a foundation to be relied upon. Bacon, who with the other crown lawyers drew up the commission, would have seen that it contained abundant openings, through which fatal bolts might be aimed at Raleigh's life, and could not therefore honestly have given the counsel attributed to him.

The first step towards deliverance was to scrape together the money to satisfy the cupidity of the chapmen, through whom he was to purchase the King's permission to breathe the fresh air. At Mitcham, in Surrey, Lady Raleigh possessed a small estate, which she had inherited from Sir Nicholas Throgmorton, her father. This it now became necessary to sell, and it was accordingly disposed of for the sum of two thousand five hundred pounds. The deed transferring this fragment of the Throgmorton estates bears the signature of Lady Raleigh between the names of her husband and son.*

During the thirteen years all but four months which Raleigh had passed in the Tower many changes had taken place among its inmates: Lady Arabella Stuart, with whose melancholy history the public have lately been made familiar,† had there, through her cousin's persecutions, terminated her life in madness, and her body had been clandestinely hurried away by night to be laid beside her grandmother's in Westminster Abbey; Lord Grey of Wilton, who had exchanged his puritanical stoicism for the poor-spirited solicitude of a half-famished penitent, had likewise gone to his account; Sir Thomas Overbury had expiated in one of its cells, by the worst sufferings that could be inflicted by poison, his connivance at the adultery of Car and the Countess of Essex; and many others of inferior note had shrunk into obscure graves, or been hurried to the gallows or the scaffold. Two captives closely connected with Raleigh's story still remained in the Tower—I

* MS. State Paper Office. February 17th, 1616.
† 'Life of Arabella Stuart,' by Miss Elizabeth Cooper. Her story is likewise told in a very touching manner by Mr. Patrick Scott in his 'Legends of a State Prison, or Visions of the Tower.'

mean the wretched Lord Cobham and Henry Percy. Much doubt hangs about several parts of Cobham's life, who is often said to have ultimately died of starvation in a miserable loft belonging to his washerwoman. Out of his estates, however, when they were confiscated by the crown, an income of five hundred a year was reserved for the use of their former owner, whom such an income would surely preserve from starvation.* It is doubtless possible, and indeed probable, that the money was never regularly paid, though funds he must have possessed, since upon his release he repaired to Bath, in the hope of restoring some degree of strength to his wasted frame. He returned, however, to London to die, and when he had paid his last debt, not to nature, but to James, his body, we are told, remained for some time unburied through want of means to provide the necessaries of a funeral.† Though he and the man he had ruined were so long inmates of the same fortress, it does not appear that they ever met.

Of the Earl of Northumberland, I may as well say now what remains to be said of him: he continued immured in the Tower till July 18th, 1621 ;‡ but captivity had neither softened his fierce temper nor taught him prudence; for in order to gall the Spanish am-

<hr>

* Raleigh, 'Prerogative of Parliaments.' Works, viii., 179, 180.
† Wynne to Carleton. MS. State Paper Office.
‡ Camden, 'Annals of James I.'

bassador, he used to drive about London in a carriage drawn by eight magnificent horses, which he doubted not the public would merrily compare with the Spaniard's " six carrion mules."*

* Wilson says it was out of contempt for Buckingham, who drove about with a carriage and six. 'History of James I.,' 720.

CHAPTER VIII.

RELEASE—THE 'DESTINY'—PROJECTED SACK OF GENOA.

ON the 19th of March, 1616, Raleigh emerged from the Bloody Tower, to walk once more through the streets of London, though still attended by a keeper. He was now sixty-four years of age; he had suffered from apoplexy and paralysis; his figure was tall, gaunt, and thin, his countenance emaciated; yet few faces were better calculated than his to command attention from the passers-by, or engrave themselves on the memory. Forbidden to repair to court,* or to be present at any great assembly, lest he should awaken too much sympathy, his amusement consisted in roaming about the capital, gazing at the changes which thirteen years had made in its aspect, and to enjoy at

---

* Sherburn to Carleton, March 23rd, 1616. Calvert to Carleton, March 25th. Chamberlain to Carleton, March 27th. MSS. State Paper Office.

the same time the unwonted advantages and pleasure of fresh air and exercise.

To arrange the incidents, minute but full of significance, that now crowded upon each other, is a task of no small difficulty, since Raleigh kept no journal, wrote no letters, and possessed no friend intent upon watching his movements and chronicling them for posterity. He was often invited to dine by Sir Ralph Winwood, principal Secretary of State, for the purpose of meeting the French ambassador, the Count Desmarets,* and other foreigners of distinction. Osborne, author of the 'Traditional Memoirs of Elizabeth and James,' was once present, though whether at Winwood's or elsewhere he omits to say, when the conversation turning on Buckingham and other court favourites, Raleigh observed, "that minions were not so happy as vulgar judgments thought them, being frequently commanded to uncomely, and sometimes unnatural employments."† He likewise allowed the impression to get abroad that he believed Prince Henry to have been poisoned, which, entering like a sting into the minds of the guilty—if there were such—excited or exasperated their enmity.

---

* Raleigh told Wilson in the Tower that Winwood had also twice taken him to Desmarets' own residence to discuss the business of Sir John Ferne's French commission. Discourse of what took place, 26th, 27th, 28th September, 1618. MSS. State Paper Office.

† Osborne's 'Traditional Memoirs of Elizabeth,' i., p. 33.

The subjecting of Raleigh to the surveillance of a keeper implied a belief in the mind of James that, instead of organizing an expedition to the western hemisphere, the captive, if indulged with complete liberty, might choose rather to effect his escape, and take refuge in France.   In this persuasion many keen-sighted foreigners concurred, among others the Venetian Secretary Lionello, who imparted to his government the conviction he entertained that Raleigh's chief motive in putting to sea was the hope of effecting his escape from perpetual imprisonment.*   Strange circumstances hereafter to be noticed strengthen this view, though there are others which appear to demonstrate that, although the idea may have been always in his mind, he nevertheless laboured to reconcile it with the ostensible aim of his policy.   Had he been guided by any other considerations, he must have passed with posterity for a fool.   Bitter experience had proved that James held him in abhorrence, and would seize on the first plausible pretext that offered itself to take his life.   Even could he have made up his mind to lie perpetually in prison, he felt that a word dropped inadvertently might any day provoke some of James's minions to obtain an order for taking him off.

* Io so assai bene che da lui non é stata eletta questa impresa con altro fine, che di liberarsi dalla preggion perpetua.   Lionello, di Londra, 14th April, 1617.   Venetian Archives.

He never, therefore, even in his cell, could be sure that he was separated from a violent death by more than a few hours, and this conviction haunting him perpetually produced, if it did not justify, those effusions of servility and protestations of loyalty which grieve us so keenly during this portion of his career.

It would be putting forward a poor apology for Raleigh, to urge that his conduct at worst was of a piece with that of the King, whose behaviour throughout life was the reverse of honourable. At this very time, while negotiating the marriage of his son Charles with the Infanta, he was steeped to the ears in intrigues, out of which, had they terminated as he hoped, a war with Spain must have instantly arisen. As far back as 1611 the Duke of Savoy had instructed Count Gabellione,* his ambassador at the English court, to propose a double alliance between the houses of England and Savoy. Against this project, Raleigh, at the instance of Prince Henry, drew up two reports, pointing out the evil consequences which could hardly fail to arise from the marriage of that prince with a Savoyard princess, or of his sister with a Savoyard prince. His chief objection arose from the belief that, as for many generations the dukes had been little more

---

* The first reference I find to this envoy in the State Paper Office is in a letter from Giovanni Francesco Biondi to Carleton, in which he says that the Prince's death having put an end to his mission, he was about to leave England. Nov. 26th, 1612.

than Spanish satraps, nothing better was to be expected of them in the future.* The events of a few years, however, had reversed the duke's policy, and impressed a new character on Raleigh's views. The steps by which this change had been effected are too obscure to be confidently followed. The English court had for some years been converted into a battle-field for simulation and intrigue by the ambassadors of France, Spain, Venice, the Netherlands, and Savoy; each of whom necessarily cherished a different design, and sought to accomplish it by unbounded effrontery and lying.

How their schemes came to be interwoven with Raleigh's story we shall presently see. When set at liberty, his first proceeding naturally was to make preparations for his westward voyage: the belief prevailed, especially among foreigners, that he was still extremely rich, though had the public been aware of the fleecing processes through which he had passed, the idea would have been soon exploded. His whole fortune, estimated by the present value of money, would have fallen short of a hundred thousand pounds, which for one who had probably enjoyed half that sum annually will be allowed to have been inconsiderable. To realize even that amount he had to call in and put to hazard all the resources which he had up to that

* See the two discourses. Works, viii., 223 and 237.

time reserved for the support of his wife and children. With indomitable energy, however, he began to draw together the elements of his fleet. and laid on the stocks the keel of his own ship, which he ominously named the 'Destiny.' A hundred noblemen and gentlemen,* with wealth at their command, and burning with eagerness for adventure, flocked to the standard of the renowned commander, the greatest that ever wielded England's power on the ocean. Through the influence of these gallant and noble adventurers, mariners gradually flocked to London from the different ports of Europe, eager to tread the deck with a commander whose name had been always associated with the plunder of Spanish towns and carracks. The terrible character of those mariners has been drawn with a dark pencil by Raleigh himself; they were, he says, a horde of sea-rovers, ruffians, blasphemers, malefactors of all sorts, reckless of everything but gold, and the coarse pleasures which it could purchase.†

Raleigh's exertions, and the success which appeared likely to crown them, were viewed with a mixture of

---

* Report of Spanish spy, of uncertain date, but written probably in the August of 1617, and signed Vadervort. Simancas. He says, many gentlemen are going on this voyage, some of whom have embarked their whole patrimonies, and all the rest are men of brave and commanding aspect. Lionello says that Raleigh's ships were *pieni di nobilta*, Feb. 10th, 1617. Venetian Archives.

† 'Apology,' p. 3.

anxiety and rage by the Spanish ambassador.* Since England took possession of Guiana in 1595, Spain, ignoring altogether the rights of our countrymen, had vigorously pushed forward her explorations and multiplied her settlements, so that, relying on the extent of her injustice, she now claimed the country as her own. Leigh and Harcourt had excited little alarm by their insignificant attempts at settlement; even the ships which Raleigh had despatched across the Atlantic to search for gold ore at the foot of the Cordillera had occasioned no uneasiness; but now, instead of mining operations, Gondomar apprehended from the formidable character of the fleet in preparation that nothing less than conquest could be projected. His representations and expostulations to James and his government were incessant and angry;† he insisted that such proceedings were inconsistent with those pacific professions which were constantly in James's mouth; and offered, in the name of his master Philip, to suffer Raleigh and his associates to explore Guiana for mines, and guarantee their safety, if they would consent to proceed thither with two ships only. But as Raleigh

* From a royal order addressed to the president of the Council of the Indies, we discover that Gondomar had sent to Philip a full account of Raleigh's proceedings, as may be inferred from Minuta de Real Orden al Presidente de Indias, 14 de Nov., 1616. Simancas.

† Gio. Battista Lionello, Despatch of February 10th, 1617. Venetian Archives.

had always argued that Guiana belonged as a colony or dependency to England, he could not agree to receive from a foreign prince, whose subjects he declared to be intruders, permission to visit and examine the country.

Things being in this state, designs were secretly formed by the agents of several neighbouring governments to blow into a flame these sparks of discord between England and Spain. The first inkling of one of the formidable schemes then in agitation was obtained by the Venetian Secretary.* Having observed that Count Scarnafisi, ambassador from the Duke of Savoy, paid unusually frequent visits to Sir Ralph Winwood and Sir Thomas Edmondes, and was often favoured with audiences by the King, he set his penetrating wit to work, in the hope of discovering the nature of their business. His usual means of intelligence—that is, his court spies and eavesdroppers—failed him now. The policy he adopted was bold and original: he went one Sunday morning for information to the count himself, and commenced operations by talking of indifferent things far removed from the

* In the Italian translation of Mr. Rawdon Brown's able and interesting Preface to the Calendar of Venetian State Papers, there are some extremely curious letters relating to this portion of Raleigh's life, addressed by Giovanni Battista Lionello to the Council of Ten, and communicated by that Council to the Senate; the first is dated Jan. 19th, N.S., 1617; the second, Jan. 26th, N.S.; and the third, Feb. 3rd, N.S., 1617. Venetian Archives.

object of his curiosity. When Scarnafisi had been warmed into good humour by a masterly display of artful eloquence, Lionello told him plainly that he knew him to be engaged in transacting some important affair with the English King. Taken off his guard, Scarnafisi admitted that such was the case, but protested that it was of so secret and dangerous a nature that he dared not reveal it. The crafty Venetian still pressed, affirming that it would be as safe in his keeping as in that of the count himself, whom by the most solemn oaths and promises not to divulge one particle of what might be confided to him he induced to betray his master.

Once in possession of Scarnafisi's secret, the Venetian, regardless of his vows and promises, immediately forwarded to the Council of Ten a full account of the projected enterprise. Nothing on record illustrates more strikingly the duplicity and faithlessness of James's character than this transaction, in which he showed himself false to his own illustrious subject, to France, to Piedmont, and to Spain.

The position then occupied by Raleigh can hardly fail to excite our wonder, even at this distance of time: wherever desperate enterprises were projected, the thoughts of men turned to him as naturally as the magnetic needle to the pole. Denmark, the insurgent princes in France, the Duke of Savoy, the Republic of

Venice, all desired to employ for their own behoof his matchless genius and daring. Common fame spread the report that, with his formidable armament then gathering together in the Thames, his design was to explore new worlds for the soothing and enriching of the English King. An attempt was now made to give a different direction to his fleet. Spain had long aimed at acquiring predominance in Italy, where, in pursuance of its aggressive policy, it had incurred the guilt of countless crimes and atrocities. Its entrance into the northern part of the peninsula had been facilitated by the Republic of Genoa, whose fleets and treasures it had made use of as its own, whose noble port was always at its command, and in whose treasury it had deposited immense riches. The Duke of Savoy, a man of Spanish blood, had inherited the ambition and unscrupulousness of his countrymen. The greatest navigator and warrior of the age was now at liberty, organizing a powerful fleet for some object not certainly known—could he not render him and his master, the King of England, subservient, for tempting considerations, to the policy of Savoy? His ambassador was instructed to move cautiously in the matter, at first, as if of himself. The plan he proposed to the British Government was this: to unite to Raleigh's fleet four ships of the Royal Navy, with as many as could be obtained from the Netherlands, after which the admiral should put to sea, as if bound for the western hemisphere; but having made a certain latitude, should change his course, enter as secretly as possible the Straits of Gibraltar, and sail directly for the coast of Piedmont, where he would be joined by the Duke's naval force. With a fleet so powerful as he would then be in command of, he was to make a sudden dash at Genoa;[*] which it was not doubted he would carry by a coup-de-main, and so become master of all the treasure accumulated in that city, estimated at twenty millions sterling.

When this design was explained to Raleigh, he at once pronounced it to be easy of accomplishment, and expressed his readiness to undertake it, not however as a private adventurer or buccaneer, but as an admiral of England, with his King's commission in his pocket.[†]

[*] It may almost be inferred from one of the despatches of Desmarets that he had obtained some inkling of this project; for having insisted on the improbability of Raleigh's expedition to Guiana, he says, " Il est a craindre que le sommaire de ce voyage ne se terminast en quelque surprise sur les voysins." Then directing his glances homewards, he adds, " C'est pourquoi il n'y aurait point de danger ce me semble d'en donner avis à nos villes maritimes afin qu'ils y prennent garde," Dép., Jan. 12th, 1617. MS. Bib. Imp.

[†] Sir Thomas Wilson, writing to James, Oct. 4th, 1618, says, " He (Raleigh) tells me also that Secretary Winwood brought him acquainted with the Duke of Savoy's ambassador, with whom they consulted for the surprise of Genoa, where they were sure to have had at least twenty millions of gold ; and that the Duke of Savoy and Monsieur de Dignére were both in the plot, and that your Majesty was acquainted with the business, and liked it well." State Paper Office.

As in all such enterprises the possibility of checks ought to be foreseen, the allies thought it prudent to demand the aid of a few galleys from the Venetian Republic, to protect the landing of the troops necessary to invest the city should it not be carried by assault. It was rightly judged by Lionello that Raleigh would be gladly engaged in such a service, which might at worst afford him an opportunity of escaping from the hands of James, whom no considerations could move to relinquish the hold he had upon his life. It may be inferred, though it is not so stated, that Raleigh was habitually present at the deliberations of Scarnafisi, Winwood, and Edmondes, though never when the King was of the party, since his inveterate hatred could be allayed neither by policy nor thirst of gold.

While this negotiation was in progress, the Prince de Rohan arrived in London* as the representative of the French insurgent princes, and had an interview with Raleigh, to whom he proposed the storming of St. Valeri, which the league desired to possess as a port through which they might receive supplies from abroad.†

* About the 9th of January, 1617, Monsieur de la Roche des Aubiers arrived in London from the Prince de Condé, then in prison, in the hope of inducing James to negotiate for Condé's liberation. The object aimed at, according to Desmarets, was to multiply the sources of discord in France. Dépêches, Jan. 12th, 1617. MS. Bib. Imp.

† James, however, though at first he seems to have favoured this project, ultimately drew back. Explaining the motives of his

This proposal also was laid before James and his Council, who had now therefore, according to the vulgar adage, too many irons in the fire. It may be inferred, from various circumstances, that James's advisers leaned to different interests: Winwood to Raleigh, whether he traversed the Atlantic, or attacked Genoa; Edmondes to the French princes, whom, before his departure from the French court, to which he had been accredited, Marie di Medici accused him of favouring.*

In the midst of this chaos of projects, James found himself incapable of coming to any decision. The wish to secure a Spanish wife for his son Charles, an alliance with which his fancy associated heaps of gold, at one moment induced him to lend a favourable ear to the advice of Gondomar; the next, his fears were awakened by the near neighbourhood of the Dutch and French fleets; then he was led to anticipate many advantages

---

foreign visitors, Raleigh said that " de Vicq came to him only for curiosity—Bonnvelt, to consult about the taking of St. Valery, to have a port to receive succours at for the princes then in action against the King." Wilson, *ubi supra.*

* Edmondes had been Ambassador in France, and quitted the French Court in January. On his departure, Marie di Medici inquired, " Strettissamamente delle sue attioni, essendo S. Mta. stata avertita di diversi mali ufficij fatti da esso in prejuiditio del servitio Regio, et in favore dé Principi del contrario partito." (See Bon Gussoni, Paris, 21st Feb., 1617). Edmondes was expected to return to Paris during James's progress to Scotland. Desmarets, Dép., Jan. 12th, 1617. MS. Bib. Imp.

from affording aid to the Prince of Condé and his friends; after which the brilliant prospect of sharing in the plunder of Genoa bewildered his imagination.

Weak minds usually seek to escape from difficulties by delay. This accordingly was James's favourite course. He had been persuaded that he was a second Solomon, and now endeavoured to give proof of his wisdom by doing nothing. On the 28th of the previous July, Raleigh had obtained a commission, but not under the Great Seal, neither was the country to which he was to sail named, nor any pardon or promise of pardon given. He remained, consequently, as uncertain respecting his fate as he had been while in the Tower. James revelled in the consciousness that he could at any moment take his head, and persuaded himself that, knowing this to be the case, Raleigh would be the more ready to obey his orders. On the other hand, Raleigh understood but too well how his authority must always be paralysed by the fact that everybody knew him to be a condemned man; a man who, in law, had no existence at all, and who, though nominally invested with the power of life and death over his subordinates, would never be able to enforce his authority. Again and again therefore did he labour through Winwood, and his other friends if he had any, to sever the chain that bound him to the block, that he might go forth to action a free man, with all the elasticity of mind which freedom gives. Nothing appears to have afforded the vindictive King so much delight as the knowledge that, by virtue of the unjust sentence at Winchester, he could murder Raleigh when he pleased.

Scarnafisi at length becoming impatient, reproached Winwood and Edmondes for what he assumed to be their procrastination, and thus extorted from the latter the humiliating confession that no movement could be made on account of the King's poverty. He acknowledged with shame, real or affected, that his master had been so prodigal in the previous part of his reign,* that he was now in want of funds to defray the common expenses of his household, and that consequently nothing requiring money could be entered upon in less than two months. Scarnafisi replied angrily, that nearly two years had been consumed by fruitless negotiations, which now seemed likely to terminate as they had begun.

Edmondes omitted to state what Scarnafisi may nevertheless have known, that the King was just then meditating a progress to Scotland,† chiefly perhaps for the

* Soon after James's arrival, Cecil observed that the expenses of Elizabeth's household had amounted to 50,000*l.* a year, and that James immediately doubled them. Lodge, iii., 34.

† The French Ambassador, Desmarets, writing from London, January 12th, 1617, informs his government that James intended to depart for Scotland about the end of March, and that he meant to remain during the whole summer in the north. MS. Bibliothèque Impériale.

purpose of escaping from the Spanish Ambassador, whose importunities wearied him, though he could not consent to relinquish, at the nod of Spain, the chances of enormous wealth to be acquired by Raleigh's expedition to Guiana.   As an indubitable proof of his reliance on this source, he contributed a large sum towards the building of the 'Destiny,'* since he most assuredly would not have done so, had he not been actuated by the *auri sacra fames*.   Gradually the truth seems to have broken on the minds of Winwood and Edmondes that the Savoy scheme would have to be relinquished, for which reason they sought to deliver themselves from the arguments and reproaches of Scarnafisi, by sending him back on a wild-goose chase to Piedmont, with letters implying the confidence of the English Government in his integrity, so that the Duke might safely intrust him with any secret purpose he might have in view.   The Count saw through their motives, and refused to stir.   To render his journey of service he must be furnished, he said, with distinct and positive instructions to settle with the Duke the whole scheme of action, the amount of the contingents to be supplied by the contracting parties, and the exact share of the plunder to be allotted to each.   On this last point James showed himself profoundly interested.   He de-

* Warrant, dated Nov. 16th, 1617, to pay seven hundred crowns towards defraying the cost of the 'Destiny.'

manded of the ambassador what security could be given him, that he should obtain his proper share of the riches to be acquired by the sack of Genoa; and was answered, that he might himself insure the equitable distribution of the money, jewels, and other property, by employing a force so large as to be overwhelming.

Whatever the motives may have been by which James was actuated, he gradually withdrew from the Savoyard scheme, of which, save a single allusion made to it afterwards by Raleigh, nothing more was heard. The project has been termed piratical; but, if so, James and the Duke of Savoy were the pirates, for Raleigh, acting under the authority of his sovereign, would have had no choice in the matter, and therefore could be by no means regarded as a pirate.

No foreign ambassador ever gave proof of so much pertinacity and overweening conceit, or exercised so powerful an influence over the English Government, as Gondomar. Imagining himself to be all-powerful, he often suffered his passions to betray him into the most unbridled insolence. Reiterating his arguments one day in the Council Chamber against Raleigh's undertaking, and dwelling on the disgust it must necessarily inspire in his master to behold his subjects and dependencies exposed to violence, the Council replied that Raleigh would go forth under the authority of a royal commission, by which his proceedings would be regulated, so that he could cause no damage to the subjects of Spain without putting his own head in jeopardy. Not satisfied with this reply, Gondomar abruptly left the chamber, but presently returned, bringing with him a book, in which were described the violence and rapine perpetrated by Raleigh in his two former voyages to the West Indies, from which could be inferred he said what might be expected of him in his third expedition. Disgusted by the ambassador's presumptuous language and bearing, the Lords of the Council deigned to make no reply, but desired Sir Ralph Winwood to let him know that he would have done well to rest satisfied with the assurances he had already received, since it was settled by the King that Raleigh should go, furnished with distinct and positive instructions, which if he contravened it would be at the peril of his life. Such being the case, the ambassador was requested to give no further annoyance either to the King or Council.

CHAPTER IX.

SECRET INTRIGUES WITH FRANCE. SAILS FOR THE WESTERN HEMISPHERE.

WANT of money meanwhile determined all the proceedings of the English Government. A caricature found its way from the Netherlands to London, representing James with his pockets turned inside out, and a Dutchman inquiring of him if he had any more towns to sell;* alluding to his having given up Flushing and other places for money. To recruit his finances there were few proposals to which, however questionable, he would have turned a deaf ear; in fact, he is believed to have seriously intended to co-operate with France in intercepting the Spanish treasure fleet,† without previously

* Lovelace to Carleton, March 11th, 1617. MS. State Paper Office.

† I submit to the reader a perplexing passage from Wilson's letter to James, in which he translates into his own vulgar language Raleigh's account of the plans he had formed in 1617 in conjunction with the Government. "That his first dealing with Captain Gage was well known to your Majesty for what cause it was; and his

declaring war; but French diplomacy was at that time extremely ill-conducted in England, where Desmarets was no match for Gondomar; otherwise it would have been easy to direct the proceedings of a court, which a handsome bribe might at any moment have induced to espouse the cause of Condé and the Huguenots, of Marie di Medici, or of Spain.

But no consideration seemed capable of reconciling James to Raleigh, whose reiterated applications and entreaties to be favoured with a pardon before his departure proved unavailing. The history of his commission is highly curious. Two objects appear to have been aimed at throughout: first, to enable Raleigh to acquire, no matter how, a vast amount of treasure, of which James might take as much as he pleased, besides his fifth, as the price of a pardon; second, to word the instrument so as that no offence should be given by it to the Spanish Government.

---

last at Plymouth about bringing French ships and men to him to displant the Spaniards at St. Thomas, that the English might after pass up to the mine without offence; that for his negotiation with the Prince of Rohan and his brother, he confessed there was a purpose with seven or eight good ships to be furnished by the French to set upon the India fleet as they came homeward, or else missing it to pass on to the mine; and he saith, the cause that this succeeded not, that your Majesty would not let him go to the Prince of Rohan, having denied him before to the King of Denmark, who would have had him for his Admiral." Oct. 4th, 1618. MS. State Paper Office.

On Raleigh's commission itself a great deal has been said; some maintaining that it was given under the broad, others under the private seal; some that it was directed to Raleigh as "our loving and faithful subject;" others, that no such words were inserted in the document. It seems impossible to throw a satisfactory light on several of these points, though others are capable of being cleared up. How the document was at first worded can never be shown unless the rough draught should be discovered. The copy of the commission found in the State Paper Office has been conjectured to be the very one which Raleigh carried with him to the New World; it is endorsed, "Sir Walter Raleigh's Commission going into the south quarters of America, 28th July, 1616," on a sheet of parchment, and signed James R. Fancy discovers on it proofs of its having been carried in a man's bosom, for it is rubbed, crumpled, and stained with perspiration. Whether this be so or not, it was critically examined and approved by Lord Bacon, who, fearing lest James might either not read it at all, or if he did, not understand its true intent and meaning, after first writing at the end of the commission, "Exd. per Fr. Bacon," goes on to say, "It may please your excellent Majesty. This containeth your Majesty's commission unto Sir Walter Raleigh, Knight, to travel and take with him into the south parts and other parts of America, possessed and inhabited by heathen and savage people, such persons as shall be willing to go and adventure themselves with him, with sufficient shipping, armour, horses, wares and merchandizes as shall be necessary for their journey, as well for the better increase of the trade of merchandize of this kingdom, as by conversation and commerce to draw those savage and idolatrous people to the true knowledge of God. It maketh him also to be commander of those that go with him, and gives him power for the appointing of captains and officers for the better ordering and government of the company and the good of the voyage, and in case of rebellion or mutiny, upon just ground and apparent necessity to use martial law; which clause hath been used to be inserted in patents of like discovery and adventure. Your Majesty doth also herein promise in *verbo regio* that the said Sir W. and his company, with all adventurers with him, shall quietly enjoy all such goods as they shall import, which is desired in respect of *the peril of law wherein Sir Walter Raleigh standeth.* . . . .

"Signified to be your Majesty's pleasure by Mr. Secretary Winwood.

"Fr. Bacon."*

Of this commission Gondomar immediately obtained a copy, and caused a translation of it to be made and

* July 25th, 1616. State Paper Office.

forwarded to Madrid, where it is still preserved. Raleigh's situation was highly critical. He had drawn together the remains of his fortune, and expended them in the equipment of his fleet, yet he had no security that James might not at any moment consign him to irremediable ruin, by countermanding the expedition, throwing him back into the Tower, or even ordering his immediate execution. On these points speculation was rife in London; some dwelling on the extent of his preparations, others on the probability that they would prove of no avail. The force under his command was variously estimated; some observing that he had six or seven good ships, with three or four pinnaces; others that his fleet consisted of twelve ships;* while there were those who maintained that it amounted to seventeen ships of war, and three or four transports, carrying, besides mariners, two thousand soldiers ready to be disembarked at the shortest notice on any hostile shore. Rumour however occasionally reduced the two thousand soldiers to three hundred. Whatever may have been the amount of his force, it was sufficient to excite extraordinary uneasiness in the Spanish Government, though certainly no way proportioned to the object said to be in view. Gondomar was indisputably right when he

---

* The French Ambassador, Desmarets, estimated Raleigh's fleet at ten or twelve ships. Postscript to despatch of Jan. 12th, 1617. MS. Bib. Imp.

argued that so formidable an armament could not be needed for mining purposes, and might have added, that if James acknowledged Guiana to be a dependency of Spain, he had no more right to send thither one of his subjects in search of gold than Philip had to equip an expedition to Cornwall for tin. Throughout the delays and discussions that took place between Raleigh's enlargement from the Tower and the date of his setting sail, the subject remained involved in doubt and obscurity. One of two things should have been cleared up then :—first, was Guiana recognised by the British Government as a Spanish possession? Second, by what right did Spain claim authority over that part of America? Discovery, as it is called, obviously confers no right, neither does the preposterous ceremony of taking possession unless the natural lords of the soil freely give their consent. Before Raleigh's voyage of 1595 the Spaniards had doubtless made several attempts to force themselves into Guiana, but had been withstood by all the power which the Caciques could oppose to them; whereas, when Raleigh landed in the country he was received joyfully as the enemy of the Spaniards, and the native chiefs voluntarily professed allegiance to Raleigh's mistress, the Queen of England. In this transaction we may discover the right of England to regard Guiana as her colony. That in the interval Spain had intruded herself into the country, and thrown up a few straggling tenements on which she bestowed the name of a town is true; but this had only happened through the remissness of James's government, which should have watched over the territory bequeathed to him by that of Elizabeth. A thief has quite as much right to the watch he has stolen as the Spaniards had to any portion of Guiana. Whatever their language may have been, this was the conviction of James and his ministers, who evidently understood and intended that Raleigh should attack and expel the Spaniards if found where they had no right to be; otherwise why was he sent out at the head of so powerful an armament? The limitations introduced into his commission were mere delusions, since they who drew it up could not have been ignorant that there was not an inch of ground from the Isthmus of Darien to the southern extremity of Terra del Fuego which the Spaniards would not have claimed.

Another question now presents itself, the consideration of which is attended by more difficulties—I mean Raleigh's connexion with France. It is a trick of historians to arrange themselves on the side of authority, and bear hard on private individuals, who in defence of their lives have recourse to the contrivances of a subtle policy. From James's absolute refusal to grant him a pardon, Raleigh logically inferred that he meant at some future day to take his life, and therefore determined to use all possible means to place himself beyond his reach. Hence his eager anxiety to bid farewell to the shores of England, and hence, as he inwardly argued, the reluctance of the Government to relinquish its grasp of him. Milton suggests that a part of the host of heaven followed Satan in his revolt through the fascination of his beauty; and many authors have thought that a large body of English noblemen and gentlemen were allured to accompany Raleigh across the ocean by the dazzling spell of his renown. This, however, is taking too poetical a view of the matter; for although they might derive confidence from his distinguished reputation, the real loadstone was gold. To them therefore, as well as to their great leader, delay was inexpressibly irksome. It afforded them no pleasure to see crowds of foreigners flocking to the docks to behold the 'Destiny;' neither did they regret the waspish enmity of Prince Charles, which led him to oppose the visit with which his mother proposed to honour Raleigh in his ship.* What they longed for was to find themselves afloat on the Atlantic, profiting by every advantage which the chapter of accidents might throw in their way, or tearing up tons of the precious metal from the banks of the Orinoco. Raleigh's faith in the auriferous nature of the Guianian soil was no less strong than theirs, but he had motives which they had

* Chamberlain to Carleton, March 20th, 1617. State Paper Office.

not for secretly making many hazardous arrangements before his departure. Desmarets,* who met Raleigh at Winwood's table, as well as at his own, and was charged by his government to enter into delicate negociations with him, visited the 'Destiny' while he held secret consultations with its commander. In his ordinary despatches he alludes to this fact, but observes that he laid no great stress on Raleigh's professions; he forwarded however, it seems probable, other despatches in which a different view of the matter was taken, since the correspondence that soon afterwards took place between Raleigh and the French Government was in all likelihood conducted through him.

About the 21st of March, 1617, Raleigh took leave of Sir Ralph Winwood, and on the 29th dropped down the river,† where the consorts of the 'Destiny' had been

---

* At what date the intrigues with Desmarets began I have not discovered. On the 12th of January, 1617, he was, or affected to be, ignorant of Raleigh's designs; for, alluding to the project against St. Valeri, he observes that it behoved the seaports of neighbouring countries to be on their guard, since it was more likely that Raleigh intended to attack some of them than that he should really propose a voyage to Guiana in the belief that it abounded in gold He thought him the first seaman of the age, and laboured, by dwelling on this belief, to inspire his government with the desire to engage Raleigh in its service. P.S. to Dép., Jan. 12th, 1617. MS Bib. Imp.

† Gio. Battista Lionello, Despatch of April 14th, 1617. 'Venetian Archives.' Chamberlain to Carleton, March 31st, 1617. State Paper Office.

impatiently awaiting the appearance of his flag. He repaired in the first instance to Dover, next to the Isle of Wight, whence, after a delay of some weeks, he sailed to Plymouth. Had the view taken of his preparations by Spain been correct, a different fate would have probably awaited him: his fleet was described as in the highest state of efficiency, supplied with provisions for a whole year, manned with the finest possible crews, and furnished with splendid and abundant ordnance. Very different however was the fact. The delays that had taken place, whether unavoidable or voluntary, had cleared out several ships of their provisions, so that while he sold his plate to supply the wants of one captain,* another rode back to London to obtain from Lady Raleigh the means of paying his biscuit-baker. Symptoms of insubordination at the same time made themselves visible; his crews were of the most disorderly and reckless description, for the mariners who had flocked to his service in better days were now either in their graves or too old and infirm for sea; their places therefore had to be supplied by pirates† and

---

* Whitney. Sir John Ferne was likewise completely out of funds, and had to be supplied by Raleigh. Apology, p. 8. Ferne had embroiled himself with the associated French merchants trading to the East Indies, and according to Desmarets, had been arrested in port at their instance. Dép., Jan. 12th, 1617. MS. Bib. Imp.

† One of these, a Frenchman, born near Dieppe, who called himself Captain Belle, stole away from Raleigh at Plymouth, went

malefactors, and even of these there was a deficiency, so that Raleigh found himself under the necessity of begging a small supply of seamen from the Prince of Orange.

Arguing the worst from these circumstances, Raleigh now determined to take all the measures in his power to protect himself from James's revenge in case of failure. That he was guilty of dissimulation I frankly admit, as well as that he had frequently been guilty of it before, since every profession of attachment he had made to James must have sought its excuse in necessity. Hatred of Spain had always inclined him to lean to France, six years of service in whose armies had almost made him one of her citizens. Philosophy had not taught him the duty of submitting to injustice and cruelty at home, rather than attempt to escape from them by accepting employment under a foreign govern-

---

to Rome, made confession to a priest there, and his story being thought likely to damage Raleigh, was advised to proceed to Madrid. There he contrived to have his statement laid before the King, who, in consideration of his extreme poverty, seems to have given him fifty or a hundred ducats for the fictions with which he sought to amuse him. The other French deserter, who called himself Captain Farge, lay sick and imprisoned for debt at Genoa. To these pirates Raleigh is said to have intrusted his letters to Montmorenci, of which, though they must have delivered them, since answers they said were sent, they yet pretended to possess the originals. Cartas Originales de Don Andres Velazquez y Don Diego Brochero á su Magestad, Feb. 12th, and March 26th, 1618. Simancas.

ment. He must have excelled saints and martyrs in charity had he not repaid with hatred the merciless persecution he had suffered during thirteen years from James, his minions, and ministers, not one of whom had shown him the least kindness or sympathy, except the Puritan Sir Ralph Winwood. Now, then, he resolved to enter into a correspondence with France, not in order to inflict any damage on England, not even to revenge his own personal wrongs on James, but, if possible, to insure his escape from that tyrant's clutches.*

* Napier seeks, through the affectation of impartiality, to inflict the deadliest wounds on Raleigh's fame, by making it appear, though with apparent unwillingness, that he was guilty of falsehood and disloyalty (p. 242). He professes to have had before him four Despatches of Desmarets'; but if so, it may be doubted whether he clearly understood them. Desmarets says that Raleigh's imprisonment was unjust and tyrannical: Napier attributes the remark to Raleigh. Desmarets relates that he saw Raleigh on board the 'Destiny,' but that because it was a place ill-suited for the discussion of serious subjects, he appointed to see him on the morrow, clearly somewhere more suitable. He nowhere speaks of visiting the 'Destiny' a second time; yet Napier represents him as saying he visited it "several" times. He speaks of a Despatch dated March 30th; the error is unimportant, but there exists no such Despatch, though there be one written on the following day. Desmarets himself commits greater mistakes; writing on the 24th April (13, O.S.), he states that Raleigh had then left the Thames five or six days: he had left it sixteen days. If he was as careless in facts as he was in dates little reliance can be placed on his statements. However, he affirms that Raleigh expressed to him his resolution to take refuge in France on his return from America; and this was true, though when pleading for his life, Raleigh, in conformity with the principles of English law, declined to criminate himself by con-

As the affair was carried on with extreme secrecy, since Raleigh knew it put his life in jeopardy, few records of what was intended to be done have come down to us —I say intended, since the design never ripened into action. How or when negociations were opened does not appear, though, as I have already suggested, the initiative was probably taken through Desmarets, who may have conveyed the intimation to his government, that the great Admiral who had just escaped from prison, under conditions the most galling and terrible, would be glad to accomplish something in the course of his expedition to South America which might insure him on his return a home in France. Few particulars of the plan were in all likelihood committed to writing, all important arrangements being made for Raleigh by a trusty friend, who in the manuscripts is named Captain Farge.* The first communication we discover is a letter from Henri duc de Montmorenci, Governor of Languedoc and Bretagne and Lord High-admiral of France, addressed to Raleigh : in it he alludes to certain

--- --- --- --- --- ---

fessing it until concealment was of no avail. Compare Desmarets' Despatches, March 17th and 31st, and April 24th, 1617. MSS. Bib. Imp., with Raleigh letters and examinations given farther on in this volume.

* If, as is possible, this be only a Spanish form of Gage, the negociation must to some extent, and in one at least of its phases, have been known to James. See the passage above quoted from Wilson's letter of Oct. 4th.

propositions made by Farge, highly advantageous to the King's service, and the best interests of the country. In consequence of the benefits to be thus conferred on France, he promises, in the King's name, to furnish Raleigh with a *brevet* or royal ordonnance, which on his return from the Indies would secure him a friendly reception in any port or harbour on the French coast to which he might be led by choice, or driven by stress of weather. Farther, in reward of the services which Raleigh undertook to perform for Louis, he was to enjoy in France not only complete protection, but was to be graced with high honours and distinctions.*   Still as the *brevet* had not as yet been drawn up and signed by the King, he could only promise that it should be forwarded as soon as possible.   Two days later, the instrument, complete in form, but without the Royal seal or signature, seems to have been conveyed to Raleigh.   This in the Spanish translation, which is alone to be found in the Archives at Simancas, is called a Commission from the Admiral of France empowering Raleigh to proceed with his fleet to Cape Blanco, Cape de Verde, Sierra Leone, Congo, and all the settlements on the western coast of Africa as far as the Cape of Good Hope.   He is thence to cross the Atlantic, to the Rio de la Plata, to sail

* Respuesta del Señor de Montmorency á don Valter Raly á acerca de alcanzar un billete del rey de Francia para quando estaria de buelta de su jornada para poder bibir en Francia.   May 7th, 1617. Simancas.

northwards by the mouth of the Amazons, and the rivers of Guiana, engaging in commercial transactions wherever he may think proper, and preserving towards all nations in alliance with France most peaceable and friendly behaviour.* This instrument, less satisfactory even than that of James himself, Raleigh esteemed of so little value, that, as soon probably as it came to hand, he again despatched Captain Farge to France to express his dissatisfaction, and press for a more ample commission. He tells the minister to whom his letter is addressed that, although on the point of setting sail, he is still so anxious to be furnished with proper credentials that he once more sends his faithful friend to explain his views and prospects, and if possible to obtain a *brevet* from the King himself. He then makes allusion to certain ships, which, according to the arrangement previously entered into, were to be sent after him ; and adds, that his trusty agent would point out the place in Guiana where he would be found working at the mines. In this communication he speaks with satisfaction of the changes which had just then taken place in the politics of the French court, by which the Spanish party had been thoroughly defeated, so that there existed little probability of its ever recovering its former influence.†

* La comision que el Almirante de Francia dio a Waltero Ralefha, 9 Mayo, 1617. Simancas.

† Carta original à Monsieur Monsieur de Bisse anc. conser. du Roy en ses conseil destat et privé. May 24th, 1617. Simancas.

To decide whether the above negociation is to be
condemned or defended, we must take fully into consideration the situation in which Raleigh stood, and
the disposition of the English court towards him. He
seems to have entertained strong doubts of the success
of his enterprise, and to have foreseen, though not of
course with absolute certainty, the calamitous termination to himself. In other years, before persecution,
imprisonment, malaria, apoplexy and paralysis, united
with the lowering effects of sixty-five years, had damped
his enthusiasm, he might have spurned the idea of
succumbing to the apprehension of death on the scaffold;
but now, looking at its terrors from a distance, he quailed
at the prospect, though, when the fatal hour arrived, no
man ever laid his head on the block with greater mag-
nanimity; still if policy could have warded off the
catastrophe, was he not justified in making the attempt?
"When they persecute you in one city," says Christ,
"flee ye to another;" and the means of flight are left
to the choice and judgment of the persecuted. If there
are others who will decide differently in this matter,
means are certainly at hand to afford a specious colouring to their decision. I regret that Raleigh resembled
Themistocles rather than Marcus Brutus; but I have
only to describe his conduct as it was, though my sympathy goes with him even when he was undoubtedly in
error.

On the 3rd of July the fleet left England, but about eight leagues west of the Scilly Isles encountered a hurricane, by which one vessel was sunk, another driven back to Bristol, and the rest compelled to take refuge in the ports of Ireland.* The 'Destiny' itself made its way to the harbour of Cork,† where Raleigh, we are told, greatly augmented his perilous force by taking into his pay formidable bodies of pirates. Here contrary winds detained the fleet till the 19th of August,‡ and this delay, caused by the elements, was, by his adversaries, objected to Raleigh as a crime.

Upon leaving Ireland, the fleet proceeded along the shores of France, Spain, and Portugal, towards the Canary Islands, and meeting by the way some French vessels, an incident occurred which led to considerable misrepresentation. Captain Baily, who afterwards deserted, seized upon a French bark, and would have appropriated her cargo to his own use without payment, but that Raleigh interposed his authority, and

* Chamberlain to Carleton, July 5th, 1617. MS. State Paper Office.

† 'Journal of Second Voyage to Guiana,' edited by Schomburgk, p. 177.

‡ The news, however, of his departure had not reached London by the 12th (23 N. S.) of September, when Lionello wrote that he was still in Ireland, adding that, " Si sia assai diminuita essendosi separati alcuni vascelli et partiti molti di quelli che vi andavano sopra." Venetian Archives.

purchased the bark of its owner.* On the 6th of
September they made the volcanic island of Lancerote,
where Raleigh's evil genius involved him in conflicts
with the Spaniards. Only a few weeks before, a
squadron of Barbary corsairs had put suddenly into
Puerto Santo, and after plundering the place,
carried off the whole of its inhabitants. When the
English fleet appeared before Lancerote, the Governor
believed, or pretended to believe, it to be the above
piratical squadron, and drew together in all haste the
forces of the island for its defence.

To augment his alarm, Raleigh landed his men, nine
hundred in number, to "stretch their legs," as he
expresses it. Upon which the Governor advanced at

* Compare Journal, p. 179, Apology, p. 9, with the following
passage from Cottington:—"The great complaint brought hither
against Sir Walter Raleigh appears, as I am certainly informed, to
be only for the taking of victuals from some few Frenchmen, and
that so small a consideration as not worthy to be spoken of."
Madrid, Nov. 4th, 1617. MS. State Paper Office.

Baily's account, drawn up probably in concert with Gondomar,
is absolutely comic: "Having first cruized," he says, "all round the
coast of England, in search of adventures and finding none, he sailed
for Ireland, where he collected all that he could find in money as
well as other commodities for his own use. . . . He took from the
prisons all the pirates who had been condemned to the gallows; and
whenever we discovered any ship we pursued it as though we had
been the enemies of all the world."

La Declaracion del Capitan Jorje Vayle que lo fue de la armada
de Gualtero Rale, sobre su jornada y designios. Diciembre, 1617·
Simancas.

the head of his troops; but instead of assailing the English, detached himself, with one officer, from the main body, and came forward with a flag of truce. In like pacific mood, Raleigh, attended by Lieutenant Bradshaw, went to meet him; and, to the Governor's inquiry, replied, that he and his followers were Christians, subjects to the king of Great Britain, an ally of Spain, and that his sole object in visiting Lancerote, was to purchase provisions and take in fresh water. To dissipate the fear that they might be Turks in disguise, he referred him to Reekes, an English factor, then with his ship in the harbour, having just arrived with a cargo of wine from Teneriffe. From what followed it is clear that it was by order, not through craven fear, that the Governor lied and equivocated, while his people were conveying their effects to the mountains, for this having been done, he prevailed on Raleigh, by falsehood, to re-embark the greater part of his mariners; after which, falling upon the remainder, he killed two and wounded others. To avenge this crime, many of the English officers demanded permission to sack the town. In Elizabeth's time the proper chastisement would have been certainly inflicted; but, in obedience to the King's orders, Raleigh curbed his resentment, and, to the disgust of his followers, left Lancerote and proceeded to the Grand Canary.

His object now was twofold: first, to supply himself with the water and provisions he needed; and second, to prefer his complaint to Don Fernando Osorio, Governor-general, of the treatment he had received at Lancerote. As might be expected, some discrepancy is found between the Spanish and English accounts, though not so much in facts as in the view taken of them. Raleigh informs us that he forwarded to Don Fernando Osorio, by a Spanish fisherman, copies of his correspondence with the Governor of Lancerote, with assurances that he had it in commandment from the king, his master, not to offer any violence, or to take any places belonging to the Spanish King. Suspecting that the Spaniards in attacking him were only obeying the orders of their government, he desired to be informed if such was the case. Osorio, with the haughtiness of an official who believes himself strong enough for self-defence, deigned no reply; but, affecting to apprehend that the English meant to storm the place, put his men under arms, and stood upon the defensive. Receiving no answer, Raleigh departed, and made for the little town of Maspaloma, where he landed a small party to take in wood and water.

Resolute in his hostility, Osorio ordered Captain Lorenzo de Torres to proceed with the troops under his command and prevent the disembarkation of the English, or, if already landed, to force them back to their ships. In this operation, approaching under cover of trees, they killed three of Raleigh's men, and took two prisoners. Torres, who performed this service, makes no mention of his own losses; but Raleigh, more honest, observes that Captain Thornhurst, Sir Warham St. Leger, Lieutenant Hayman, and his son Walter, hastening to the rescue, killed three Spaniards, and put the rest of the valiant Torres's company to flight.*

It would have been indeed strange if an English admiral, in command of a formidable fleet, should have borne patiently such treatment as Raleigh met with in the Canaries. The peace existing between Great Britain and Spain entitled him at least to civility, and the privilege of purchasing provisions for his money; but instead of a friendly reception, he everywhere encountered hostility and treachery. Profound irritation, bordering upon revenge, pervaded the whole armament, so that slight offence would have been needed to provoke a general massacre of the islanders. This was on the very eve of being supplied on their arrival at Goméra, for as they approached the lofty rocks that overhang the harbour's mouth, the natives opened their batteries upon our ships; to silence which, since forbearance could no longer be maintained,

* 'Journal,' p. 182; 'Apology,' p. 15. Carta Autógrafa del Capitan Lorenzo de Torres à S. Md. May 12th, 1618. Simancas.

the contents of twenty demiculverins were sent rattling through their houses. The firing then ceased, and a Spaniard was sent on shore with a letter to the Governor, informing him that the English came as friends, exclusively for the purpose of obtaining fresh water, which, however, they stood so much in need of that it was impossible they could dispense with a supply. The proceedings at Goméra formed an agreeable contrast to those which had preceded. The Governor, a member of the noble Flemish family of Horn, with his lady, a descendant of the English Staffords, immediately accorded to Raleigh all he demanded; and their intercourse, though short, formed a pleasing episode in the narrative of Raleigh's calamitous voyage.

Of the particulars no correct information had reached the Grand Canary by the middle of the following May, since Torres, in his statement, then assured the King that Raleigh, having no money, obtained what he required in return for two brass pieces of ordnance. Quite different were the facts. Desirous of obliterating from the minds of the English all recollection of the insults and injuries they had received at the other islands, the Governor and his lady were profuse in their kindness and hospitality, not only permitting them to take in fresh water in abundance, but loading them with the most welcome presents. To men suffering from the fevers engendered in autumn by the sultry calms of those latitudes, fresh fruits appeared like fountains in the desert; knowing which, the Governor's lady sent on board baskets of lemons, oranges, delicate grapes, pomegranates, and figs, together with loaves of fine sugar, manchets, and poultry. Raleigh himself, however, had begun the process of hospitality by presenting the lady with "six exceeding fine handkerchiefs and six pair of gloves," writing to her at the same time, that if there were anything worthy of her in his fleet, she should command it and him. To the above were added, as a parting gift, two ounces of ambergris, an ounce of the delicate extract of amber, a large glass of rosewater in high estimation there, with a very excellent picture of Mary Magdalene, and a cutwork cuff.

In testimony of the friendly intercourse which had taken place between the English and the inhabitants of Goméra, the Governor intrusted Raleigh with a letter to the Spanish ambassador in London, in which he spoke in the highest terms of the Admiral's pacific and honourable bearing.

On his departure from Goméra, Raleigh pursued a south-westerly course, through a succession of sultry calms, squalls, and storms. Disease soon broke forth in the fleet, and day after day fresh victims were sewn up in their shrouds and committed to the deep. On board the 'Destiny' alone forty-two persons died and among them some of Raleigh's nearest and dearest kin. Describing to his wife what he suffered, he says :—" Sweetheart, I can write unto you but with a weak hand, for I have endured the most violent calenture for fifteen days that ever man did and lived . . . . Remember my service to my Lord Carew and Mr. Secretary Winwood. I write not to them, for I can write of nought but miseries."*

As the adventurers proceeded, gorgeous rainbows threw their arches over the ocean, and all the splendour of the Southern sky burst upon them. One evening, about eight o'clock, they caught the first glimpse of the Magellanic Clouds, vast concentric circles of pink and opalescent stars, resembling, from their countless multitude, a portion of the Milky Way, and constituting the most splendid and mysterious phenomenon in the heavens.†

On the 11th of November he reached Guiana, and experienced some slight improvement in health, partly through the influence of the land-breeze, partly from the refreshing fruits which two caciques who had been with him in the Tower sent on board. His hopes being still unquenched, he now strove, by their aid, to banish the recollection of his sufferings as he drifted down slowly towards the Orinoco, between clusters of islands, on one of which Defoe has laid the scene of Robinson Crusoe.

* Works, viii., 630, 631.   † Sir John Herschel's ' Astronomy,' 895.

CHAPTER X.

MACHINATIONS OF HIS ENEMIES AT HOME.

THE above, though brief, is a faithful account of Raleigh's proceedings in the Canary Islands: it will now be necessary to consider the effects produced in Great Britain and Spain by those transactions.

One of the principal actors in this part of the Raleigh drama was the Spanish ambassador, Gondomar, a man of audacious and turbulent spirit, devoured by self-conceit and animated by an inconceivable hatred of Raleigh. According to his own representations to Philip he constituted the central figure at the English court, about which everything revolved, king, favourite, and ministers. Next to Raleigh, Winwood was the chief mark against which his rancour directed itself, which, if we may credit his own statement, terminated in the humiliation and death of his victim. When a Spaniard hates, he seldom does it by halves. Gondomar at any rate would have realized Johnson's idea of a good hater, and, like Hobbes and Shakespeare, might have put the question—

"Hates any man the thing he would not kill?"

When intelligence reached England from Lancerote, Gondomar made a simultaneous attack on the weakness of James, and the vindictiveness of Philip. Nothing occupied the mind of the former but field-sports and the craving after gold, which involved him in the meshes of Spain, because he viewed the marriage of Charles with the Infanta, Donna Maria, in no other light than as a wicket leading into the treasury of El Dorado. A man of discernment would long ere this have seen through the delusion; but James was not a man of discernment, and accordingly suffered himself to be tossed to and fro like a tennis-ball by the agents of the Escorial. In the autumn of 1617 the great business at court was the appointment of commissioners to treat of the marriage, and Winwood, we are assured, desired to be one of the number. As James thought him qualified to be Secretary of State, he could have felt no objection to gratify the minister's wish, if the repugnance of Gondomar could be subdued. Winwood, therefore, it is said, endeavoured, through the intervention of Buckingham and his mother, to blunt the edge of the Spaniard's animosity; but instead of succeeding, only exasperated his malignity. Persevering in season and out of season in exciting James's wrath by dwelling on the acts of piracy of which he accused Raleigh, Gondomar not only succeeded in causing his fictions to be accepted for facts, but turned the tide of royal resentment so fiercely against Winwood, that through vexation he was thrown into a burning fever, which carried him off in a few days. As fevers were then often produced by artificial means, especially by Rome and Spain, and as the post-mortem examination of Winwood's body pointed to such an inference, it may not be too uncharitable to suspect that James's supposed indignation was not the main source of Winwood's malady.

I have already alluded to the fact that Captain Baily, though, as he says, he had invested his whole fortune in Raleigh's enterprise, deserted from the fleet at Lancerote, and returned to spread through England calumnious rumours against his commander. Was it through cowardice that he acted thus, or had doubloons or pieces of eight anything to do with his desertion? It is certain that he enjoyed the sympathy and support of Gondomar, who, when he drew up a slanderous declaration, full of falsehoods against Raleigh, caused a translation to be made of it into Spanish, which I have now before me, and appears to have vouched to his government for its accuracy. There were, however, some awkward circumstances opposed to Baily's success; the crew of his own ship gave the lie to his accusations, for which reason he evinced much reluctance to make his appearance in London; and when at length he repaired thither, and was subjected to examination by the Privy Council, his evidence broke down, and he was committed to the Gatehouse for desertion and calumny against his General, though of these facts not a whisper appears to have been wafted to Madrid.

Gondomar's next move was to embarrass the English government, and betray the nation into hostility towards Raleigh, by putting a sudden stop to our commerce with Spain. With intemperate haste he forwarded to Philip terrible accounts of Raleigh's excesses in the Canary Islands, where he was accused of committing every kind of atrocity; nay, so audacious it was said had he grown in his wickedness that, writing to the Earl of Southampton, he not only boasted of his crimes, but frankly proclaimed his intention of stationing himself in the group to intercept the American fleet on its way to Spain.

When these representations were laid before the Council of State at Madrid they occasioned an important debate, at which, after the lapse of two hundred and fifty years, we may almost imagine ourselves present. The old Council Chamber is no longer standing, having been pulled down in the eighteenth century, when the present unrivalled palace was erected by an Italian architect. In accordance, however, with the taste of the age, of which we may form a just conception from several ancient buildings, the apartment was spacious and gloomy, with which the costume and grave bearing of the councillors were in harmony. The question under consideration being whether or not it were advisable to lay on all English vessels at Seville the embargo recommended by Gondomar, the Duque del Infantado opened the discussion by advocating the views of the ambassador.

He said that since the Conde de Gondomar, a man of prudence and discretion, was the moving spirit in the whole matter, he could not reject the counsel he gave to his Majesty respecting the embargo. No fear need be entertained that it would interrupt the peace existing between the two countries or lead to any other sinister consequences, because, with the experience he had acquired by a long residence in England, the ambassador would have been withheld from giving such advice had there been any danger to be feared. At the same time the Chief Justice of Seville should be commanded to observe great caution in carrying out the measure, so that no injury might be inflicted on individuals or any damage sustained by property. Simultaneously with these proceedings notice ought to be given to the English ambassador at Madrid and forwarded to Gondomar in England, in order that, being acquainted with all the circumstances of the case, he might be able to ward off untoward consequences.

Don Agustin Mesia observed that he would willingly adopt the policy of the Conde de Gondomar, but was deterred by considering that the only news hitherto received of the said Walter Raleigh was that his fleet had touched at Lancerote; but it was not known that he had committed any damage, and until news to such effect should be obtained he would oppose the embargo.

The Marquis de la Laguna argued in favour of the measure proposed by Gondomar, and improving upon his policy, recommended that the embargo should be extended to the other ports of Spain as well as Seville.

Philip's confessor spoke next, declaring that he agreed entirely with Gondomar, and that as a point of conscience he should feel more scruple in abstaining from offering such advice to his Majesty than sorrow for giving it; because it was evident that Gondomar was acquainted with Raleigh's proceedings, and knew of the letter he had written to the Earl of Southampton, stating that he meant to station himself at the Canaries for the purpose of intercepting the homeward-bound fleet. He then referred to Captain Baily's declaration, which, agreeing, he said, with the advices received from Lancerote, inclined him to put faith in his whole story. Having advanced clearly thus far, the confessor's ideas became confused, so that he mingled facts and fictions strangely together. Being ignorant that Baily had been sent to prison for his statement, he took advantage of his own ignorance, and contended that he would have been punished in England if his story had been false, especially as Lady Raleigh and her friends made loud complaints against his report.

Don Baltasar de Zuniga closed the debate with a brief but convincing speech; since no harm, he said, could arise from delay, it might be as well to observe proper forms in laying on the embargo. Instructions should be sent to the Chief Justice of Seville, and the other authorities there, directing them to inform themselves minutely of the damage that Walter had done in the island of Lancerote, or in others of the Canaries, of which doubtless there would be in Seville very particular news; and upon this investigation he thought it might be well to have recourse to an embargo; but he did not consider it very probable that Raleigh, being so good a seaman, and having with him so many who were the same, should be waiting in the Canary Islands for our fleet to come from the Indies, since on the voyage out they pass near the Canaries, but on their return take a route very distant from them.*

A report of this discussion having been laid before Philip, he appears to have considered the arguments for and against the embargo, and to have been swayed

* Minuta de consulta del consejo de estado 7 de Diciembre 1617. Simancas.

by the advice of Zuniga to postpone action to inquiry.
Instructions were accordingly sent to the Chief Justice
of Seville,* directing him to examine with secrecy and
despatch the grounds of the rumours circulated against
Raleigh, that the King might be put in possession of
accurate information. As no such information existed
at Seville, the Chief Justice applied to Don Fernando
Osorio, Governor-general of the Canaries, who directed
Lorenzo de Torres to draw up a report containing the
particulars of Raleigh's visit, to which I have already
referred.†

If the Spanish government and most of its agents
exhibited the dignity of sluggishness, Gondomar could
by no means be complimented for the same virtue.
His hatred of Raleigh urged him to sleepless vigilance;
his letters, despatches, representations, may be said to
have trodden on each other's heels through the eagerness of their author to compass the destruction of the
great Englishman. To this end the juggle of the
Spanish match was skilfully protracted, and while
Gondomar dwelt secretly on the reports of Raleigh's
misdoings which he himself had fabricated, he eschewed
speaking openly on the subject, because several members
of the English Council who remembered the vehemence

* Real despacho al asistente de Sevilla, 27 de Diciembre, 1617.
Simancas.

† Carta Autografa del Capitan Lorenzo de Torres, 12 de Mayo,
1618. Simancas.

with which he had opposed Raleigh's departure suspected his designs.*

For some time there was a lull in the storm of persecution, because no intelligence reached England which might seem to justify its continuance. Still, Gondomar and the Secretary Ulloa supplied Philip and the Council of State with irritating reports, in the hope of producing an embargo, by which they trusted that James's anger against Raleigh might be blown into a flame. They were very confident, however, that he would secretly have felt little regret for the interruption of commerce, since it would have seemed to justify the punishment of those who had urged him to permit Raleigh's departure entirely against his own conviction. Sir John Digby, English ambassador at Madrid, ranked among the foremost of Raleigh's enemies, and by his despatches exasperated James's hostility, of which he artfully represented his own dislike to be only an echo.

While the above correspondence was in progress, Captain Alley, who left Guiana on the 14th of November, landed in England.

Before the contents of his letters could be known, the bare announcement that he came from Raleigh sufficed to awaken public enthusiasm. In our own day the discovery of a new gold-field is hailed with rapture,

* Parrafo de una carta del Conde de Gondomar à S. Md., 30th de Diciembre, 1617. Simancas.

because all persons secretly expect to derive some mysterious advantage from it. Far more widely spread was this extravagant expectation in Raleigh's day, so that Captain Alley, had his nervous system been of the toughest, might have been thrown into a vertigo by the babel of inquiries in the midst of which he found himself. Instead, however, of rendering more intense the fever of cupidity, the intelligence he brought was well calculated to allay it. He no doubt related that Raleigh was in Guiana, moving inland towards the mines; but from the sufferings and loss of life encountered on the voyage, reflecting persons augured unfavourably of the whole enterprise. Yet there were those who retained their original faith, and expected the speedy arrival of other messengers to announce the acquisition of untold treasures.

Meanwhile the Spanish government more than participated the harassing uncertainty experienced by James. Gondomar, indeed, though encouraged by Philip to persevere in the course he was pursuing in England, felt his ardour somewhat damped at being told by his king, that though Raleigh had indeed landed in the Canaries, he went his way without inflicting any damage on the islands.*

The ground of apprehension was then suddenly shifted; now the news reached Madrid that the great

* Real despacho al Conde de Gondomar, 9th de Feb., 1618. Simancas.

Corsair had been beheld passing by San Domingo, towards Guiana and Trinidad, with fourteen ships of war ;* and now it was confidently affirmed that he contemplated the taking of Margucreta or Jamaica, where, being a fugitive from England, he intended to establish himself, and by offering an asylum to the sea-rovers and buccaneers of all nations, to aim at sovereign power.

Some of these reports originated with a French pirate, who in Spain called himself Captain Belle, and said he was a native of Dieppe. According to his statement, he had been known to Raleigh for six or seven years, and, in conjunction with Captain Farge, had been employed by him in conveying letters to and from France. Though a pirate, however, he cherished all the scruples of a good Catholic, and deserted treacherously from Raleigh's fleet, because he disliked the society of Huguenots. To purify himself from the taint acquired by an intimacy of six or seven years, he repaired to the great sink of Christendom, Rome, where he confessed his sins—which were doubtless numerous —and received absolution ; but his confessor, instead of enjoining amendment of life, counselled new acts of guilt. Hastening with the papers he had stolen to Madrid, he was there to betray his former master. Following the directions of the priest, he passed over

* Despatch of Piero Gritti, May 30th, 1618. Venetian Archives.

into Spain, and on reaching the capital, told his story to Don Andres de Velazquez, who repeated it to the King.* As the ex-pirate was in a poor plight, Velazquez thought it probable that his disclosure might be a fiction, especially as he prayed to be favoured with a hundred crowns, though he offered to remain as a hostage till the truth of his statement could be inquired into. Philip gave him the money, and referred his examination to Don Diego Brochero, who appears to have conducted it with intelligence and fidelity. Belle admitted to him that in parting with Raleigh he had been guilty of treachery; for being at Plymouth, he and Captain Farge informed the Admiral that some officers of their acquaintance were getting ready at Dieppe and Havre four or five ships to join him in Guiana, but would wait until they received directions from him and Farge. Believing what they said, Raleigh gave them a written description of the route they were to follow, together with a chart of navigation in order that they might find him with more certainty. That both Belle and Farge intended from the first to betray Raleigh is clear from the fact that they opened the packets they were engaged to convey to and from France, and made transcripts of the enclosed letters, copies of which now lie before me. Both the miscreants

* Carta Autografa de Don Andres de Velazquez al Rey, 12 de Feb., 1618. Simancas.

afterwards met with their deserts, for Belle reached Madrid in the condition of a beggar, while Fargo seems to have rotted in jail at Genoa, where he was imprisoned for debt.*

It has been often affirmed that Raleigh himself believed in the existence of no mines in Guiana, or believed it without any ground and in opposition to the testimony of all well-informed persons; but Gondomar and his secretary, who ought surely to have possessed exact information, entertained no doubt respecting the existence of those mines. They were fully persuaded, however, that through the arrangements made by the Spanish government, Raleigh's enterprise would end in disaster.†

To this statement of Ulloa another, conceived in the same spirit, was soon afterwards added by Gondomar, who concluded rightly enough that the chances of failure were multiplying fast about Raleigh. His letters occasionally, from being wanting in names, dates, and circumstantial details, suggest the suspicion that he often amused his catholic majesty with fictions of his own invention. Just at this juncture a ship arrived quite *à propos* at Portsmouth, bringing about Raleigh's proceedings news so strange that it reads like

* Carta de Don Diego Brochero sobre asuntos de Gualtero, 20 de Marzo, 1618. Simancas.

† Don Sanchez de Ulloa à Ciriza, Feb., 1618. Simancas.

an extract from Sir John Mandeville. Having lost on the voyage many of his best men, the master of the 'Destiny' among others, he missed the mouth of the Orinoco, and entered a port where the current ran inland with such force that it would be a work of much difficulty to sail out again. Suspecting the designs of his officers, Raleigh, it was said, seized and opened the letters they had written to England, through which he discovered the general disaffection existing in his fleet, and the resolution *all* had formed, if their condition did not speedily improve, to cast their Admiral into the sea, and return to England. When Raleigh ordered one of the most violent of these prophets to be placed under arrest, the mariners refused to obey his commands; so that it was obvious nothing but disappointment and calamity was to be looked for. Gondomar himself still clung to the belief he had entertained from the beginning, that Raleigh's crews would turn pirates; and this persuasion appears to have been shared by several other persons.[*]

[*] Carta del Conde de Gondomar à su Majestad, 26 de Marzo, 1618 Simancas.

CHAPTER XI.

HIS GOLDEN VISION IS DISPELLED.

IF facts and events could, in spite of reason, establish the doctrine of fatality, I might suspect that the Three Sisters had now clutched Raleigh in their inextricable grasp, since everything he planned or did shaped itself into a means of destruction. Whatever enthusiasm or buoyancy survived in the fleet connected itself with his person, so that where he led all would fearlessly follow, and in the surge of their valour bear down everything before them. Conscious of this, and that success in his enterprise was synonymous with life, he was yet, through the prostration produced by sickness, constrained to relinquish the lead to another.

Owing to the insufficient depth of water on the bar, it was found impracticable to force the larger ships into the river, on which account the ' Destiny ' and its bulky consorts remained cruising between the mouth of the Orinoco and the island of Trinidad, under the command of Raleigh, who through weakness had to be carried from one place to another in a chair; while five of the smaller vessels, with a considerable force of soldiers and mariners, ascended the river under the command of Kemys and young Raleigh.

The fact having transpired that the Spaniards had reinforced all their settlements in Guiana, the party under Kemys would hardly have ventured inland had not Raleigh remained on the coast to prevent their retreat from the country being cut off by the arrival of a fleet with fresh troops from other parts of America. Raleigh himself fully expected that he should have to encounter the galleons, but assured his friends that, under all circumstances, they should find his ships or their ashes at Punto de Gallo, for that he would fight while there remained a deck to stand on. That an attack was meditated by Spain is certain. If Sir Walter Raleigh, says Gondomar, should have gone direct to Guiana without touching at Jamaica, as is rumoured, it will be easy to crush him, since it will be necessary for him to leave his vessels and stores in Trinidad, while he ascends the Orinoco in boats and barges.*

Meanwhile Kemys, furnished with clear instructions, proceeded up the Orinoco with an adequate number of mariners and three hundred soldiers, under the com-

---

* Carta del Conde de Gondomar à S. Md., 10 de Agosto, 1617. Simancas.

mand of Walter and George Raleigh. His orders were to make for the mines without offering the slightest molestation to native or Spaniard; but if attacked, to repel force by force. It has been already seen that, by directions from Spain, the authorities in Guiana had made preparations for crushing the English, whom they regarded as invaders. When, therefore, Kemys and his mining party disembarked and bivouacked for the night at a point midway between the mines and San Tome, they could hardly have calculated on peaceful slumbers. Their movements had in fact been watched by the Spaniards, who, as soon as stillness prevailed in the camp, made a rush upon the sleepers, in the hope of surprising and cutting them to pieces; but the English, being on their guard, repulsed the assailants, who, facing about, retreated towards the town, closely pursued by young Raleigh at the head of his men. On the brow of the hill a personal encounter took place between him and Erineta, a Spanish captain, who, having fired off his piece, felled his youthful antagonist with a blow of the stock. In another moment Plessington, the sergeant of Raleigh's company, ran Erineta through the body with his pike; after which, the English, rushing forwards, slew Palameque the governor, with his principal officers, and then set fire to the town.

Though defeated and dispersed by this sudden onset, the Spaniards, who were far more numerous than their assailants, retreated to the woods close at hand, whence at brief intervals they issued to alarm and harass the English. That there existed mines in the neighbourhood was now proved, since four gold refineries were found in San Tomé. Kemys however had lost heart. Everything had fallen out contrary to his expectations: during the previous twelve months Spain had multiplied and strengthened her position in Guiana; the passes of the mountains were in her hands, her troops swarmed in the forests and along the rivers, so that in whatever direction he moved his followers were shot down at his side without his being able to catch even a glimpse of the enemy. In this hopeless state of affairs, he resolved to brave the reproaches of his General and abandon the enterprise. Returning slowly and sorrowfully down the river with news which he doubtless felt would be received almost as a sentence of death, he found Raleigh at Punto de Gallo with the fleet.

What follows stands perhaps less in need of apology than of explanation. Kemys, born and nurtured amid the winds on the Wiltshire downs, had in him the soul of an ancient Roman, and to serve his country, or satisfy his leader, would any day have leaped into as hopeless a gulf as Curtius did. He had stood by Raleigh in every turn of fortune, good or ill; had been with him in the Tower, had been shown the rack without flinching, had been always ready, in order to shield his leader from censure, to take any amount of blame upon himself.

Nothing therefore but the overwhelming grief by which Raleigh's mind was at this time stunned—for he could and did bear the prescience of the axe with equanimity—can excuse the harshness of his behaviour towards Kemys upon the failure of the inland expedition. It is true that upon that failure hinged his own fate; it is true, and there was no disguising it, that to return to England empty-handed was to return, like Regulus, to certain death; but if the death was not to be shunned Raleigh should have so conducted himself towards this gallant gentleman, who erred, if he did err at all, more through desperate sorrow for the loss of his young leader than through any reluctance to face hardships or dangers—Raleigh, I say, should have so conducted himself that he and Kemys might have laid their heads on the same block, and left life as they had passed it together. There was nothing of which Kemys was not capable, and he may be cited as one of the noblest examples on record of the pure and heroic love of man for man. Of all the names connected with Raleigh, his is the brightest, and it is impossible to repeat, or to read his story without deep emotion. It is true he fell, like Brutus at Philippi, by his own hand; but he fell in despair, not only of any longer serving his country, but of preserving the approbation of the great man, to be whose lieutenant had been the sole ambition of his life. That Raleigh loved and valued him as he deserved cannot be doubted, but it was because of this very love and esteem that he gave way to that tone of reproach which entered like iron into Kemys's soul and made him loathe existence.

In Raleigh's own accounts of Kemys's death—for there are two—we find some discrepancies, which, however, considering the state of mind in which he wrote, we may easily understand and forgive. He had just lost his son, a loss which at the moment seemed the greatest he could sustain; he saw in the countenances of all around him unmistakable marks of disappointment and alienation; he could not therefore doubt that in many cases, from friends and followers, they would soon be converted into accusers; over his seditious and savage crews he felt that his power was at an end, and consequently that, instead of leading them to any new enterprise, he was in truth their prisoner. Had he been joined by the promised French squadron he might have been still his own master; but Montmorenci had proved as little reliable as James, and he would now therefore have to return to the Tower and the block, unless by some subtle manœuvre he could effect his escape from those who were eager to wreak upon him the loss of the riches on which they had confidently reckoned. Raleigh was now an old man, broken down in health, maddened by grief, embittered by disappointment, bewildered by the prospect of the troubles and sorrows which he beheld grouping themselves before him. When Kemys therefore stated his reasons for not repairing to the site of the mine, he refused to accept his explanation, upon which, in despair, that gallant officer put an end to his life.

Writing from St. Christopher in March, Raleigh says, " I was no sooner come from him into my cabin, but I heard a pistol go off over my head, and sending to know who shot it, word was brought me that Kemys shot it out of his cabin window to cleanse it. And his boy going into his cabin found him lying upon his bed with much blood by him, and looking in his face saw him dead. The pistol being but little, did but crack his rib, but turning him over, he found a long knife in his body all but the handle."*

Four months later, at Salisbury, covered with pustules, blains, and blotches, he wrote amid the noise and bustle of an inn, in a brief snatch of leisure obtained by artifice, the same story with some variations. After detailing the particulars of his discussion with his old friend, Raleigh says, " He replied in these words, ' I know not then, sir, what course to take;' and went out of my cabin into his own, in which he was no sooner entered, but I heard a pistol go off. I sent up (not suspecting

* Letter to Winwood, Works, viii., 632.

any such thing as the killing of himself) to know who shot a pistol. Kemys himself made answer, lying on his bed, that he himself had shot it off because it had been long charged, with which I was satisfied. Some half-hour after this, the boy going into his cabin, found him dead, having a long knife thrust under his left pap, through his heart, and his pistol lying by him with which it appeared that he had shot himself; but the bullet lighting upon a rib had but broken the rib and went no farther."*

Arguing from these differences in the two statements, Sanderson, in his ' History of Charles I.', accuses Raleigh of assassination. To such an accusation no reply is needed.

Thick obscurity now gathers about Raleigh's story. I am not his apologist; whatever may be thought of his conduct, my duty is clear; I have to state the truth, and nothing but the truth, and leave the reader to base his decision upon it. In the circumstances of extreme difficulty in which he stood, a straightforward policy would probably have forestalled the executioner. We speak of him as an abstraction, as a name now; he was a man then, invested with all a man's attributes, love of life among the rest. It has been seen that among the desperadoes in his fleet, the idea of casting him into the sea widely prevailed, and against this catastrophe he considered himself authorised to provide.

* ' Apology,' p. 39.

With this view he fell back upon his French commission, which accorded to him, he said, more ample powers than that he had received from James. According to some accounts, which I know not whether to regard as facts or calumnies, he suggested to his mutinous followers the project of making up for their losses on shore by capturing the Spanish treasure fleet, which must either have involved England in a war with Spain, or have thrown him and his associates into the category of pirates. He is made by one report to confess such a design in his examination before the Privy Council, when Bacon, we are told, observed, " Then, Sir Walter, you would have been a pirate:" to which he replied, " Did you ever know of any one being a pirate for millions? I would have silenced all objections by a lavish distribution of treasure."*

But this anecdote rests on too slender a foundation to be accepted as a disclosure of what took place in the West Indies. All that appears to be known with certainty is that, soon after the failure of the mining enterprise, Raleigh's fleet broke up, some ships proceeding in one direction, some in another. The peril of law, in which, as Bacon expresses it, Raleigh stood, deprived him of authority, and, among men incapable of estimating personal greatness, converted him into an

* Conversations with Wilson in the Tower, September 26th, 1618. State Paper Office.

object of derision. No trustworthy narrative of what took place between his departure from the West Indies and his arrival at Plymouth has been hitherto discovered. For a while four ships seem to have followed his flag, but whether or not they accompanied him to Newfoundland I have been unable to ascertain. The probability is that by the time he reached that island two ships only remained to him, the 'Destiny' and the 'Jason,' commanded by Captain Pennington. His intention to put into some French port having apparently transpired, a mutiny took place at Newfoundland, when a majority of the sailors insisted on returning to England. All exact dates are lost. Turning their prows eastwards, they reached Kinsale some time in May, where, for reasons which I have never seen explained, Pennington's ship was seized by the Lord-deputy, while the 'Destiny' continued its voyage, and made Plymouth Sound early in June.

Here, to intimate that his Odyssæan wanderings were at an end, Raleigh dismantled his ship and sent her sails on shore. At no great distance on the Devonshire coast lay that Hayes Farm, from which, half a century before, he had departed to commence, under the greatest of English sovereigns, his studies and his toils, and now, broken down by calamity and disease, he was returning to lay his head at the feet of the most worthless. "His friends," says Contarini, " are now endeavouring to obtain a free pardon for him from the king, that he may be at liberty to come to court, and not go back to the Tower."*

Instead of conceding to Raleigh's friends the pardon they sought, James, on the 11th,† issued a proclamation, denouncing the proceedings at San Tome as a breach of instructions, and inviting all persons who might be able to supply information to give evidence before the Privy Council.

In spite of the hostility discoverable in this document, Raleigh set out for London, but had proceeded only twenty miles, when he was met at Ashburton by his relative Sir Lewis Stukeley, Vice-admiral of Devon, who had been commissioned to arrest him, and take possession of his ship. Stukeley possibly saw nothing particularly base in the office he had undertaken; but the judgment of his contemporaries was so different, that he was thenceforward distinguished by the appellation of Sir Judas Stukeley. More sure, perhaps, than he wished of his victim, the Vice-admiral was eager to obtain possession of his property, and therefore, instead of repairing with him at once to London, went back to Plymouth, where the two relatives lodged in the house of Sir Christopher Harris.

* Despatch of June 21st (N.S.) Venetian Archives.

† The proclamation is dated June 9th, though it seems to have been issued on the eleventh. State Paper Office.

I have said that Stukeley felt, perhaps, only too sure of his prisoner, since he seems at first to have purposely held him with a loose rein, that, if he would, he might effect his escape and leave him master of the ' Destiny.' To suggest the course that should be followed, he made visits into the country, sometimes remaining absent two or three days. Reflecting on this, Raleigh formed the design of escaping to France. Through Captain King, who still clung to him, he hired a bark bound for Rochelle, and directed it to lie to till he should come on board.

Late one night he repaired with King to the beach, and pushing off in the dark, approached to within a quarter of a mile of the ' Rochellois;' then, yielding suddenly to the force of some other motive, put about the boat and returned to land. His conduct may by many be thought wrong; but, in my opinion, he acted wisely and fortunately, since it was better that he should die—better for us, as well as for himself, when and how he did—than that he should have drawled out his life as a fugitive in a foreign land, with a great abatement of the admiration with which mankind now regard his career. The love of life, it is true, prompted one more effort at escape; but I am glad the purpose was defeated, first by reflection, next by accident, otherwise the life of Raleigh would have lacked its great moral, and missed the blaze of glory in which it set.

On the 25th of July, Raleigh, with a considerable suite, left Plymouth, and arrived in the evening at the house of Mr. Drake, where Stukeley received letters from the ministers ordering him to advance with greater speed. At sight of the pursuivant, Raleigh is said to have changed countenance, and to have exclaimed bitterly against Fortune; the desire, also, to effect his escape revived and gained strength in proportion as it became more difficult. He spent the Sunday at Sherbourne, at the house of Sir Edward Parham, and on the following day set out with his wife and attendants for Salisbury, a distance of thirty-five miles. On approaching this city he alighted from the carriage, and walked down the hill, accompanied by Manourie, a French quack in Stukeley's service, in whom, not suspecting him to be a spy, he began, we are told, to repose some confidence.

Wishing to obtain leisure in order to draw up an account of his proceedings, he here determined to feign illness or madness, or both. By Manourie's aid he covered himself with blains and blotches, so that for the appearance of sickness he substituted the reality, and being ignorant of the nature of the medicines he took, may have had his brain purposely disordered. In this diseased state the idea of escape returned with redoubled force; Lady Raleigh was sent forward on Tuesday to prepare his house in London, and Captain King to hire boats and a vessel in the Thames.

He then applied himself to the writing of his
' Apology,' but became so ill, that Stukeley, despairing of
his life, consulted the Bishop of Winchester, a kind and
good man, who sent three physicians to attend the
illustrious prisoner.

On Saturday, the 1st of August, James visited Salisbury, and in all likelihood saw Stukeley and the spy,
and learned from them whatever they had to communicate. It may even be suspected that these worthy
agents received instructions to conduct themselves so as
to win upon their prisoner's confidence, in order the
better to betray him.

That Raleigh expected to be sent for on this occasion by James we may infer from the following
passage in a letter from Chamberlain to Carleton:—*
"Sir Walter Raleigh was at Salisbury, but he had no
audience either of the King or Council; by reason he
was so sick and weak, and withal so broken out all
over, that it is verily thought to be a leprosy, or else he
hath taken a dram of something to do himself harm."

Leaving Salisbury, they travelled on by way of
Andover, Hartford Bridge, and Staines, to Brentford,
where, at an inn, Raleigh was visited by La Chêne, a
French gentleman, who informed him that Le Clerc,
the agent of France at James's court, desired to speak
with him on his arrival in the metropolis.

* August 8th, 1618. State Paper Office.

On the evening of Friday, the 7th of August, Raleigh arrived in London, and was once more under the same roof with his wife and only son. His friends, meanwhile, had been using their utmost exertions either to obtain his pardon, or, failing in that, to secure him, through the assistance of Le Clerc, a passage to France. In these kind offices many persons of the highest distinction—James's queen among the rest—were actively engaged; and to oblige them the envoy was willing to hazard the utmost resentment of James and the displeasure of his own sovereign. Lady Carew saw M. Le Clerc, and ascertained from him that, in his endeavours to serve and save Sir Walter Raleigh, he was not acting by the direction of his Government, but on his own authority, in order to meet the wishes of the great commander's friends in this country, particularly Anne of Denmark. To understand why the queen should interest herself so strenuously on Raleigh's behalf, it must be borne in mind that she was opposed to the marriage of her son Charles with a Spanish princess, and desired rather to obtain for him a wife in France. Could Raleigh, therefore, succeed in making his way into that country, he might be able to further her designs at the French court. The means by which Anne carried on her negociations with Le Clerc are indicated rather than explained; but it seems that it was by the agency of a French gentleman, who had access to the backstairs of the palace. The full particulars of this intrigue may never perhaps be made known, but a contest was certainly going on between James and his consort.

The negociations with the French envoy were in progress during Raleigh's journey from Plymouth to London, but there is no ascertaining the exact date of Lady Carew's interview, an account of which was afterwards extorted from her when the court was engaged in fabricating some pretext for shedding Raleigh's blood. The French Government, it was known, would welcome the great commander, partly to cause uneasiness to Spain, but chiefly with the design of profiting by his services in America. Yet these things were rather understood than expressed. Lady Carew maintained to Sir Thomas Wilson, that when she inquired of Le Clerc what Raleigh would do in France, he replied, *Il mangera, il boiera, il sera bien.*

On the day after Raleigh's arrival in town, while Captain King and his subordinates, Cotterell and Hart, were hovering about the Thames, Raleigh's friends flocked to him at his house. The jeopardy in which he stood no one could disguise. Since the death of Winwood not a friend remained to him in the Cabinet, while the person who had succeeded that upright statesman was, next after the Stuart, his bitterest enemy. At eight o'clock in the evening the French envoy, with his secretary, La Chêne, repaired secretly to Raleigh's house, where, having been admitted, he passed through the great hall, and was led up-stairs to the gallery and requested to wait. Raleigh then went forth from the parlour that he might converse with the envoy without being overheard. Le Clerc's sole object in this visit was to explain the plan he had formed for insuring Raleigh's escape from England, and his good reception in France. He had a bark, he said, in readiness, apparently at the mouth of the river, and had arranged all the means by which the illustrious prisoner might safely convey himself on board. He was then to make all sail for Calais, where La Chêne would be ready to receive him with a passport, and letters to facilitate his journey and insure him an honourable reception.

For reasons not easy to be understood, Raleigh preferred trusting to the arrangements made for him by Captain King. In discussing these plans, the whole interview with Le Clerc was consumed. In order that as few persons as possible might be acquainted with the coming of the French agent, Raleigh called no servant to attend him to the door, but went himself down the stairs, which with the habitual politeness of his country Le Clerc opposed; Raleigh persisted, however, though he stopped at the foot of the stairs, and peeped into the hall, to discover whether there were any persons there who might observe him.

On the following day, which was Sunday, Raleigh was sitting in the parlour with his wife and a number of friends, among whom were Mr. and Mrs. Pagenham, Sir Edward Gorges, Sir Lewis Stukeley, Mr. Craddock of Westminster, Mr. Emanuel Gifford, Mrs. Thynne, Raleigh's niece, who had been maid of honour to Queen Elizabeth, and many others, some, acquaintances made by Bessy in his absence, and some his or her relatives, when La Chêne came and passed through the parlour, but whether noticed or unnoticed does not appear. This interview with La Chêne probably took place, like the one of the preceding day, in the gallery, but with no result.

Adhering with fatal tenacity to his own plan of escape, Raleigh remained quietly in his house till night, when it had been agreed he should repair to the Tower Dock, where King was to wait for him with two wherries. He had flattered himself into the belief that he had secured the services of Stukeley by the promise to make good to him whatever loss he might sustain in furthering this design; but in truth the Vice-admiral had disclosed the whole contrivance to James and his ministers, who ordered William Herbert, with a number of men, to keep watch unobserved about Raleigh's house.

Ignorant that he was moving in the midst of enemies, Raleigh, as the hour of departure drew near, disguised himself in the hope of slipping out unobserved, by putting on a false beard, and a hat with a green hat-band. His papers and effects were deposited in a cloak bag, which, with four pistols, was all the luggage he took with him. Accompanied by Sir Lewis Stukeley, young Stukeley, and his own page, he then took leave of his wife and son, and passing over the threshold which he was never to cross again, proceeded towards the place of rendezvous. There the faithful King and the traitor Hart were found with the wherries. To the question if all things were ready, King replied in the affirmative, and that the cloak bag and pistols were in the boats. Wishing probably to discover whether or not he were suspected, Stukeley now saluted the captain, and asked whether he had not hitherto con-ducted himself like an honest man; to which King, who seems to have been not quite free from doubt, replied, " that he trusted he would continue so." The whole party then stepped into the wherries, and the watermen began to pull.

What appearance the Thames presented on that memorable August Sunday night, it would be difficult to figure to ourselves. In these days it would be crowded with steamers, boats, and craft of all kinds, fringed thickly with gas-lamps, and swarming with pleasure-seekers. It was different then. Here and there the dark hull of some lugger, brig, or collier, helped to thicken the shadows on the water, while the eyes of the fugitives detected the presence of a single wherry shooting through the darkness.

From an observation of the boatmen, it soon appeared that Mr. William Herbert had transferred his vigilant watch from the land to the water, for they said he had just taken boat, and made as if he would go through bridge, but returned down the river after them. Part of the truth now flashed athwart Raleigh's mind; he saw clearly that his project had been discovered, but clung nevertheless to the hope that, availing himself of the ebb tide, he might, if the watermen would co-operate, resist all attempts at capturing him, and make his way by force to the bark at Tilbury.

To ascertain the amount of his chances, he observed that a foolish quarrel with the Spanish ambassador had made it necessary for him to absent himself awhile from Court, and pass over into the Low Countries. Instead, however, of displaying the daring natural to English sailors of all classes, the miserable boatmen, inspired with terror by James's despotism, burst into tears, protesting they durst not oppose the king's authority, and declining the ten pieces of gold which Raleigh offered them for their pains.

Knowing it to be immaterial where his victim should be seized, Stukeley encouraged the watermen to row on, as did likewise Captain King, who was in the other boat with the younger Stukeley. They passed Deptford, and were drawing near Greenwich, when they were crossed by another wherry, which Raleigh felt persuaded was come in pursuit of them ; but King, who seems to have still cherished a favourable opinion of the Vice-admiral, urged their pressing forward, affirming that if they could but reach Gravesend he would stake his life they might pass over to Tilbury. The stoppages occasioned by their frequent consultations spent the tide just as they came opposite what are now the great gunpowder magazines of Purfleet, and here, the watermen protesting it would be impossible to reach Gravesend before morning, Raleigh conceived the idea of landing, and pursuing his way to Tilbury on horseback, a plan which Hart and Stukeley encouraged; the former engaging to procure nags, while the latter said he would himself, if necessary, carry the cloak bag half a mile or more. Captain King, however, insisting on the impracticability of this scheme, they rowed on, probably to a reach called the Galleons near Plumstead, about a mile beyond Woolwich.

In the only account left us of this night's adventure there is much confusion and contradictory statement. Sometimes we are led to believe that the wherries were to bring Raleigh to the bark at Tilbury, or at least to Gravesend, but when they neared the Galleons, we discover it had been concerted that they should at this point quit the wherries, and perform the rest of the voyage in Hart's ketch; for we are told that several small vessels of the same class coming in sight, Hart began to express his doubt whether any one of them were his. Raleigh now saw they were betrayed, and gave orders to put about the boats in the hope of reaching his own house before morning, at the same time questioning Hart strictly respecting the arrangements he pretended to have made. From his quibbling and equivocating one inference only could be drawn, which was converted into certainty when, having rowed back a few hundred yards, they saw and hailed a wherry, obviously in chase of them, the crew of which declared they were there for the king.

Raleigh, who to some extent had been active hitherto, now became passive—the game was up, and he saw it—every one around him grew to be an object of suspicion, save King, whose integrity could not be doubted. The remainder of the night was passed in that despondency which had settled upon him at Plymouth, and been more or less his companion from the moment of his disembarkation until now. Still he would not entirely relinquish the hope of escape, for which reason he sought earnestly to return to his own house, from whence alone he could have any chance of effecting it. He therefore besought Stukeley, who had hitherto conducted himself so artfully as not to awaken in his kinsman the least suspicion, to declare to the king's officers that he was his prisoner, which, Stukeley's rank and authority being superior to theirs, would prevent his being handed over to them. To this the traitor, running no risk by the stratagem, cheerfully consented, and in order to obtain substantial proofs of his captive's gratitude, hugged and embraced him with all possible show of affection. They likewise for a considerable time conferred together in whispers apart, and Captain King saw Raleigh take something from his pocket—probably jewels—and give it to his betrayer.

On arriving near Greenwich, the Vice-admiral saw that the moment for throwing off the mask had arrived. He therefore declared bluntly that, it being impossible to take Raleigh back to his house, they must land here, and when they had done so, and stood on Greenwich Bridge, Stukeley proposed to Captain King that he should affect at least to forsake his master, and range among his accusers, which, though Raleigh himself seemed to think it might be expedient, King refused to do. He was then arrested by Stukeley's orders and given in custody to two of Sir William St. John's and Herbert's men, that no communication might take place between him and the chief prisoner. Here at a tavern they passed what remained of the night ; and in the morning, while proceeding towards the Tower, King overheard Raleigh say, " Sir Lewis, these things will not redound to your credit ;" to which, whether the caitiff made any reply or not, the captain has omitted to relate. At the entrance to the Tower King was separated from his master, who, in parting, said to him, "Stukeley and Cotterell have betrayed me;" adding, "for your part, you need be under no apprehension, it is I am the mark that is shot at."

Then Captain King, in what frame of mind may be easily imagined, took leave of Raleigh for ever, inwardly committing him to the care of that Power, with whom, at the conclusion of his narrative, he says, "I doubt not his soul resteth."*

* See King's Narrative in Oldys, pp. 533–537.

CHAPTER XII.

IMPLACABLE RANCOUR OF SPAIN.

ONCE more in the Tower, with little or no chance of emerging from it, except to ascend the scaffold, Raleigh displayed, as was natural, many fluctuations of spirits and temper—now buoyed up by transient hope, and now reluctantly giving way to the conviction that his days were numbered. They were so, indeed; for when seventy-nine should be added to the course of his life, he would be at rest.

Hitherto no full account of this last portion of the hero's career has been laid before the world, and yet it may in many respects be regarded as the most interesting, if not the most important. For more than two thousand years mankind have perused with unabated curiosity and emotion the narrative of the brief interval which separated the Athenian philosopher's sentence from his death. Being imprisoned, however, among a civilized people, and in a free state, though subjected for the moment to capricious oppression, he suffered no insult, but, like a captive at large in his own house, was visited by his wife and children, and by his friends, who came and went at their pleasure. It was different with Raleigh. All who approached him were enemies, spies, traitors, instructed by a cruel Government to wring from him by cajolery, by simulated kindness, by false promises, by threats, such information as might seem to palliate the murder it contemplated.

I say *murder*, because, finding nothing in his recent conduct which would appear to justify the infliction of capital punishment, James and his ministers were driven back upon the sentence of 1603, which, I trust, I have proved to have been iniquitous. But why put him to death at all? Did James find it impracticable to breathe the same air with the great Admiral? Why not connive at his escape into some foreign country, by which the guilt of shedding his blood would have been avoided? It is very certain that, however unappeasable the king's hatred may have been, he discovered in the aspect of public opinion indications which for some time made him shrink from the crime he was urged to perpetrate. But what were the circumstances which created the urgency for Raleigh's assassination? The leading fact that he was sacrificed to gratify the vindictiveness of Philip and the rancour of his ambassador has been all along known; but hitherto undeniable proofs that such was the case have not been laid before the public. I shall adduce them now. While bringing them forward, however, I do not desire to keep out of sight the truth that Raleigh had been engaged in very questionable negociations with France, which I have already described; but those dealings, though they exasperated James, were not the ground on which Raleigh's life was sought and taken. At the risk of being betrayed into some repetitions, I must preface what I have further to relate by recapitulating certain circumstances: first, when James granted Raleigh a commission, he knew it was to Guiana he intended to proceed; second, he was fully competent to decide whether he regarded Guiana as a British or as a Spanish dependency; third, if he looked upon it as a British possession, he must have felt that no reference need be made to Spain in the matter; fourthly, if he believed Guiana to belong to Spain, he must have known that, in aiding Raleigh to prosecute his voyage thither, he was implicating himself and his Government in a piratical undertaking. In whatever light viewed, the enterprise took place in the manner and with the results I have described. Wherever, in the course of it, there was any collision between the English and the Spaniards, the latter were the aggressors, while the former only made use of force in self-defence. From my narrative, which I believe to be fair, the reader will, I persuade myself, have been led to this conclusion;

he will, at all events, be able to estimate the amount of falsehood and malignity discoverable in the statements of the Spanish Government.

While Raleigh's fleet still lay in the Thames, that Government, acting upon information received through its ambassador and spies in England, sent orders to the Council of War for the Indies to strengthen the defences, and reinforce those garrisons in Guiana and the neighbouring countries which might be thought to lie most open to attack. The assurances given by the English king and ministers that Raleigh would abstain from all acts of violence towards the king of Spain's subjects and territories were treated as of no value, though securities had been entered into by Raleigh's friends to make good any damage he might occasion. No sooner, however, had the news of what took place at San Tome reached Spain than, without inquiring into the correctness of the statement they had received, the most violent and indefensible proceedings were recommended by the Council of State to the king. Two days later, that king, basing his orders on the Council's views, forwarded a despatch to Gondomar, directing him what steps to take in England for the purpose of obtaining from James the sacrifice of Raleigh and the seizure of his property, together with that of his securities, as compensation for the damage and injury sustained by Spanish subjects in America. These papers, though prolix and confused, are very craftily drawn up. Two sentiments prevail throughout—apprehension of a quarrel with England, and the double desire of money and vengeance. Gondomar, or his representative if he should be absent, was cautioned not to employ threatening language, lest it should occasion war, for which Spain was by no means prepared. The policy secretly resolved upon, should the English Government decline punishing Raleigh, was to make reprisals on all English property found ⸲in any part of Philip's dominions; but this was rather to be suggested than broadly laid down. Relying on James's ignorance of the real facts of the case, Philip and his ambassador affirmed that no preparations whatever had been made for the defence of the Spanish possessions in South America, in consequence of the trust they had reposed in the promises of England; though two days before the date of this solemn assurance peremptory orders had been issued by Philip to double the forces which, during the preceding year, had been sent to America. Much stress was laid on the report that preparations were making at Plymouth to add large reinforcements to Raleigh's fleet, which was false, and on the statement, which may have been true, that the English in Seville were much elated at the intelligence of Raleigh's achievements in Guiana.*

* Minuta del consejo de Estado à S. Md. sobre loque contienen

For some time a plan had been in agitation for uniting
a squadron of English men-of-war with what was pom-
pously called the Ocean fleet of Spain, with a view to
protect the coasts of the peninsula from the ravages of
the Barbary corsairs.   As far back as the previous year,
the idea had been entertained by both Governments,
with the addition of stationing a naval force at the
entrance to the harbour of Algiers to cut off the pirates
in their attempt to put to sea.   From this enterprise
Philip now shrank, not knowing what consequences
might flow from the admission of English ships of war
into the ports and harbours of his kingdom.   Gondomar
was therefore instructed to defer entering into any
agreement on this subject till the way in which James
meant to deal with Raleigh should be known.

Meanwhile, the greatest possible solicitude was felt
at Madrid lest the English should take offence, rush to
arms, attack the Spanish settlements in America, capture the homeward-bound fleet, and annihilate Spanish
commerce almost at a blow.   No symptom of this
apprehension and solicitude was however to be suffered
to appear to the British Government, which, on the

---

dos consultas de la Junta de guerra de Indias acerca de lo ejecutado
por Gualtero Rale enlas Islas de Barlovento, 7 de Junio 1618.
¿ Minuta de Real despacho al Conde de Gondomar con la relacion de
lo que habia hecho Gualtero Rale enlas Islas de Canarias.   Madrid,
9 de Junio, 1618.   Simancas.

contrary, was to be assailed by strong and incessant representations of the outrages, devastations, and massacres perpetrated by Raleigh's fleet in America; together with the resentment felt by Philip, and his firm resolve to insist on reparation.*

Gondomar, whose natural bloodthirstiness was sharpened by ill-health, went on unceasingly harrying James and his ministers to hasten Raleigh's execution, a point which Philip had evidently more at heart than any compensation in money. Alluding to the despatch of which I have spoken above, Contarini observes, " The Spanish ambassador has received an express, with orders from his King not to leave this until he witness the thorough completion of the punishment of Sir Walter Raleigh ; so he had to return to his Majesty, and complain of the excesses committed by him on the island of St. Thomas † in the West Indies, without any regard for persons or holy places : he had audience the day before yesterday, whereupon the proclamation against Raleigh was repeated, and he is understood to be now under arrest at Plymouth, but in a bad state of health."‡

A few days later, the intelligence reached England that the Spanish Government had actually issued a

---

* Minuta de Real despacho al Conde de Gondomar, 9 de Junio, 1618. Simancas.

† The writer here confounds the island of San Tomé with the town of the same name on the main.

‡ Contarini. Despatch of July 5th, 1618. Venetian Archives.

proclamation commanding the seizure of all English ships in the kingdom, upon which Gondomar had another audience of James, in which he gave great offence by "his resentful and harsh language." Upon this, the Spaniards, never popular in England, became doubly hateful, especially among the mercantile classes, whose irritation was probably increased by the rumours now prevalent of the arrest of Raleigh.*

Meanwhile Gondomar's maladies, whatever they may have been, assumed a character which, in spite of the orders he had received, determined him to return to Spain. On the 25th of July, therefore (N.S.), he set out from London with his countess, and proceeded to Dover, whence he passed over to Flanders in an English ship of war.

The day before he departed, however, he enjoyed an opportunity of learning with what feelings he and his countrymen were regarded in London. "One of his gentlemen," says Contarini, "riding through the street, went over a little child who was incautiously at play in the middle of the road, and although more frightened than hurt, so great a mob collected and followed the Spaniard, that, notwithstanding his galloping at full speed, he had much ado to reach the embassy at Ely House, where the crowd and uproar increased in lieu of diminishing, and in a short time

* Contarini. Despatch of July 12th, 1618. Venetian Archives.

all the neighbouring streets swarmed with people, who in the foulest language commenced cursing all Spain, and most contemptuously abusing the subjects of that crown; after which, with a shower of stones, they broke all the windows in the house, and were proceeding to force the door, which it would have been impossible to defend against so violent an attack, had not the Lord Mayor made his appearance, and in virtue of his office quieted the people, though he experienced great difficulty in causing them to disperse."*

When James, who had often complained to Gondomar that he was unable to keep his subjects in order, heard of the tumult in the City, he commanded the Mayor to wait upon Gondomar with the assurance that the rioters should be severely punished. With this ovation, Gondomar, it was hoped, would be satisfied; but the Venetian remarks that the circumstance proved the hatred of the English people for Spain, and how keenly they would resent the marriage of Prince Charles with the Infanta. In the hope of diminishing popular aversion for the Spaniards, James issued a proclamation, in which it was affirmed that the rioters had been pardoned entirely through the intercession of the gentlemen of the Spanish Embassy.†

Ulloa, who had been left by Gondomar to conduct

* Contarini. Despatch of Aug. 2nd, 1618. Venetian Archives.
† Idem. Despatch of Sept. 28th, 1618. Venetian Archives.

the business of the embassy, carefully avoided touching
in his despatches upon the circumstance of the riot,
and enlarged instead on the extraordinary affection and
esteem with which the Count was regarded by all classes
of persons. He alluded however incidentally to the
fact that, in spite of the professions he might choose to
make, James was actuated by no love for the King of
Spain—still less, he might have added, for his insolent
ambassador—but simply by fear, which, he significantly
adds, is " very powerful with him."*

Towards the end of July, James, the sole business of
whose life consisted in the enjoyment of coarse pleasures,
found himself encountered by his usual difficulty—want
of money. The means by which he escaped from the
dilemma were curious and characteristic. The sale of
honours is a practice of ancient date in England, and
was resorted to on this occasion by James. To appear
in proper state at Salisbury, where the meet of the grand
stag-hunt was to be held, no less a sum than forty thousand pounds would be needed. How was it to be raised?
After much deliberation, James's ministers hit upon the
plan of elevating a wealthy alderman's son to the peer-
age for fifteen thousand pounds, and of creating four
new earls—among whom the husband of Raleigh's niece
Barbara was one—for twenty thousand more. The

* Carta Autografa de Julian Sanchez de Ulloa, 26 de Julio, 1618.
Simancas.

supply, however, still fell short of the demand, so that five thousand pounds had to be raised by forced contributions from the officers and servants of the royal household. With pockets thus filled, James with Baby Charles and a glittering retinue set out for Salisbury, where he arrived while Raleigh, dejected and covered with sores, was employed in writing his 'Apology' at a miserable inn. At the same time, James's unhappy wife passed through London on her way from Greenwich to Oatlands. As the new Earl of Leicester held the place of Chamberlain to the Queen, both he and his Countess may be fairly presumed to have exerted their influence —though none may perhaps have been needed—to keep Raleigh in her affectionate remembrance, since throughout the dark period upon which we are entering she stood unfalteringly by the man who had been the friend of her favourite son, and who cherished the same political aspirations with herself.*

To understand the peril in which Raleigh now stood, it will be necessary to consider attentively a report which the Council of State at Madrid addressed to Philip, based on two despatches of Gondomar, one dated June 24th, the other July 15th. From this report it appears that the ambassador, having laid before James the Spanish view of Raleigh's proceedings in

* Carta de Julian Sanchez de Ulloa à Su Majestad, 30 de Julio, 1618. Simancas.

Guiana, had extorted from him a promise which must, I think, be acknowledged to be the most base and iniquitous concession ever made by one sovereign to another. When Lord Carew, the steady and affectionate friend of Raleigh, knelt before James, and besought him to extend pardon to his kinsman, the reply he received was, that the accused for whom he pleaded should have a fair hearing. How far he could have meant what he said, may be seen from the report under consideration, which says, that in compliance with the requisition of Gondomar, Raleigh and his accomplices should be thrown into prison, and their property confiscated; that with regard to their persons, he would deliver them up in order that they might be punished in Spain, or, if Philip desired it, be hung in England. As the choice had thus been left to the King of Spain, the Council urged that the odium of the execution ought to be left to James, under pretence that where the crime had been perpetrated punishment should be inflicted. To illustrate Gondomar's sentiments towards Raleigh, we must consider the various means to which he had recourse, in order to precipitate James into the perpetration of the desired crime. Reckoning confidently on his fears, which throughout life exposed him to the contempt of the world, he apprehended no chance of war from the most offensive proceedings, and therefore recommended not only the laying of an embargo on all English vessels in the Azores and Canaries, but that the fleets of Spain should capture and make prize of whatever English ships they might meet at sea, which would expose James to the complaints and outcries of his whole people.*

Acting upon the advice of his Council, Philip forwarded a despatch to Count Gondomar, in which occurs the following ominous passage : " You will write to your Secretary Ulloa, desiring him to make use of all possible means in order that that King may at once punish Walter Raleigh and his accomplices as he has promised you ; since for many reasons this seems more advisable than that they should be sent here. Let it also be understood that satisfaction for damages must be given from the property of Walter and his securities, the amount to be assessed by my ministers, which I consider the most proper course to be followed." He then informs the Count that the seizure of English ships had been postponed ; but that it should be immediately carried into effect if the King of England showed any remissness in inflicting punishment on Raleigh.

* Minuta del consejo de Estado à S. Md. sobre Waltero, 11 de Agosto, 1618. Simancas.

CHAPTER XIII.

WILSON'S MISSION.

WHEN, on the 10th of August, Raleigh found himself once more in the Tower, the first step taken by the authorities was to search his person and take possession of his papers and effects. His old lodgings being occupied by the Earl and Countess of Somerset, he seems to have remained in Sir Allan Apsley's house for a few days, after which he was removed to Lord Cobham's former apartments in the Wardrobe Tower.

On Wednesday, two days after Raleigh's commitment to the Tower, Lord Bacon, with a number of other Commissioners, repaired thither to examine him respecting his motives for attempting to escape into France. No record of their questions or of his answers has been preserved; but he is said to have admitted that he had been wrong in attempting to escape. Being able to make nothing of such an admission, another meeting of the Commissioners was appointed for the following

Monday at Whitehall, when Lord Carew, Sir William St. John, and Sir Lewis Stukeley, were commanded to attend, to investigate probably Anne of Denmark's complicity with Raleigh, for it was said to be "on some business of the Queen's."[*]

While the examinations, frequent and protracted, were in progress, Raleigh put forward his 'Apology,' respecting which, as might have been foreseen, opinions were divided; they who judged from the English point of view approving, while all members of the Spanish faction remained unconvinced.[†]

Nearly a month having been consumed in fruitless examinations, the Court, baffled and profoundly irritated, appears to have formed a design which carries us back to the times of Alexander VI. and Cæsar Borgia. The mysterious proceedings of a French gentleman, who, while the royal family were at dinner, forced himself into the palace, threw James into paroxysms of terror. Some second Ravaillac, he perhaps thought, hired by Raleigh or by his Queen, had come with the intention, which heaven must have averted, of hurrying his sacred person to Windsor vaults. What was there he would not do to preserve himself from the assassin's knife? He consulted with the caitiff Naunton, with the libidi-

* Archbishop of Canterbury to Sir Thomas Lake, August 14th. MS. State Paper Office.

† Chamberlain to Carleton, August 20th, 1618. State Paper Office.

nous and truculent Buckingham, and a plan seems to have been agreed upon between them which they at once proceeded to carry into execution.

There was at that time about the Court an individual named Wilson, with the countenance, sentiments, and language of Abhorson, whose very appearance suggested the idea of some horrid crime, and inspired the wish to commit it. This wretch was now admitted by Naunton to a secret audience with James, at which it appears to have been agreed that Raleigh should be preserved from the executioner by such a death as the blood-boltered Banquo met with. Eager to give proof of his devotion to his employers, Wilson hastened to the Tower, where his gait and aspect inspired universal horror and loathing. A whisper passed among the officers of the fortress that Raleigh's days would certainly be few.

Shocked at the evident object of Wilson's coming, Sir Allan Apsley, father of Mrs. Colonel Hutchinson, was put by instinct upon his guard, so that he at once determined not to be trepanned into the fate of Sir Gervase Elwes, whose gallows may have been still standing on Tower Hill. With the revolting familiarity of an executioner, Wilson stepped into Raleigh's apartments, accosted the prisoner, and then studied the hindrances and facilities furnished by the nature of the place. Several objectionable peculiarities presented themselves. The room had two large windows, looking on one side towards the Mint, on the other into the great court, over passages into which letters might be thrown, and from which prying persons might also possibly discern what took place within—an arrangement which presented obstacles to his purpose. Still, if at night he could get into his hands the keys of Raleigh's apartments, the thing might be done, and he therefore demanded them abruptly from the Lieutenant. As he at the same time required that Raleigh's personal attendant should be removed, and a man of his own, bearing likewise the same name with himself, substituted in his place, Apsley saw at once the whole drift of his scheme, and peremptorily refused compliance.

What was to be done? In Venice, the maxims of whose government were in that age much studied in England, State prisoners whose public execution was thought objectionable were often dealt with secretly by poison or the stiletto, and James appears to have lulled himself into the belief that, if Raleigh could be disposed of after a similar fashion, it would save him from the obloquy of publicly sacrificing an illustrious subject for the purpose of obtaining a Spanish wife for his son. The Venetian Council of Ten seldom, we may be sure, had obstacles thrown in their way by the impracticable consciences of their gaolers; but, in England, every Lieutenant of the Tower was not an Elwes, though no midnight assassin that ever traversed the subterranean passages of the Piombi surpassed Wilson in bloody recklessness.

The hatred that instinctively springs up between greatness and baseness, when forced into proximity, warmed immediately into life in Wilson's heart, so that he fiercely longed for the opportunity of dealing with Raleigh. Offended by the refusal of Sir Allan Apsley, who he saw clearly suspected his intentions, he, in a tone of injured innocence, laid his complaint before Naunton, who explained it to the King. The matter now assumed an awkward character. It was obvious that the nature of their project was understood in the Tower, and the apprehension suggested itself that, if anything should happen suddenly to Raleigh, the whole country, and the world, would comprehend by what agency he had been taken off. Naunton, therefore, was ordered by James to return for answer to the belligerent officers that his Majesty referred them " to the old custom to be adhered and abided by."*

It seems clear that Wilson had never heard the story of Raleigh's attempt at suicide in 1603, otherwise he would surely have referred to it while chronieling his conversations with Raleigh, who, he affirmed, often spoke of suicide, and maintained that, under certain circum-

* Naunton to Wilson, Sept. 14th, 1618. State Paper Office.

stances, a Christian might have recourse to it and be forgiven. The assassin in intention, who had small faith in Raleigh's Christianity, would only have been too glad could he, by taunts and sneers, have provoked him to put his theory in practice. Raleigh, however, whose desire it always was to die in the light, and not by his own or Wilson's hands in the Tower, spurned the suggestions of the tempter, and used all reasonable means to prolong the life which God had intrusted to him.

Meanwhile, Sanchez de Ulloa, to whom particulars of the examinations to which Raleigh was subjected were communicated, was sedulous in transmitting an account of them to Madrid. Knowing in what tone Philip and Gondomar, who had by that time reached the Spanish capital, would expect him to write, his style brimmed over with malignity and virulence. "I have already spoken," he says, "of the evasions which Raleigh has invented to avoid the punishment of his crimes, which he fears and merits. They are now examining him in earnest on the intentions and designs with which he left England for Guiana, and on the insolences, cruelties, robberies, and murders that he committed in the countries of the King our Lord, chiefly in San. Tome."*

* Carta de Sanchez de Ulloa à Don Juan de Ciriza, 12 de Setiembre, 1618. Simancas.

But though the occurrences in Guiana constituted the chief subjects of accusation against Raleigh, greater subtlety and pertinacity were displayed by the Commissioners in the endeavour to implicate Raleigh in the intrigues which Anne of Denmark was carrying on with France for the purpose of thwarting her husband's desire to secure the hand of Donna Maria for Charles. Under any other circumstances, less importance would have been attached to his dealings with the French agent and his secretary; but, suspecting that his chief object in attempting an escape to France was his wish to further in that country the designs of his benefactress, James's petty jealousy was fanned into a flame. "Tell, him," he exclaimed, with vehemence, "that he owes allegiance to no one but to me!" Anne, it appears, secretly admitted French agents to her presence by the back-stairs, and Raleigh, after one examination, expressed his fear that, by the disclosures into which he had been betrayed respecting his interviews with Le Clerc and La Chêne, he might have alienated the Queen's affections.

With these facts before him, which, however briefly stated, are undoubted, the reader will understand the feverish eagerness of James and his Commissioners to wring from Raleigh every minute particular of his interviews with the French agent. Whatever Philip, Gondomar, or Ulloa might fancy, it was perfectly understood by Court and Commissioners that the outcries against the proceedings in Guiana originated in political jealousy, and were irreconcileable with facts; but as they might, nevertheless, obstruct his darling design of obtaining a consort for his son, James's passion became more vehement as the obstacles to its fulfilment multiplied.

By the law of nations, Le Clerc was placed beyond James's reach, but his secretary occupied no place within the charmed circle, so that, when his visits to Raleigh had been discovered, he was immediately arrested and thrown into prison. When first called before the Council in the palace of Whitehall, he was accompanied to the entrance by the envoy Le Clerc, and a number of other French gentlemen, who continued lingering about the lobby till the angry Councillors sent their secretary to order them to depart.*

To what extent La Chêne's examinations were pushed, I am unable to say; but if the reader happen to be gifted with sensitive nerves, he will probably shudder at one of the questions put to him at Whitehall—he was asked if he were a gentleman. Had he replied in the negative, he might have been instantly made acquainted with the rack and the Scavenger's Daughter; but the employés above a certain rank of a foreign sovereign could not be so treated without serious

* Carta de Ulloa à Ciriza, 24 de Setiembre, 1618. Simancas.

offence, though James's own subjects, even when
ministers of the altar, might with impunity be torn
to pieces by the rack. This point having been cleared
up, the examination proceeded.*

Commissioners. How long have you known Sir Walter
Raleigh?

La Chêne. More than seven years.

Com. Have you seen Sir Walter frequently, and if so,
what is the nature of your business with him?

La Chêne. I saw Sir Walter frequently before his
voyage, and always found him courteous and friendly,
because he was partial to the French. We never
spoke, however, on any but familiar subjects.

Com. How often have you seen Sir Walter since his
return, and what was the object of your visits?

La Chêne. Merely to confirm our former friendship
by sympathising with him in his troubles.

Com. Where did you visit him?

La Chêne. At his house.

Com. How many days after Sir Walter's arrival?

La Chêne. On the second or third, I am not certain
which.

Com. Who was present at the interview?

La Chêne. I do not remember.

---

* Throughout these examinations I have substituted the first for
the third person, but in other respects have given a literal translation
of the original documents.

Com. Were there many present, or not?

La Chêne. Six or eight, but I do not recollect their names.

Com. In what language did you converse?

La Chêne. In French.

Com. How many letters have you written to him or other persons on the subject of his escape?

La Chêne. I have not written any.

He was then told that they could show him some, to which he answered, that they must be forged.

Com. How could you be so presumptuous as to visit Sir Walter Raleigh, he being under criminal prosecution, and in disgrace with the King?

La Chêne. I visited him no otherwise than as a friend.

Com. How could you, being a foreigner, presume to visit a criminal; and do you not think that by so doing you have offended his Majesty?

La Chêne. No; because I never spoke of his Majesty in a way to give offence.

Com. Do you wish to say anything respecting the letters you have written?

La Chêne. No.

Upon this La Chêne was sent back to prison.*

* Las preguntas que los señores del consejo de Estado de Inglaterra hicieron al Señor de la Chêne caballero Frances y respuestas de éste, 19 de Setiembre (N.S.), 1618.   Simancas.

Three days later his examination was resumed.

Com. Do you know Dr. Turner?

La Chéne. Yes.

Com. Have you known him long?

La Chéne. Four or five years.

Com. What business have you had with him?

La Chéne. When I went to see him it was on no particular business or design.

Com. How often have you gone to see him?

La Chéne. I don't know.

Com. How long is it since you last saw him?

La Chéne. Not long.

Com. Do you remember the time?

La Chéne. About a fortnight.

Com. When you were together did you speak of the affairs of Sir Walter Raleigh?

La Chéne. We did.

Com. What did you say?

La Chéne. Only expressed our sorrow for his misfortunes.

Com. Did you converse on any other subject?

La Chéne. No; we spoke of nothing else.

Com. Did not Dr. Turner confide to you his fears for having shown favour to Sir Walter Raleigh?

La Chéne. Yes.

Com. Were you at Oatlands when a pursuivant came to summon Dr. Turner before the Council?

La Chêne. Yes.

Com. Did the Doctor inquire of you what answers he ought to make ?

La Chêne. He did.

Com. What advice did you give him ?

La Chêne. The best that I could give him for his good.

Com. What was that ?

La Chêne. I advised him to tell the Council that Lady Raleigh, who is a relative of his, had requested him to obtain an audience of the Queen, and beg her to intercede for her Ladyship with the King. I gave him no other advice.

Com. How many letters have passed between you and Dr. Turner ?

La Chêne. I have never written to him.

Com. What will you say if we show you some of those letters ?

La Chêne. I remember nothing about any such letters, so that I have nothing to fear.

With this reply, the second examination closed, and La Chêne was reconducted to prison. Out of the circumstances of this case, it was hoped at Ely House that causes might arise which would lead to a rupture with France. The exultation therefore of the Spanish Secretary was great, especially as James every day gave fresh proofs of his entire devotion to Spain. While the diplomatic agents of Louis Treize were treated

almost like felons, and Raleigh in the Tower was subjected to daily insults and persecution, Ulloa exerted
an influence scarcely inferior to that of Gondomar himself; by this his Castilian pride was so much gratified,
that he thought it necessary to draw a picture of his
success to his master, Philip; and while so doing, he
affords us a curious glimpse of James's Court. Repairing early to Buckingham's apartments in the palace,
and expressing a wish to see the King if not incon-
venient, the Marquis replied in the negative, "and
leading me into his chamber," says Ulloa, "went into
the presence of the King. Returning a moment afterwards, he conducted me into the private closet of his
Majesty, whom I found near a window reading some
papers. On seeing me enter, he lifted his hat, and
advancing two steps from the window, with great kindness took me by the hand, in the presence of the
gentlemen of his chamber, and those of the Council.
I told him that notwithstanding the good news I had
received of his health, I was extremely glad to be an
ocular witness of it, that I might be able to certify to
your Majesty that it was excellent, because I knew
your Majesty would be very glad to hear such news; to
which this King, lifting again his hat, replied that he
respected no one in the world more than your Majesty,
and that, consequently, he merited your love and friendship. . . . . . . He told me I might be assured

that in the matter of Walter Raleigh, and whatever else he had promised to the Count Gondomar, he would keep his word. . . . . . To this I bowed very low, and expressing my sense of gratitule for it, took my leave."*

Finding Raleigh's apartments in the Wardrobe Tower unsuited to his purpose, Wilson made loud complaints; he thought Sir Allan Apsley must have forgotten himself, to indulge Raleigh with comfortable chambers, while he located him and his man in a bare prison room over head. Affecting politic reasons, he wished to have the arrangement reversed, so that while he lay below, his illustrious captive might be thrust up into the bare room, which, though objectionable for him and his man, he thought quite good enough for Raleigh. Tractable as the prisoner was on most points, he displayed some obstinacy on this, saying he would not go up thither unless they would carry him by force.†

While some captives were treated with harshness and rigour, a strange laxity was observed towards others. The Earl of Northumberland and the Countess of Shrewsbury, for example, now monopolized all the best lodgings in the Tower, so that the Lieutenant found himself in much perplexity to decide where he should

* Carta de Sanchez de Ulloa à Su Majestad, 24 de Setiembre (N.S.), 1618. Simancas.

† Wilson to Naunton, Sept. 12th, 1618. MS. State Paper Office.

locate Raleigh. With Wilson by his side, he went up and down the whole fortress in search of suitable rooms, but could find none without dislodging Lord Carew from the Brick Tower, which was assigned to him as Master of the Ordnance. One of its apartments, indeed, was from time to time given up to young Lord Percy when he came to visit his father, a mark of respect to the old Earl which Wilson considered preposterous. His opinion prevailed. With an innate propensity to scatter insults, Naunton snatched eagerly at the occasion to humble the proud Percy and annoy the Master of the Ordnance, and directed the appropriation of the Brick Tower to Wilson and his captive, adding soon after a female to the list of Raleigh's gaolers, in the person of Lady Wilson.

It is impossible to proceed with this story without often contrasting the feelings and behaviour of educated men in those days and in these. If the erection of a State scaffold were possible now, the sympathy of all that is generous in England would surround and cling to the sufferer, no matter what might be his offence, whereas it was then common in persons of the highest position to jeer and scoff at the fallen. In a fit of dejection caused by Wilson's arrival at the Tower, Raleigh had exclaimed, " Let the King do even what he will with me, for never man was more desirous to die."*

* Wilson to Naunton, Sept. 11th, 1618. MS. State Paper Office.

This being repeated to James's chief Secretary of State, raised to that eminence by his relative Buckingham's profligacy, that polished individual replied, "I hope you will every day gain ground of that hypocrite that is so desirous to die—mortified man that he is!"

It seems evident that Wilson had suggested in a letter, which it was thought politic to destroy, some mode of proceeding with Raleigh which promised to further the design of the Court: "The King," says Naunton, "is well pleased with your *prescription*, and will, I think, long for the ripening and mellowing of your examinations and conferences by which you are to" . . . Then follow words which obviously argue a foregone conclusion—"the best comfort I can give you is that *you shall not be long troubled with him.*"*

As soon as arrangements could be made, Raleigh, with such property as he possessed, was removed to the Brick Tower, which afforded Wilson an opportunity of examining and cataloguing all articles of curiosity or value that had been left to him. The report having been circulated that Raleigh still carried about his person a diamond of great price given him in other days by the Tudor Queen, a strong desire to obtain possession of it appears to have sprung up among the principal officials. Wilson was therefore commissioned

* Naunton to Wilson, Sept. 14th, 1618. MS. State Paper Office.

to make inquiries respecting it, but without success. The only jewel of value he could discover was a sapphire ring which the captive used as his seal. The removal occupied a whole day, but when it was completed, Wilson was filled with exultation. "Since my last letter of yesterday morning," he says, "I have been wholly employed in removing this man to safer and higher lodgings, which, though it seems nearer heaven, yet is there no means of escape from thence for him to any place but hell."*

Allowing Sir Thomas Wilson to be, on the subject of suicide, a fair exponent of the sentiments of his age, we must infer that it was generally regarded as an offence which placed those who were guilty of it beyond the sympathy of men or the forgiveness of God, for though hardened beyond most of his worst contemporaries, Wilson's notion was, that all persons who destroyed themselves were not only doomed to eternal punishment, but entailed utter ruin on their posterity. Affecting the solicitude of inquisitors, Raleigh's persecutors told him, they must take away his drugs and extracts, that he might not possess the means of poisoning himself; upon which he contemptuously observed that, if he wished, he could find death by running his head against a post. Meanwhile, the great point aimed at was to elicit some information respecting the dealings of Raleigh and James's

* Wilson to Naunton, Sept. 17th, 1618. MS. State Paper Office.

Queen with France, for which purpose Wilson appears to have been authorised to hold out the usual bait of a promise of life in case of compliance, which he was afterwards, with affected regret, to confess he had no right to give. In the performance of this duty he gave proof of subtlety which would have done no discredit to a Jesuit. Putting on the mask of genial simplicity, sympathy, interest, and even affection, he protested that he would peril his fortune and his life for the promotion of Raleigh's welfare, while in his communications to the Court he overwhelmed him with the coarsest ridicule and abuse, described his stately courtesy as astuteness and glozing, suggested that nothing but a rack and a halter could bring him to speak the truth, and chuckled at the conviction that he could only escape from the Tower to the bottomless pit.

CHAPTER XIV.

EXAMINATIONS AND CONFRONTATIONS.

SYNCHRONOUS with these proceedings took place the examinations of the captains who had sailed with Raleigh to Guiana, of which I have met with no account, together with those of La Chêne, of which I believe the only record in existence is found at Simancas. The third examination began with the question—

Is it true that in Brentford you offered succour and help to Sir Walter Raleigh in case he wished to escape?

La Chéne. I never spoke of it, but merely expressed my commiseration and compliments.

Commissioners. What promises did you make to Walter when you visited him at his house a second time, and what induced you to go thither?

La Chéne. When I visited him at his house, it was only to assure him of my sympathy and console him in his misfortunes.

Com. If it be true that you had no design or power

to help him, why did you write to assure him of your assistance and friendship?

La Chêne. It is true that I have written, but my letters have been only those of friendship and sympathy.

He was then told that the time would arrive when letters should be shown him expressing great promises, to which he replied that, when his letters should be produced, they would be found to contain no such promises.

Com. Why then were you not satisfied with sending him one letter; wherefore did you write him a second and a third?

La Chêne. I do not think I have written more than one on that subject.

Being told that he would not now confess having written such letters, because in his former examinations he had denied it, he replied that he had no recollection of having written them.

Com. Have you so depraved a memory that you cannot recollect what you did so recently?

La Chêne. The said letters were of so little importance that I do not remember anything about them.

Com. Did the agent of France send you to Raleigh to assure him of his friendship and aid?

La Chêne. I went to see him as a friend, and no otherwise.

Com. Do you know whether the agent wished to furnish him with letters to France after his escape?

La Chéne. I know nothing of such a circumstance.

Com. Do you know to what persons in France the said agent wished to recommend him?

La Chéne. No.

Com. What pensions did the French agent promise him from the King his master if he could effect his escape?

La Chéne. I have never heard of any arrangement of the kind being made between them.

Com. Why, then, has Dr. Turner spoken to you so often on that subject?

La Chéne. He has only spoken to me respecting his own exoneration, and what he should answer to the gentlemen of the Council.

Com. Did the French agent think of employing Raleigh in reviving the treaty of marriage between the Prince of Wales and a princess of France?

La Chéne. If such a thing were to be negociated, it would be done by a prince, and not by Raleigh.

Com. Is it true that, through the influence of the last ambassador of France in England, Raleigh had a commission from the Most Christian King, or from his admiral, to go to sea?

La Chéne. The said ambassador never communicated anything of the kind to me, nor did I ever hear him talk about it.

Com. Do you know that a Frenchman named Captain Farge went to France with that object?

La Chéne. I have heard it said, but don't know the truth of it, because I had nothing to do with that business.

Com. Did the said Farge present himself to the Admiral of France, or to some other person?

La Chéne. I know nothing about it.

Com. Did you see the said Captain Farge after his return from France?

La Chéne. No.

Com. Did the said Farge obtain the commission or not, and did he give it to Raleigh?

La Chéne. I know nothing about it.

Com. Did Raleigh put to sea before the arrival of the said Farge in London?

La Chéne. I understood that Raleigh had departed before the arrival of Farge.

Com. Do you know whether the said Farge and Raleigh afterwards met, or not?

La Chéne. I have heard it said that they met at Plymouth.

Com. Do you know whether he gave the said Farge the command of any ship?

La Chéne. I have understood that Raleigh gave him the command of a vessel of forty or fifty tons' burden, but that he never returned.

A few days later, the Council having met at Hampton Court, resumed the examination of La Chêne at ten o'clock in the morning. After what fashion he had been treated since his last examination is not known, but his whole manner was now changed, so that he seemed ready to confess anything and everything.

Com. Will you deny that you have treated three several times with Sir Walter Raleigh?

La Chéne. It is true, and I confess it to be so.

Com. Did you not promise him a vessel, and everything necessary to effect his escape?

La Chéne. I did.

Com. Did the French agent send you with messages of that kind?

La Chéne. The French agent did order me to do those things, otherwise I should not have done them.

Com. How many times did you see Sir Walter Raleigh by order of the agent?

La Chéne. Every time I went to see him it was by his order.

Com. Why, in your first answers, did you always affirm the contrary?

La Chéne. Because I understood the time had not come for declaring it, but now my conscience compels me to do so.

Com. Do you know the handwriting and signature of the said Raleigh?

La Chéne. I know it very well.

Com. Did you believe what the said Raleigh wrote in his letter ?

La Chéne. I cannot say otherwise, since I have already confessed it.

The gentlemen of the Council then caused certain letters of Sir Walter Raleigh to be read to La Chêne which contained an account of the whole matter, and La Chêne confessed that it was all true.

Com. Is it not likewise true that you and Dr. Turner have often conversed on the same subject ?

La Chéne. Yes.

Com. Do you not believe that you have greatly offended the King by such proceedings ?

La Chéne. I was compelled to do all I did by my master's orders.

Com. Is it not true that when you last visited Raleigh the French agent was present to confirm the promises you had made ?

La Chéne. Yes.

Com. Will you maintain all you have advanced in presence of the agent of France, if confronted with him ?

La Chéne. Yes.

In the afternoon, when business was resumed, the first question was: Have you anything to alter in the statement you made in the morning ?

La Chêne. No.

Com. Do you remember what you said?

La Chêne. Perfectly well.

Com. When you see the French agent, will you adhere to what you have advanced?

La Chêne. Yes.

At this point the French agent was brought in, and in his presence the statements made by La Chêne were read. He was then asked whether or not he admitted them to be true. The agent answered that there was no truth in them; that he had never seen Raleigh or sent any one else to see him; that La Chêne's head was turned by his imprisonment, so that he knew not what he was saying or doing, but was seeking to escape from prison by accusing him.

Here the members of the Council left the apartment to wait upon the King and learn his decision; and on their return Lord Bacon, addressing the agent, said his Majesty was much surprised that such proceedings should have been carried on by him in violation of the friendship existing between the two crowns, which no one desired more to preserve than his Majesty; and now that the agent had endeavoured to break it, he forbade him to exercise his official functions, since he no longer recognised him as an agent; he was therefore commanded to live privately till his Majesty should have informed the French King of his proceedings, and learned his decision respecting them. The Council then, on its own authority, ordered La Chêne to be conveyed to the Tower by four of the King's Guards,* but when the barge was on its way a countermand overtook it from the King, consigning La Chêne to his former prison.

Perceiving with how little consideration the members of the Privy Council were inclined to treat him, Le Clerc's temper was aroused, and he determined to stand upon his dignity. When summoned therefore to Whitehall, he caused it to be understood that he expected to be treated with the same ceremony and distinction as were shown to the English agent in France, meaning that when he entered the Council Chamber all the members of Council should stand uncovered as he did, which was conceded to him.† When Le Clerc arrived at the palace, he was accordingly received by the members of Council uncovered in the hall, near the gallery where the King usually gave audience to ambassadors. No new topic was discussed, and Le Clerc denied in the most absolute and peremptory manner having been at all engaged in Sir Walter Raleigh's attempted escape. He was then requested to walk in the gallery while the Council retired to consult together. Presently after he was called into the

* Carta de Sanchez de Ulloa a Ciriza, 5 de Octubre, 1618. Simancas.

† Contarini to the Signory, Oct. 12th, 1618. Venetian Archives.

Council Chamber and confronted with Sir Walter Raleigh, who repeated his statement concerning the offer made to him by Le Clerc. With intrepid coolness, the Frenchman replied that what he said was only in the hope of saving his own life by endangering others. Raleigh then endeavoured to prevail upon the agent to admit what was undeniable, especially since no danger could thereby arise to him, since he was not a native of England or subject to its laws. The examiners then said to Le Clerc that there was no need of any further proofs, since both Sir Walter Raleigh and his own secretary La Chêne contradicted him in their presence. The Lord Chancellor Bacon added, " Remember what you were told last Wednesday at Hampton Court. I now repeat to you that the King no longer recognises you as the agent of France, and will receive nothing through your hands." Le Clerc replied that he had been installed in the office he held by the King of France, and that no one could prevent his attending to his duties except that King on whom alone he depended ; then attempting to revert to business, he said, " Sir, remember what I told your lordship the other day about the poor French gold-wire-makers, who are suffering very great injustice, and who hope that through the instrumentality of your lordship they may secure their rights according to the agreement made between France and England." But the author of the

'Novum Organum' turned his back on him, and walked away without making any reply, upon which the agent also departed.*

By one authority it is affirmed that Le Clerc admitted, in presence of the Council, a part of Raleigh's statement, namely, that he had called on him at his house in Broad Street, in consequence of having received a letter from him stating that he had something of importance to communicate for the service of the King, his master; but that, on his arrival, Raleigh observed that, when he should be in France, he would explain the nature of the business to the King himself. Other admission than this Le Clerc refused to make. On returning to his house, and reflecting upon the proceedings of the Council, he drew up a concise declaration,† exactly agreeing in substance with the above statement, said to have been made verbally, and to that declaration he set his name and seal. He then despatched to France a courier bearing to his sovereign a circumstantial narrative of all that had taken place.‡

Finding that nothing more was to be extracted from the agent, the gentlemen of the Council resumed the

* Discurso de todo lo que paro en el consejo de S. Md. en Whitehall, 6 de Octubre, 1618. Simancas.

† Declaracion de M. le Clerc, agente de Francia, 6 de Octubre (N.S.) 1618. Simancas.

‡ Contarini, Despatch of Oct. 5th, 1618. Venetian Archives.

examination of his subordinate, La Chêne; which they did after they had dined.

Com. Did you speak the truth in the last answers and declarations you made before Sir Walter Raleigh and the agent of France?

La Chêne. Yes.

Com. Is it true that, when you last went to see Sir Walter Raleigh, the agent of France went with you, having changed his dress that he might not be known?

La Chêne. It is very true.

Com. Is it true that the said agent promised Raleigh a French vessel in which to make his escape, and confirmed all the promises you had previously made him?

La Chêne. It is true; and the said agent cannot deny it.

Com. Do you know what are the agent's reasons for denying the truth so obstinately, in the face of so many proofs, in addition to your own testimony?

La Chêne. I cannot tell: but all that I and the said Raleigh have testified is the truth.

Com. Will you confirm all you have said if confronted with Raleigh?

La Chêne. I cannot deny it.

Sir Walter Raleigh was then called in, and confronted with La Chêne, when their testimonies were found to correspond exactly. Then the gentlemen of the Council, who by the King's order had come post haste from Hampton Court expressly on this business, returned to give James an account of what they had accomplished.*

* Las preguntas que los señores del consejo de Estado de Inglaterra hicieron al Sr. de la Chêne caballero Frances, y respuestas de este, 19 de Setiembre, 1618, en Whitehall. Simancas.

CHAPTER XV.

DEFEAT AND CONFESSION.

Of Raleigh's life there yet remained a month and three days, during which England, France, and Spain were kept in a state of perpetual turmoil by the changing aspects of his fate. It was one point of James's policy to interpose between the great prisoner and the public that screen of impenetrable stolidity, Sir Thomas Wilson, who might not only intercept the brightness of his genius from flashing forth upon his contemporaries, but prevent that endless trail of glory which his thoughts, if embodied in fitting words, might have thrown along the vista of his country's history.

For some time the Spanish Secretary Ulloa cherished the hope that Raleigh's negociations with Montmorenci, Desmarets, and Le Clerc might involve England in a war with France, and the view he took of the matter was by no means inconsistent with probability. By his conduct in the affair of Raleigh's attempted escape Le Clerc had certainly infringed the law of nations;

but, without breaking through immemorial usage, James could not have subjected him to punishment. To insult and contumely it was thought proper to expose him, for nothing could be more contemptuous than the act of the Lord Chancellor Bacon, who turned his back upon him in the Council Chamber, or that of James himself, who, when the intrepid agent had ridden down to Hampton Court for the purpose of presenting to him a letter from his Sovereign, refused to receive it at his hands.

The English Government, which has seldom assumed an aspect so pusillanimous and ignoble as it then exhibited, appears to have drifted into the position it occupied through the credulous intemperateness of the King, who, without inquiry, without even allowing himself time for deliberation, had been betrayed by his personal hatred of Raleigh into the pledge he gave Gondomar, that his illustrious subject and his associates should be put to death. To the fulfilment of this promise the Spanish King and ministers strenuously laboured to hold James bound; though he was not long in discovering that the pledge had been given in ignorance that the occurrences in Guiana were not such as he had been brought to believe when he gave it, and that accordingly he might have honourably retracted his word. But in that case he foresaw he would have to accept two consequences highly distasteful—the relinquishment of the Infanta, and the suspension of all commerce with Spain. Being ignorant of the real weakness and poverty of that country, his timidity may even have induced him to fear an immediate appeal to arms. He, therefore, long after the truth had broken in upon his mind, pretended to put faith in the statement of the Spaniards, that Raleigh had perpetrated revolting outrages, cruelties, and murders in South America, in territories which he now resolved not to call his own.

Affecting to be possessed by this persuasion, he, on the 29th of September, addressed two letters to Louis XIII., in which we discover the utmost virulence against Raleigh, together with much indifference as to whether the complications arising out of his case should lead or not to hostilities with France. We ought, no doubt, to be prepared to find falsehood cropping out abundantly in such documents, yet it is impossible to avoid smiling at James's reference to the love he had felt for Louis's father, whom he abhorred so thoroughly that he could not even avoid the indecency of attacking him before his guests at table. However, the point for consideration now is, his simulated belief in the Spanish account of Raleigh's proceedings. To prove to Louis how blameable his agent Le Clerc had been, he describes as follows the individual to whom he offered succour :—

" Sir Walter Raleigh, a person condemned as a traitor

to our crown, and recently returned from the West Indies, where, expressly against our instructions and orders, he practised such insufferable cruelties upon the Spaniards as to furnish cause for breaking the peace and great friendship existing between the Spanish crown and ours." *

James then proceeds to view the conduct of the French agent from the point of international law, insisting that he might legally have punished him, but that through courtesy to Louis he had left his chastisement to him. Immediately on the receipt of this unfriendly missive, Louis replied in a tone still more unfriendly, insisting that his agent had been improperly dealt with, and by no means recognizing the right of the King of England to act as he had done. " We have been informed," he says, " that our agent there has not been dealt with in so favourable a manner as has been customary, and that the Council of England has proceeded against him *for things of very small consideration,* by ways unheard-of until now." Then, setting aside James's testimony, Louis proceeds to inform him that he has recalled his agent, in order to learn the truth of the whole matter from him.†

* Carta que el Rey de Inglaterra, escribio al Rey de Francia, enviada por el Marques de Buckingham, al Conde de Gondomar; y traducida de Frances en español à la letra, 29 de Setiembre, 1618.   Simancas.

† Traduccion de una carta que escribio el Rey de Francia, al Rey de Inglaterra, 13 de Octubre, 1618.   Simancas.

About the same time, an incident occurred in France which co-operated in embittering the relations between the two courts. James had sent over Dr. Mayerne, a man of unfortunate repute in his profession, to transact some business with the Huguenots, but his presence in France no sooner became known than he was banished the kingdom. Becher, our agent in Paris, was directed to complain of this affront, and to demand why Mayerne had been expelled like a bandit; to whom the French Council replied, that "the King of France was not accountable to the King of England for his acts, neither was he in a condition to be in fear of any one; and that the King of England should govern his own kingdom, and not meddle with that of France." At this language, which it must be owned was somewhat rough, James was extremely indignant, and it was generally understood that Le Clerc's treatment was quite as much intended as a set-off for that of Mayerne, as on account of his interference in Raleigh's affair.*

Princes less tame than James and Louis might have converted this epistolary skirmish into a cause of national hostility, especially as they recalled their ministers and adopted a tone of bluster in their correspondence; but, as was foreseen from the first by the

* Carta de Sanchez de Ulloa à Ciriza, 5 de Octubre, 1618. Simancas.

representatives of Venice and Spain, the matter went
no farther.

Raleigh, meanwhile, having been subjected to incessant persecution, to examinations and confrontations
before the Council, to personal insults from James and
Naunton, conveyed to him through Wilson and Sir
Allan Apsley, seems at length to have grown weary
of carrying on the struggle. If he requested permission
to write a few lines to his wife, Naunton and James
had to be consulted before so poor a favour could be
granted, and when written—though this he did not
know—his letters were subjected to the scrutiny of both
secretary and monarch before they reached their destination. In fact, his seal was broken, and the letters
having been read were resealed and returned to Wilson,
who then sent them to Lady Raleigh, whose answers
were subjected to the same examination.

Sir Thomas Wilson, it cannot be doubted, received
both from the King and his Secretary orders to extract
from Raleigh, by solemn promises of pardon, such
admissions and confessions as, in the opinion of those
who were to judge of them, would compromise his life:
in doing this he was to insinuate, though not positively
to assert, that he had high authority for the language
he employed: if the bait took, his masters were to
disavow his proceedings, and overwhelm him with
censure, but to base nevertheless upon his artifices the

destruction of their victim. Naunton acknowledges frankly that such was the practice; and the number of heads which were thus brought under the axe was doubtless considerable. I have before me undeniable proof that it answered its purpose with Raleigh, for twenty-four days before his death he wrote to the King as follows :—

"Sir,

"Having been imprisoned by order of your Majesty, and several times questioned respecting the commission I had from France for crossing the seas, as well as in respect to the hope of aid which the French had promised me, I have always feared to speak the truth, lest I might give pain and trouble to those who had vouchsafed me many favours, and afterwards wished my liberty. But, seeing that your Majesty desires extremely to know the truth, and has strictly commanded me to reveal it; not wishing any longer to keep your Majesty in doubt and suspense, and in conscience feeling myself obliged to please my natural King and Prince, and no other—hoping, as I have always desired in other things, to give satisfaction in this, that he may have compassion on my hard and critical condition, and on my old age—I will now speak the truth to your Majesty.

"I received a commission from the Duc de Montmorenci, Admiral of France, to go to sea, which was given to me by a Frenchman named Farge, who told me that the French ambassador, Desmarets, would favour me with his letters to the Duc de Montmorenci for that end; and on the other point, of which your Majesty so much desires to know the truth, I will declare it. It is true that a French gentleman named La Chêne came to see me at three different times; the first time at Brentford, and the other two at my house in London; at all which times he promised me, in the name of the French agent, that he would assist and favour my escape to France, and would place at my service a vessel for this purpose, and would furnish me with very favourable letters, in order that certain gentlemen in France might receive me well and recommend me to the Most Christian King, who would employ me honourably, and give me reason to be well satisfied. The same agent came with him the third time to confirm all this. And I have now resolved to make an effort to save myself in the best manner I can by disclosing the truth to your Majesty, seeing that my enemies in this kingdom have great power to do me harm. I pray you humbly, therefore, to pardon and have compassion on me, and if it may please your Majesty to grant my life, even in imprisonment, I will reveal things which will be very useful to the State, and from which there will result great wealth and advantages, at the same time that my death could occasion nothing but gratification to those who seek it with so much vindictiveness and anxiety, contrary to the natural disposition of your Majesty, who has always been inclined to goodness and clemency, on which I base all the hopes I have in this world; and praying to God that he would give your Majesty as much happiness as I could wish for myself, I am, Sir, your Majesty's most humble and most unhappy subject,

" WALTER RALEIGH." *

Had Raleigh known the true nature of James's feelings towards him, he would have spared himself the humiliation of appealing to his compassion; but sorrow, captivity, and the infirmities of premature old age had broken his spirit. Though not fully aware of the King's complicity with Spain, and how completely he had put it out of his own power to be either merciful or just, he understood perfectly well the fierce hungering after his death by which Philip and his ministers were devoured. No doubt they contrived to palliate to their own minds the bloodthirstiness that inspired their proceedings, to which it would be difficult to find a parallel. Diego de la Fuente, one of the priests

* Tower of London, October 5th, 1618. Whether or not the original be still in existence, I have been unable to discover; the above is a re-translation from the Spanish version, to be found in the General Archives of Simancas.

attached to the Embassy, who enjoyed the privilege of writing familiarly to Philip, furnishes several proofs of James's folly and subserviency to the Escorial:—"He (James) told me again that he desired or valued nothing so much as a true union with your Majesty, and that on all occasions he would give proof of this disposition, as would now be seen by the punishment of Sir Walter Raleigh, at whose examinations remarkable things were daily disclosed, chiefly from the correspondence and understanding he had with France, whose King expected by means of Raleigh to rob your Majesty of your Western Empire. The King then indulged with seeming pleasure in lively satire against France."*

Early in October, Sir Thomas Wilson, finding his mission at the Tower as unpleasant as it was unprofitable, since he could make but little way with Raleigh, while the Lieutenant and his friends loathed his presence, and gave the most sinister interpretation to his practices, prayed to be permitted to resume his labours at the State Paper Office. From the date of his application we learn nothing of Raleigh for about ten days, which he probably employed in reconciling himself to the conviction that the struggle was over, and that he must prepare for death. The town was full of conjectures

---

* Carta de Fray Diego de la Fuente sobre Gualtero, 12 de Octubre, 1618.   Simancas.

respecting his fate, which changed and melted into each other like a series of dissolving views. The friends he still possessed exerted themselves in vain to turn aside the shafts of Spanish malice; while in the same proportion, and with greater energy, his enemies, Baby Charles, his evil genius Steenie, Secretary Naunton, John Digby, above all Ulloa and the priests of the Embassy at Ely House, strained every nerve to hasten his execution.

Philip, ensconced in gloom and ferocity at Madrid, devoted a large portion of his time to the task of bringing about Raleigh's death. In obedience to his peremptory orders, Ulloa followed James to Royston, where, being granted an audience, he exhausted his powers of persuasion in the attempt to subordinate James's conscience to the revenge of Philip. The King of England had then in reality degenerated into a Spanish satrap, displaying no will of his own, but consenting to take the guilt of blood upon his head at the behest of another. Though Ulloa, familiar with the Plaza de Toros, felt doubtless much delight in cruelty, he only performed his duty in stimulating James to the murder of his subject. "I spoke very urgently," he says, "as your Majesty commanded me, in the matter of Walter Raleigh, and after referring to the promises he had made to Count Gondomar, respecting the punishment of Raleigh and those who accompanied him to Guiana, I told him how much reliance your Majesty placed in his promises, and that, since Raleigh's crimes were so evident and public, he, the King, ought to see at once that justice should be done upon him and his accomplices. . . . The King answered me favourably, saying that he had already, on account of Raleigh's affair, lost the friendship of France, whose government had incited him, if he could with its assistance effect his escape, to lie in wait on the ocean for the Indian treasure fleet, and take refuge in France with the spoils."*

Writing on the same day to Ciriza, principal Secretary of State at Madrid, Ulloa says, "I am using every possible effort in order that Walter Raleigh may speedily be brought to justice, in inflicting which they seem to be very dilatory. Towards the satisfaction for damages which he did in the Indies, I use the same urgency, and I hope that when this King returns to London, something will be done."†

The government was at this time engaged in carrying on inquiries into the conduct of several officials, who at the time of James's accession were thought to have appropriated to themselves the property of the crown. Raleigh, as cognizant of these doings and unfriendly to

---

* Carta autografa de Julian Sanchez de Ulloa à S. Md., 26 de Octubre, 1618. Simancas.

† Carta de Ulloa à Ciriza, 28 de Octubre, 1618. Simancas.

the actors, was expected, it is said, to be able to throw light on their proceedings. "He has now," says Chamberlain, " good means to redeem his demerits, if he can speak to the purpose in a cause wherein he was lately examined, about the conveyance of jewels and such like matters at the King's first coming, and for which, and for the sale of lands, there is a commission come forth, which, it is thought, will shrewdly reflect upon the Earls of Suffolk, Salisbury, and others." *

Chamberlain, however, was either misinformed on this subject, or Raleigh possessed no information which James would consent to receive as an equivalent for his life. Indeed, the probability is, that if any hopes were held out to Raleigh, they were like those put forward by Wilson, mere delusions to allure him into disclosures which, though advantageous to the court, were to be productive of no good to himself. From what James said to Ulloa at Royston on the 15th, and from the whole tenor of his language since Raleigh's return, it must have been clear to all who were in his confidence that he had resolutely determined to become an accomplice in the murder of Raleigh. No assignable political motives will suffice to explain how a man having a real belief in the existence of God could voluntarily participate in such a crime ; so that we are compelled to suppose in his mind the prevalence of a

* Letter to Carleton, Oct. 24th, 1618. State Paper Office.

hatred so fierce and powerful that it entirely blinded his sense of justice. He could not lay the least stress on the professions of friendship made to him by Philip, because he was conscious, as all those who approached him were, that his own professions to that individual were false. To gratify his petty resentment, he had brought his country to the verge of a rupture with France, and he may therefore, as Ulloa suggested, have been assailed by fear lest, if he faltered now, he should bring upon himself the vengeance of Spain also. His matrimonial scheme for Baby Charles would, had he been capable of reflection, have appeared to him, as it did to all sensible men in the kingdom, rather as a well-spring of calamity than as a source of good, since they foresaw that in the actual temper of the nation any Catholic connexion would almost certainly occasion those terrible events which were afterwards stamped upon our annals in characters of blood.

To this dark prospect James shut his eyes, and with the gay recklessness described by Fray Fuente, at length gave the fatal order that Raleigh should prepare for death. As far back as the 22nd the die was cast, though the public knew it not, for on that day, Raleigh having been taken from the Tower to Whitehall, was told what had been resolved respecting him. For some particulars of what took place in the four hours during which Raleigh pleaded for his life, we are indebted to a foreign witness, who however has omitted others which we should have been glad to learn. It was Bacon's ill-fortune to be under the necessity, as Lord-chancellor, not only of acquiescing in Raleigh's execution, but of sprinkling over his spirit those bitter waters of reproach and contumely by which James thought proper in his case to herald the pangs of death. "I have been told," says Ulloa, "that the Lord-chan_cellor of England censured him greatly for the injuries he had done to the vassals and territories of your Majesty, and dwelt on the manner in which he had abused the permission to put to sea, granted him by this King, when his professed object was to discover a gold-mine, which he had affirmed he knew where to find. In conclusion, he informed him that he must die." Ulloa then adds what is inconsistent with all other accounts of Raleigh's last days, that on hearing this he was stunned, losing his senses for a moment; after which, coming again to himself, "I am told," the Secretary continues, "that he spoke wanderingly. They then took him back to the Tower, changed his room, servants, and dress, placed over him a guard that was changed every hour, whose business it was to remain night and day in his room and observe all his words and actions, which was necessary to prevent his taking his own life by poison, knife, or in any other manner."*

* Carta Original de Julian Sanchez de Ulloa, 16 de Noviembre, 1618. Simancas.

Though up to the last James's neglected and unhappy Queen made use of her utmost efforts to save Raleigh's life, maintaining that her own depended on his prescriptions, she soon discovered the bitter truth that the reason she alleged may have been among her husband's chief motives for ridding himself of her physician.* The Spanish Secretary certainly drew upon his imagination for some of the details he forwarded to his master, since Raleigh's servants were not changed, nor is there any reason to believe in the reality of the guard, or in the removal from one set of apartments to another. He may have been equally ill-informed respecting the part played by Lord Bacon, upon whom however, by virtue of his office, devolved the unpleasant duty of drawing up and forwarding to the Lieutenant the warrant commanding Raleigh's removal from the Tower to the King's Bench, preliminary to his execution.

* Chamberlain to Carleton, Oct. 31st.   MS. State Paper Office.

CHAPTER XVI.

PALACE YARD.—CONCLUSION.

WE have now reached the eve of the blackest day in
James's black reign, and the brightest perhaps of all in
Raleigh's life. For some time he had been suffering
grievously from dysentery, fever, and ague, engendered
by breathing the miasmata exhaling from the stagnant
and fetid waters of the Tower ditch; but still more
from the conflict with his enemies, which nature urged
him to carry on in defence of his life. That warfare
being over, the certainty of death cleared away the
mists of weakness from about him, and he was himself
again—never prouder, never more stately in his bearing,
more gay, gracious, or resolute, when he wooed Elizabeth in the bowers of Windsor, or trod the rocking
deck in Cadiz Bay.

He had been all his life an early riser, but on the
lowering morning of the 28th of October, when the
pursuivant brought to the Tower Bacon's warrant to

Sir Allan Apsley, the physical debility caused by illness detained him still in bed. It was eight o'clock, not a very late hour for that dreary season of the year. He rose immediately, dressed in all haste, and then, as cheerfully as if going forth to battle, joked with his barber, who observed as they issued from the gate, "Sir, we have not combed your head this morning." "Let them comb it," he replied, "that shall have it;" and then, going on in the same lively vein, "Peter," said he, "canst thou give me any plaster to set on a man's head when it is off."*

Entering his carriage, it is to be presumed, with Peter, he proceeded under a strong guard to the King's Bench, where James's legal accomplices, Montague and Yelverton, were to complete what Coke and Heale had begun at Winchester. Upon being asked if he had anything to urge why sentence of death should not be pronounced against him, Raleigh answered, "That the King had employed him in his service, and given him a commission wherein he styled him his 'loyal subject,' and withal gave him *potestatem vitæ et mortis*, which did amount to a pardon; for in all reason he must be master of his own life who hath power over other men's. The judges replied, that there is no pardon for treason by implication; wherefore, he must find a better plea or undergo the sentence. Then Raleigh spoke of his trial

* Porey to Carleton, Nov. 7th.   MS. State Paper Office.

at Winchester, and maintained that all, or the far greater part of those present, did acquit him in their consciences; and that the King's gracious forbearing him so long, and but for this late accident longer would have done, even to a hundred years, if nature would have drawn out his life so long, did show his Majesty did approve his innocence." But the Lord Chief-justice, knowing what was expected of him, replied, "If Sir Walter Raleigh hath none other thing to allege for himself, the former sentence must stand good, and that the Lieutenant, by virtue of a writ, ought to deliver him to the sheriffs of Middlesex." At the stair-foot coming down from the King's Bench, stood the Clerk of the Crown, with the same writ directed to the Lieutenant to deliver him, and another to the sheriff to receive him, and carry him thence to the Gate-house.*

On the way from the King's Bench, as the carriage with his guards made its way slowly through the multitude that thronged the streets to behold the great prisoner of the Bloody Tower, Raleigh noticed in the crowd his old friend, Sir Hugh Beeston, and invited him to come to Palace Yard on the morrow to see him die.

On reaching his new prison, he is said to have employed some time in writing letters to the King and others; and afterwards being joined by Dr. Tonson,

---

* Porey to Carleton, Oct. 31st, 1618. State Paper Office.

Dean of Westminster,* he prayed with him awhile. Weekes, then Governor of the Gate-house, appears to have been a kind and indulgent man, who put no restrictions on the visits of Raleigh's friends to him; for on this sad evening many, we are told, came to sit up with him. Unfortunately, such of his contemporaries as have left us an account of his last hours were not persons of taste or discernment, but thought more of chronicling sallies of sprightliness than of giving us such a picture as they might have drawn of his whole bearing that night. Late in the evening his wife came to him, but of what they said to each other nothing is recorded but this: she mentioned as some consolation that the Government had granted to her the disposal of his body. "It is well, Bess," he replied, "that thou shouldst have the disposal of that dead, which thou hadst not always the disposing of living."†

Shortly after midnight took place the parting scene, of which nothing has been, or perhaps need be said: it is related he dismissed her then, when he saw probably that feelings which he might not be able to keep in check were beginning to burst up from the depth of his heart. From these he sought refuge in sleep, and probably found it; since on the threshold of their last

* Chamberlain to Carleton, Oct. 31st, 1618. MS. State Paper Office.

† 'Court and Times of James I.,' ii., 104.

sleep, when it would almost seem that they needed it not, men have generally a foretaste of that rest towards which they are hastening. At four o'clock, one of Raleigh's cousins, Charles Thynne, arrived at the prison, and when they began to converse, observing Raleigh to be more than usually cheerful, he expressed some fear lest his enemies should accuse him of affectation. "Good Charles," he said, "let me be merry for this once—it is the last merriment I shall enjoy in this world; but when I come to the sad part thou shalt see I will look on it like a man." *

The Dean of Westminster having come to the prisoner at five, Raleigh prayed with him, and according to his own conception made his peace with God. He then prepared for the axe and the scaffold, and as usual breakfasted at eight o'clock. His frame had been wasted by long confinement and malaria, which had brought on fever and ague, and to support his physical strength to go through the trying scene on which he was about to enter, "there was a cup of excellent sack brought him, and being asked how he liked it; 'as the fellow,' said he, 'that drinking of St. Giles' bowl as he went to Tyburn, said that was good drink if a man might tarry by it.'"

To lessen the crowd, which it was expected would be very great, the Government chose that Raleigh's ex-

* Percy to Carleton, Nov. 7th. MS. State Paper Office.

cution should take place on Lord Mayor's-day, that the curiosity of the public might be somewhat divided; yet the multitude was so great that persons of distinction, with letters to the sheriffs from a Secretary of State in their hands, could scarcely make their way through the dense throng. The Captain of Elizabeth's Guard was known to everybody old enough to remember the great Queen, so that he might now be said to be surrounded by familiar faces. In the crowd he observed Beeston, whom on the previous day he had invited to be present, and seeing that he was unable to make his way forward, Raleigh bade him farewell, saying, " I know not how it may be with you, but I shall be sure to find a place." A little further on, he noticed an old man with a bald head, pressing eagerly towards him, and inquiring whether he would have aught of him, the old man answered, that he only " desired to see him, and pray God to have mercy upon his soul." " I thank thee, good friend," said Sir Walter, " and I am sorry I have no better thing to return thee for thy good-will; but take this nightcap "—which was a very rich one—" for thou hast more need of it now than I."

The scaffold having been erected near dwelling-houses, Raleigh observed when he ascended it several noblemen and gentlemen who had stationed themselves at a window of Sir Randal Crewe's to witness his death, and because his voice was weak, he requested them to come out and stand on the scaffold, as he had something to say to them : when they had done as he desired, he made a short speech, the meaning of which has scarcely been preserved. What we possess under that name it is impossible he should have uttered, unless we assume the letter to James of the 5th of October, together with his examinations and those of La Chêne, and all his communications with the French authorities, to be forgeries. Had he denied, as he is said to have done, that he ever saw any commission, letter, or seal, from the French King, his admission to the contrary in his own handwriting would doubtless have been produced on the scaffold, to confound and silence him. We must consequently believe, either that the documents referred to were mere fabrications, or that several gentlemen who were present at his death, and heard him deliver his farewell address to the world, either misunderstood his language, or purposely misrepresented it. On this point, as on so many others connected with different stages of Raleigh's career, it seems all but impossible to ascertain the truth ; the evidence on record being contradictory, though the witnesses in many cases who testified in his favour can be suspected of no intelligible motive which could have biased their judgment. If the English originals of the letters to James, and of the minutes of examinations taken at Whitehall could be found, some approximation to certainty might be made; but, in the meantime, we are left to draw what conclusions we can from the conflicting reports that have come down to us.

The reference he made to Essex's death may have imported no more than this, that he never spontaneously sought his destruction, though the Earl had fallen by the means he had been constrained to employ to preserve himself against his machinations. He thanked God, however, that he was permitted to die in the light, that he might clear himself of many heavy imputations which had been laid upon him. The Dean of Westminster then inquired in what faith he died: he replied, in that of a Christian as professed and taught by the Church of England. The cold being sharp that morning, the sheriff kindly invited him to descend, and warm himself: to which he answered, "No, good Mr. Sheriff, let us despatch; for within a quarter of an hour mine ague will come upon me, and if I be not dead ere then, mine enemies will say I quake for fear." Before laying his head upon the block, he gracefully bowed to the spectators, and taking the axe from the executioner, and feeling its edge, said, "This is a sharp, but sure remedy against all miseries and diseases." He then knelt down, and having said a short prayer, gave, as had been agreed upon, the word to the executioner, "Strike!" and at two blows, his head was severed from his body.

The effect produced by Raleigh's death upon the world differed widely from that which the Government appears to have expected. A Spanish Dominican, more clear sighted than James or Philip, foresaw that by the execution of the great Admiral the unpopularity of Spain in England would be augmented. Nothing was talked of throughout London but Raleigh's perfect death,* to avoid hearing which James retreated to Royston; though his conscience may not have been much the quieter on account of the distance.

When Raleigh's head had been held up, and shown to the people as that of a traitor, it was put into a leathern bag and borne to a mourning coach, which Lady Raleigh had in waiting near at hand, and conveyed no one exactly knows whither. According to some the headless trunk was interred in St. Margaret's, Westminster; according to others, his remains were deposited in the church at Beddington; while there is a tradition

---

* Mr. Forster, in his able 'Life of Sir John Eliot,' quotes from a MS. work of that great patriot a passage on Raleigh's death, equally honourable to the writer and to the martyr. " Matchless, indeed," says Eliot, " was his fortitude. It was a wonder and example, which, if the ancient philosophers could have witnessed, they had acknowledged as the equal of their virtue. . . . . His mind became the clearer as if already it had been freed from the cloud and oppression of the body; and such was his unmoved courage and placid temper, that while it changed the affection of the enemies who had come to witness it, and turned their joy to sorrow, it filled all men else with admiration and emotion." Life of Sir John Eliot, i., 34, 35.

which maintains that Lady Raleigh, who certainly embalmed her husband's head, performed the same office also for the whole body, and kept them near her through life. Whatever credit may be accorded to this story, the embalmed head gradually became an object of public interest, to behold and kiss which people appear to have sometimes travelled many a mile. That strange Protestant, Bishop Goodman, tells us in his strange book, "I know where the head is kept, and I have kissed it."* For twenty-nine years Lady Raleigh survived her husband, and during that period seems. wherever she went, to have carried about with her the head of the man she had loved. The relic then passed into the hands of her son Carew, with whose remains it is supposed to have been deposited in the earth.

Such as I have described him in the foregoing pages was Sir Walter Raleigh. For many years after his death the paramount influence of the Stuarts rendered it unsafe to do him justice; since, to defend his memory was to criminate them. As the love of freedom spread, reverence for Raleigh's genius, and pity for his misfortunes, spread with it, through the efforts partly of such men as Hampden and Milton, who set a high value on his writings, and laboured to revive his fame. From the period of the Commonwealth to the present

* 'Court of King James I.,' 69.

day, Raleigh has gradually risen in public estimation, until he has almost come to be considered as the great type and representative of his race—adventurous, daring, insatiable in the pursuit of power, and not over-scrupulous in the use of it, contemptuous of foreigners, remorseless in his patriotism, and recklessly eager to stamp an English impress on the whole action of the world. Through these characteristics, whether good or bad, he is seldom regarded otherwise than with deep enthusiasm by those who have familiarised themselves with his career.

To penetrate into the secret of his philosophy it is necessary to scrutinize the entire body of his writings, in some places so enigmatical as to defy positive inter-pretation. The position he ought to occupy among great men is hard to be determined; but perhaps they who look upon him as the greatest on record of real Anglo-Saxon origin may have formed the truest con-ception of his intellect and character.* One quality he had in common with the loftiest intelligences that have taken up their abode in clay—he absolutely rejected the authority of other minds, and thought himself as much at liberty as the first man to think and judge for himself on all subjects of inquiry or speculation.

* Hallam, by no means friendly to Raleigh, adopts the national opinion that he was the bravest and most renowned of Englishmen. 'History of England,' i., 355.

Ceaseless study carried on in the camp, on the ocean, in palaces and in prisons, had acquainted him with all that man from the beginning has dared to utter or think; and on looking back, even to periods dimmest and most remote, he beheld few individuals of his species who, had all his energies been concentrated on philosophical investigation, would have been found to go beyond him in subtlety, originality, or grasp of thought. But, aiming at conferring great practical benefits on mankind, he was content to forego his claim to be reckoned among the foremost of those who have marked and laid out the tracks in which men's ideas and opinions are to advance for ever.

By the ignorant and prejudiced * among his contemporaries, Raleigh was sometimes accused of atheism; but, possessing a sound mind in a sound body, he never at any period of his life furnished the slightest pretext for such an accusation. He had familiarised himself, as I have said, with the process by which systems of philosophy are constructed, partly with materials visible and tangible, partly, if I may so speak, with blocks of thought, hewn out of the metaphysical universe which, in darkness impenetrable, wraps about the diminutive sphere made luminous to us by knowledge. It is to that limitless storehouse of mystery that the

---

* Archbishop Abbot to Sir Thomas Roe, February, 1619. MS. State Paper Office.

founders of creeds and systems resort for powers and sanctions with which to overawe and coerce the minds of men. Law is will embodied in words: "Thou shalt not kill; thou shalt not bear false witness; thou shalt not steal." Why? That is what no one dares to inquire. The law carries its own sanction with it: it is an emanation of the will that brooks no opposition, but binds up inextricably punishment with transgression. In the track of duty there is light, there is warmth, there is vivifying energy: step out of it, and you feel at once the cold dark touch of the infinite, which thrusts you back shuddering to your place.

To estimate the power of a man's character, we often need little more than to witness the amount of terror with which he inspires his enemies. Lucius Sylla, after the proscriptions, standing up in the Roman senate, bareheaded and with folded arms, to defend the cruelties he had perpetrated with patriotic intentions, was gazed at with less dismay than that with which Spain and the England of the Stuarts regarded Raleigh. History supplies no parallel to the fierce thirsting for a man's blood displayed by Philip and Gondomar; or to the base subserviency of James and his craven ministers. They looked at Raleigh through an atmosphere of bewildering fear, from the pangs and pressure of which they endeavoured to deliver themselves by his death. Accordingly, when his blood had been shed, they drew a long breath, like persons escaping from the stifling weight of a nightmare, and began to entertain each other with the farce which they thought fit to enact after the tragedy. Writing to his master, Nov. 5th (16th N.S.), while he was an object of execration to all London, Ulloa observes that he continued to press for compensation for the ravages committed by Raleigh in America: "I have spoken," he adds, "to the King himself about it. After relating to me all the appeals made to him for Raleigh's life, he promised that reparation should be made, and said that he had caused a ship* with much property to be confiscated in Ireland towards making up the sum. He then delivered to me two small pieces of mineral gold, which, he said, was all that had ever come to his hands. For these I gave him my receipt."† As this document is characteristic I subjoin it :—

"I have received from the hands of his Majesty the King of Great Britain two pieces of rough gold that Sir Walter Raleigh brought from the Indies."‡

Two months after James, in humble submission to Spain, had shed the blood of his greatest subject, he received a letter of thanks from Philip, drawn up in

* This probably was the 'Jason,' commanded by Pennington.

† Carta Original de don Julian Sanchez de Ulloa, à Su Majestad, 16 de Noviembre, 1618. Simancas.

‡ Recibo que don Julian Sanchez de Ulloa dio al Rey de la Gran Britaña, 16 de Noviembre, 1618. Simancas.

obscure language, referring at the outset to long past dates, but suffering the joy he felt at Raleigh's assassination to pierce through the reserve which he thought it politic to affect. That the heavy burden lying on James's conscience was much lightened by this communication is what we may be permitted to doubt. It ran, however, as follows:—

"I am much gratified to learn by the letter of your Serene Highness, dated June 18th (which I received by the hands of Mr. Francis Cottington), the satisfaction given by the Count of Gondomar, my Ambassador, in the affairs which he has transacted in my name with your Serene Highness and your ministers; all which proceedings have been in conformity with my best wishes. The said Count has mentioned to me the goodwill that he has always found in your Serene Highness towards us; and in the demonstration made respecting Walter Raleigh, which has been such as might have been expected from our brotherhood and friendship, for the just settlement of the affair. Your Serene Highness will always find in me the same goodwill in return, as you will understand more particularly from my servant Julian Sanchez de Ulloa."*

Thus terminated the sanguinary correspondence between the Kings of Great Britain and Spain. Raleigh

* Minuta de Carta del Rey de España al de la Gran Britaña. Madrid, 30 de Diciembre, 1618. Simancas.

had passed out of their power into the domains of history and fame; and while every succeeding age has accorded to them additional scorn and contempt, it has, in the same proportion, encircled the name of their victim with additional glory, which, I am persuaded, will go on increasing as long as genius and intellect shall continue to command the admiration of mankind.

THE END.

LONDON: PRINTED BY WILLIAM CLOWES AND SONS, STAMFORD STREET
AND CHARING CROSS.